Death on a Hillside

Gary J. George

ISBN-13:978-1532930003
ISBN-10: 1532930003

For Ginny.

My Life. My Love.

Death on a Desert Hillside

CONTENTS

Prologue

The wind was blowing toward them out of the east. *In the ghostly gray light of the cold, pre-dawn December day, the pack neared the end of a night of hunting as it approached the broad mouth of the sandy wash. The hunt had been unsuccessful. The dogs were hungry. The previous night had been only marginally better, yielding only one small dog and a cat. Not nearly enough to feed the massive alpha male and the three other dogs.*

The pack was beginning to turn west to run close to the edge of the steep, southwest escarpment when the alpha caught the scent. Meat. Smoky meat. He stopped. Saliva began to dribble from his jaws as he turned his head from side to side to pinpoint the source.

There!

The big dog bolted at a dead run. The three smaller dogs followed in his wake, struggling to keep pace.

In a few minutes, the dogs saw the source of the scent.

It was a man.

The smaller dogs slowed to a tentative trot.

Men were dangerous. Men should be avoided.

But the alpha male did not slow. He continued over the soft ground, throwing up great gouts of sand with every leap forward. His thick chest heaved with each ragged gulp of cold air, but he managed to summon a final burst.

The man suddenly heard him, turning his head in alarm and taking flight. He dug hard toward a stairway leading upward from the desert floor.

The huge dog caught him on the fourth step, but his enormous jaws closed mostly on cloth. The cloth ripped as he tried to pull the man down. The man jerked free. He pounded to the top of the stairs and disappeared through a door.

With the meat.

With the delicious, smoky meat.

The alpha male howled in frustration and hurled himself over and over again against the door while the other dogs milled and whined below.

CHAPTER 1

DESERT DOG PACK

Lieutenant Carlos Caballo, known throughout the Lower Colorado River Basin in the tri-states area simply as "Horse," loved his job. Except for the paperwork. He was grinding his way through a stack of it early on a Monday morning in December of 1961 when his dispatcher's voice came over the intercom.

"Lieutenant, Deputy Chesney has a problem he'd like to talk to you about."

Delighted to have an excuse to get out from behind his desk, he went into the outer office. The dispatcher turned his chair over to his boss.

"Go, Andy."

"Lieutenant, I'm out here at the rodeo grounds with Willy Gibson. He's real upset about something, and I'm making it worse because I can't understand him. Over."

"Any idea at all what he's trying to tell you? Over."

"Can't make heads or tails of it. He got so frustrated he started growling at me. Lieutenant, you can understand him better than anybody. Any chance you could come out here? I know it would help. Just now when he heard your voice on the radio, he stopped growling and sat down on the ground. Over."

The Lieutenant's face lit up.

"Sit tight, Andy. I'm on my way. Clear."

He hurried to his office, pulled his gun belt off the back of his chair and jammed his Stetson on his head. He was buckling on his gun as he headed for the substation door.

"You've got the fort, Fred. Unless it's World War Three, I don't want to hear about it until I get back."

He started his unit and drove down the long driveway to Highway 95 and turned left toward Smoke Tree. At the stop sign where Route 95 merged with Route 66, he turned on his light bar and hit his siren to create a break in the traffic so he could get onto 66. As soon as he was in the stream, he turned them both off. A half mile later he dropped down the hill into town. As he drove along the section of the highway with the Santa Fe tracks on his right and a string of gas stations and old, one story motor courts on his left, he thought about Willy Gibson.

Carlos Caballo was sixteen the first time he saw Willy. Carlos was walking across the little park in front of the Santa Fe Depot in Smoke Tree. A cold, winter wind was kicking hard across the stiff, brown, dormant Bermuda grass in the park, flinging trash and dust and yellow leaves from a giant cottonwood into the air. In the middle of the park, he saw a man having a conversation with the World War One field gun that sat on a raised, concrete slab enclosed by a wrought iron fence.

As he got closer, he realized the skin on the man's face was a mass of scar tissue. It looked like melted tallow stained with red ochre and flecked with bits of iron oxide had been poured over a dented oval. His ears had been badly burned and were curled tightly against the side of his head. They were the size, shape and color of tiny, dried apricots. He had neither eyebrows nor any other hair on his head. The only unmarked features of his face had a singular beauty: kind, clear, gray eyes and oddly full and girlish lips that looked like they belonged on someone else's mouth.

He was a small man. He was stooped, and his shirt hung loosely on his frame. He was so thin, in fact, that a pair of suspenders, incongruously covered with pink polka dots, helped a wide belt keep his worn, khaki pants from sliding down over his hips. But in spite of the narrow torso, his forearms strained the fabric of his shirt and his wrists were so thick the sleeves were unbuttoned. At first Horse thought it was because the man had just a thumb and one finger on one of his badly scarred hands and only a ring finger and pinky on the other and could not do up the buttons. But then he realized the rest of the buttons on the blue flannel shirt were done up, including the small collar button.

Whatever the man was saying to the gun seemed very important to him. And apparently the gun was answering because he kept pausing to listen and nod his head. When he noticed a boy had stopped to look at him, the man included the boy in the conversation.

"Guh!" he said, loudly.

Even though he was practically shouting, Carlos was not afraid of the man with the scars, the missing fingers on his bent and twisted hands and the disheveled clothing. He did think it was a little strange the man was having a conversation with a gun Carlos had walked past hundreds of times without really seeing. But Carlos didn't leave, and perhaps just as importantly, he didn't look away. He thought he knew what the man was saying.

"That's right," said Carlos. "Gun."

There was suddenly a delighted smile on the man's face.

"Oom!" he shouted. Then he pursed his full lips and came out with a loud, high-pitched whistle that gradually descended in pitch until it ended in another "Oom!"

"Boom!" said Carlos.

The man was so happy he started dancing from foot to foot. Then he stopped and pointed at himself and said something that sounded like "Weeyee."

Carlos realized the man was giving his name. Carlos had never heard of anyone named Weeyee. Then something clicked, and Carlos understood.

"Willy?" asked Carlos, pointing at the man.

The man's smile grew even bigger. The rest of his badly burned face did not move when his lips and eyes smiled.

Carlos pointed at himself.

"Carlos."

The man stopped dancing and gestured at Carlos.

When he tried to say the name, it came out as "ahr yos."

When Carlos nodded, the man stuck out his right hand, the one with a finger and a thumb on it.

9

Carlos hesitated, but only briefly, and then extended his own. The small man lightly squeezed the boy's hand between his thumb and middle finger. Then he withdrew the hand and bobbed his head.

"Bah!" he shouted.

"Bye," said Carlos

The man walked off across the park, turning twice to wave and smile.

In the months that followed, Carlos often encountered Willy Gibson, sometimes in Smoke Tree, sometimes in the desert outside of town and sometimes sitting above the Colorado River watching the water flow. Over time, the man and the young boy became friends. In a way Horse could not define, the man reminded him of his father, the father who had not returned home from the Pacific in World War II. Perhaps it was the kindness Carlos saw in Willy's eyes. And for Willy, young Carlos was someone who wasn't frightened by Willy and, more importantly, didn't make fun of him.

Carlos soon understood that Willy could not make hard sounds like "k" and "d" and "t". He also had trouble with "l" and "r" sounds, but he could approximate them. Once Carlos understood the limitations of Willy's speech, he could usually parse what the man was trying to say.

Before long, Carlos realized whatever had happened to Willy had damaged his mind as well as his body. Some days were better than others. Some days his eyes were clear, and he seemed alert. But some days, Willy seemed to look at the world around him without comprehension. As if he weren't sure exactly where he was. On those days, it sometimes took Willy a while to recognize Carlos. In fact, in those first few months, Willy sometimes introduced himself again; going through the same routine he had that day by the field gun.

But after the first year, Willy no longer made that mistake. There was a mind at work behind those gray eyes; a mind struggling to make sense of the world; a mind that longed to communicate with and be accepted by others. Once, after Carlos had known Willy long enough to be sure Willy could understand him completely, Carlos asked Willy if he could write, thinking that would be a way for the two of them to communicate. It was on one of Willy's better days: a day when he seemed to be in touch with his surroundings. Willy held up both of his badly twisted and burned hands and shook his head. He looked as if he were going to cry.

It was all Carlos could do to keep from crying himself.

By the time Carlos graduated from high school, he and Willy had forged a lasting bond. Carlos often went out of his way to seek the man out and make sure he was all right. Willy was always glad to see him. And it made Carlos angry when people treated his friend badly. People stared and pointed at Willy as if he were an exhibit of some sort. And they laughed at him.

Then the Smoke Tree Police officers joined in the fun. In a late-evening ceremony behind the station, they pinned a dime store badge on Willy's shirt and gave him an old STPD hat. They strapped a holster to his waist that held a revolver so badly rusted the cylinder wouldn't turn and gave him a big flashlight.

Willy took it all very seriously. Late at night, he would walk the downtown armed with his rusted revolver, wearing his badge, hat, and star and carrying his flashlight. He would go to every business that had closed for the night and rattle the doors to make sure they were locked. Then he would shine his flashlight through the windows before he moved to the next place.

It wasn't long before news of the ceremony and Willy's self-appointed role reached the town's two barbershops. That's all it took. Soon, everyone in town knew Willy on sight, although very few of them ever spoke to him.

Carlos thought the whole thing was mean-spirited. But Willy seemed completely unaware the cops were laughing at him behind his back. And he only wore the badge and the hat and carried the gun and flashlight when he did his rounds. No one knew where he stored them once he had completed his nightly routine.

As Horse drove through town, he noticed the Smoke Tree Chamber of Commerce had tacked wreaths on the streetlight poles and hung a few sparse strands of tinsel and strings of Christmas lights over the highway. Many of the big city people travelling through Smoke Tree probably saw the decorations as tacky and pathetic. Horse thought they were perfect. The worn decorations felt just right for Christmas in a hardscrabble, blue collar town in the middle of the Mojave Desert. Anything finer would have been out of place.

Horse left the motels and gas stations of town behind and continued north on Highway 66. There were discarded beer cans and bottles and other trash on both shoulders of the road. In fact, discarded trash lined 66 from at least Holbrook, Arizona to the bottom of Cajon Pass in San Bernardino. For most people, that was all the desert represented: a place to throw beer cans. Horse sometimes pictured the highway from far above: a band of junk extending ten yards from both sides of the road, bleeding into a clean and untrammeled desert just beyond the tossing range of thoughtless motorists.

Before he reached the turnoff that led to the rodeo grounds, he saw a sheriff's department unit parked partway up the dirt road. Horse turned on his light bar and hit his siren to create a traffic break and turned west onto the road.

He pulled in behind Andy Chesney's cruiser. Andy was leaning against his unit. When Horse got out, Andy walked toward him.

"Mornin', Lieutenant."

"Good morning, Andy. Where's Willy?"

"Sitting over by the car."

As Horse walked over, Willy got up.

"Hello, Willy."

"Orse!" yelled Willy, looking relieved.

"Willy's been calm ever since I told him you were on your way."

"Tell me what happened."

"Well, sir, I was coming in toward town when I saw Willy down there by the highway. It almost seemed like he was waiting for me. Anyway, he started waving his arms and jumping up and down, so I pulled onto the shoulder. He was beside my door before I could get my unit stopped. I persuaded him to follow me onto the dirt road so he wouldn't get hit by the traffic.

He really, really didn't want to follow me very far up the road. In fact, right here was as far as I could get him to go. As soon as I got out, he started yelling at me.

I'm sorry, Lieutenant, but I couldn't understand him. The harder he tried to tell me something, the more upset he got. And so I called you."

"You did right."

Horse turned to Willy.

"What were you trying to tell Andy?"

"Og!" shouted Willy.

"What kind of dog?"

Willy made large gestures with his injured hands.

"Big dog?"

12

Willy nodded.

"And what about this big dog."

Willy shook his head and started making slashes in the air.

"More than one dog?"

"Ehss."

"How many, Willy. Two, three?"

Willy made a 'keep going' motion.

"Four?"

Willy held both hands up, palms out.

"Four big dogs?"

Willy shook his head and held up a finger.

"One big dog?"

"Ehss."

"How big were the other three?"

Willy indicated a medium size with his crippled hands.

"Where did you see them last?"

Willy pointed west with his thumb.

"How far?"

"Roh eee oh."

"If we take you to the rodeo grounds, can you show us?"

Willy nodded.

Horse opened the back door of Andy's unit, and he and Willy got in. Andy drove slowly through the soft sand and stopped the car near the bleachers. He started to get out.

"Un!" shouted Willy.

"Andy, he wants you to get your gun out before you open the door."

Andy drew his service revolver and held it up for Willy to see.

"Sho un," said Willy. "Sho un."

"He says you need your shotgun."

13

Andy released his shotgun from its holder and got out with it. He opened the back door for Horse and Willy.

It had been months since the rodeo, but when a gust of wind kicked up sand in the arena, the smell of manure with a vague undertone of hot dogs and popcorn rose into the air. The bleachers partially surrounding the arena were laid out in a horseshoe shape with stands on the south, east and west sides. The north side of the fenced oval contained the stock pens and chutes where the animals were released to be roped or bulldogged. There were also chutes where cowboys climbed onto the backs of broncos or bulls before the animals were turned loose in a cloud of whirling, dangerous and dusty mayhem.

Willy surveyed the area carefully and then motioned for Horse and Andy to follow him. He walked around the south side of the bleachers toward the steps that led up to the announcer's booth. As they walked, Horse said to Andy, "Willy lives in that booth up there when there's no rodeo."

"Don't they keep it locked?"

"Yeah. But I have the key."

"Oh."

Just below the steps, Willy stopped and pointed at the ground. Horse could see the deep impressions left by Willy's boots where he had run through the sand toward the steps. Mixed in with the boot prints were the tracks of a number of dogs. The prints of one of the dogs were huge. Willy made growling noises and snapped his teeth. He pointed at himself and then at the steps.

"The dogs were chasing you, and you ran up the steps?"

"Ehss!"

Willy growled and snapped his teeth again and mimed a running dog.

"The dogs came after you?"

Willy shook his head and held up the only remaining finger on his right hand.

"One dog came after you?"

Willy turned to the steps and began to climb. As he and Andy followed, Horse noticed Willy's frayed and faded pants were ripped just below his calf. He could see blood leaking down the back of Willy's sock.

The door to the announcing booth was nothing more than a slab of plywood hooked with crude hinges to the other slabs of plywood that formed the rectangular booth. There was a hasp for a lock and above the hasp a simple handle screwed into the wood so the makeshift door could be pulled open.

Willy pointed to the door, and Horse looked closely. There were deep scratches in the plywood. Horse was over six feet tall and the scratches were chest high on him. Beside him, Andy let out a long, low whistle.

"Man, that's a big dog."

Willy turned away and pointed at the tear in the left leg of his pants Horse had noticed as they climbed the stairs.

He growled and snapped his teeth again.

"My God! That big fella got ahold of you?" asked Andy.

Willy put the back of his hand to his forehead and grimaced.

"I'll bet it hurt!" said Horse. "Can you let me have a look at that?"

Willy pulled his pant leg up above his calf. His sock was ragged but clean, except for blood from the bite.

"That's a bad bite, Willy. I'm going to run you over to the hospital."

Willy shook his head.

"No, don't argue with me on this one, partner. This is serious."

Willy hung his head, but finally nodded agreement.

"So, Willy, you managed to get inside and close the door after the big dog bit you?"

Willy growled and made barking noises.

"But the dog wouldn't go away.

I see. How long do you think it stayed?"

Willy pointed at Horse's watch. Horse held it up. Willy tracked halfway around the face of the watch with the finger on his right hand.

"About half an hour?"

"Ehss."

"Okay, then what did you do? Walk down to the highway?"

Willy shook his head, then held his hands behind his ears and turned his head from side to side.

"You listened for the dogs for a while before you climbed down.

How long?"

Horse held up his watch again.

Willy traced all the way around the watch.

"So, this all started about sunrise. Where were you when you first saw the dogs?"

Willy gestured toward an area a few yards from the bottom of the steps.

"Okay, Willy. Let's get you over to the hospital.

Andy, go back to the office and go through the logs with Fred. We've had calls lately about people losing pets in town. We always lose a few to coyotes, but there have been more than usual lately.

Stick around until I get back. I want to talk this through with you."

"I'll get right on it, Lieutenant."

Andy turned to Willy. "I'm sorry you got bit, Willy. And I'm sorry I couldn't understand you."

Willy shrugged and smiled.

The three men went down the steps and headed for Andy's car. Horse noticed that Willy never stopped looking around as they walked. It was obvious the dog attack had left him badly rattled.

Andy drove Horse and Willy back to Horse's unit.

Horse opened the passenger side door so Willy could sit in the front seat with him. He backed onto the shoulder of 66 and left enough room for Andy to back out in front of him.

Horse stayed in the room while the doctor examined the bite on Willy's leg. The flesh around the bite marks was badly lacerated. Dr. Hayden flushed the area with alcohol and antiseptic, sutured two of the tears and covered the others with butterfly bandages. Through it all, Willy never winced or made a sound.

"Any idea how long it's been since Willy had a tetanus shot?"

"Can you remember, Willy?"

"Ah me."

"In the army."

"You mean Willy's a veteran?"

16

"That's where he got all the injuries."

"Well, if it's been that long, we'd better take care of that.

And another thing. You're going to have to quarantine the dog that bit him to make sure it's not rabid."

"I think it's a feral dog, probably part of a pack. We'll try to find it."

"When you do you're going to have to kill it and take it over to Horace Creighton. He'll remove the head, get it under refrigeration, and send it to San Bernardino County Veterinary Public Health for testing.

"How long does it take to get results back from them?"

"They'll phone you with the information the day after they get the head.

If you don't find it and get test results before five days from now, we're going to have to start Willy on a series of rabies shots."

"I've heard those are painful."

"Excruciating would be a better word."

"Okay, I'll find it."

"By the way, who's paying for this?"

"Put it on the county tab."

"How do I describe Willy?"

"Willy Gibson. Five foot seven, brown hair, gray eyes, one hundred and thirty pounds. No known address. Dog attack victim."

"Can you wait here with Willy a minute?"

"I'm his ride."

Dr. Hayden left the examining room. It was only a minute or two before a nurse came in.

"Morning, Betty."

"Morning, Horse. Can you roll up Willy's sleeve for me?"

When Horse complied, the nurse swabbed Willy's upper arm with alcohol and gave him the injection. She covered the area with a bandage. Once again, Willy showed no reaction.

17

When they were walking toward the parking lot, Horse asked, "Did you follow all that, Willy?"

"Ehss."

"Now look. Don't worry too much about those shots just yet. I'm going to find that dog, okay?"

Willy smiled and made a "thumbs up" gesture with his only thumb.

"In the meantime, let's get you out of that announcer's booth. It's not safe out there with those dogs around."

Willy looked worried.

"It's okay, Willy. I've got a better place in mind."

Horse left the hospital parking lot and merged with the eastbound traffic on Broadway, which was both the main street in Smoke Tree and Highway 66 as it passed through town.

Willy had a puzzled look.

Horse drove through town to the Highway 66/Highway 95 split and took Highway 95 south. After a few miles, he turned onto a dirt road that led to the County of San Bernardino landfill. He was still in sight of the highway when he stopped at a flat-roofed, squat, square building made of cinder block and discarded materials.

"Willy, do you remember Sixto Morales?"

Willy twisted his lips in disgust.

"Ehss."

"Yeah, a lot of people felt like that."

Sixto was shot in the fall of last year after robbing a liquor store in Bullhead. He died two days later at the House of Three Murders out in the river bottom. Sixto's mom, Lucinda, the woman people in Smoke Tree called 'Landfill Lucy,' lived in this building. Mrs. Morales went up to Bullhead one day and killed the man who shot her son. She's serving life in prison over in Arizona, so nobody is using this place, and it doesn't belong to anyone."

Willy held up his hands, palms up.

"I'm telling you this because I want you to move in here. Those dogs might come back to where you were before. I don't want you to get hurt again. Take a look inside. The door is open."

Willy got out of the car and walked to the makeshift door. He pulled it open with his thumb and middle finger and peered inside.

He turned around and smiled at Horse.

"We'll get your stuff from the booth and bring it out here."

Willy went inside the shack.

Horse reversed his unit, made a 'K' turn and headed back to the highway.

When Horse got back to the station, Andy was waiting for him.

"I've got the information you wanted."

Horse led him into his office.

"Good. Let me get set up here."

He got a piece of white poster board and propped it on an easel. He drew an arrow for north in the upper right hand corner and put a circle in the middle of the paper. He labeled it "rodeo grounds".

"I took Willy to the hospital. Doc Hayden cleaned and stitched the bite. It was a lot worse than I thought it was when Willy showed it to us. Doc told me if we couldn't find the dog that bit Willy for testing within a couple of days, Doc's going to have to start him on rabies shots. Big needle in the stomach, a series of shots over days. We've got to find that dog.

What did you find out about the missing pet incidents?"

"They're mostly from along the edge of the big wash coming down from Eagle Pass."

"Which streets?"

"Mesquite, Acacia, Cottonwood, Cactus Flower and all the housing tract streets that dead end into Edge Street."

Horse stood up and drew a curving line on the poster board that represented the north side of town. He drew short lines representing the streets.

"Tell me about the pets."

"Mostly cats and small dogs. Even a couple of big dogs that were badly injured but managed to make it home."

"Nothing from the south side of town?"

19

"Nossir."

"Good. That narrows the search.

I put Willy up in the shack Lucinda Morales was living in. Maybe he'll be safe there for a while.

So, the dogs are running the wash along the northweswt edge of town."

"And the pack that chased Willy killed those missing animals."

"Bet on it."

"You don't think they might be town dogs?"

"No, these are feral," said Horse. "And more than that, recently feral. We haven't been getting these reports for long. So, what we have is a few dogs that belonged to someone who has turned them loose. And dogs that have recently gone feral aren't hunters. They raid garbage cans and pick off small animals at the edge of town because if they moved into the open desert they'd starve to death."

"How do we find them?"

"Track them."

"That won't be easy."

"Not for you or me it wouldn't. I can track people, but tracking dogs over sandy, rocky ground? Way beyond my skills. But I know someone who can do it.

Remember Chemehuevi Joe?"

"You mean the guy who officially wasn't there when we caught Harvey Vickers last year?"

"Yep. Joe can track anything that doesn't fly or swim.

I'll call Keith Halverson at Smoke Tree Hardware. He'll know if Joe is doing carpentry work here in town. If he isn't, I'll head out his way and see if I can find him."

"Want me to come along?"

"No. I'd like you to run back out to the rodeo grounds and pick up Willy's stuff from the announcing booth. Everything he owns will be in a duffle bag. I left the door unlocked, so snap the padlock when you're done. Take the bag out to Lucinda's shack.

Willy's not used to you yet. Just put it outside the door and holler at him. Tell him who you are and what you've done. Once you've done him a favor, he'll feel like he knows you."

Fifteen minutes later, he knew Joe wasn't working anywhere in Smoke Tree. Horse left the office and headed south on 95. Just beyond the tiny Smoke Tree Airport that was just a hangar, a windsock and a runway graded out of the desert, Horse turned onto a dirt road.

The road cut west and led to the foothills of the Sacramento Mountains where Horse lived with his wife, Esperanza. He had built their simple, small, home of stuccoed cinder block topped with a sloped, tarpaper and white-rock roof on five acres bought for next to nothing in 1954.

As the house came into view, he could see the long row of cottonwood trees he had planted on the north side of the property as a windbreak for the relentless winds of January, February and March. Behind the house was a substantial corral that took up one of the acres. It was built of railroad ties cemented into the ground and connected by heavy pipes set into holes cored through the ties. Caps screwed onto the end of the threaded pipes held them in place. Cheaper than a fancy, metal fence, but just as substantial.

Just below the corral was his tack room. It was built of eight-foot-long, eight-inch-square railroad ties. Working with the two hundred pound ties had not been easy, but Horse sometimes liked to think that long after the town of Smoke Tree had disappeared into the sands of the Mojave Desert, his tack room would still be standing.

As he came up the whitewashed-rock-lined driveway, he could see his palomino gelding Canyon and his wife's Roan mare Mariposa looking his way. The bougainvilleas on the big trellises he had built on the north and south sides of the house were blooming red and purple. A rain bird was spraying his front lawn. It was deep green in the morning sun. He was one of the few people in Smoke Tree who planted winter rye when his Bermuda grass went dormant each November. He could see smoke from the fireplace being pushed to the west in the wind typical of December on the Mojave.

He parked his cruiser behind two other vehicles: his wife's '57 Chevy Bel Air and his '55 Chevy pickup. As he got out and walked around to the back door to avoid the sprinkler, he smelled sweet smoke from a mesquite wood fire.

When he opened the back door, his wife smiled the smile that never failed to gladden his heart. Esperanza had been born a Narvarro, and there was much more Spanish blood in her family than in his, a fact her mother, Esmeralda, had always been quick to point out to anyone she talked to, no matter how many times they had heard it before. In fact, her mother had tried to persuade Esperanza not to marry Horse, claiming he was far too dark. A light brown in comparison to Horse's deep mahogany, Esperanza was a small, slim but surprisingly strong woman with long black hair that dropped halfway to her waist. Her hazel eyes were the color of sandstone flecked with mica. Her teeth were so white they sparkled when she spoke. And she placed no credence at all in her mother's talk of "Spanish blood".

"I'm a Mexican," she always said. "Just like my Carlos."

Esperanza's mother was bitterly disappointed when her daughter married "that Mestizo". Esperanza's father, who looked much more Spanish than his wife, thought Carlos Caballo was a wonderful young man. But when Umberto Navarro died of cancer two years after Horse and Esperanza were married, Esmeralda began to become more Spanish by the day. She was soon one hundred percent Spanish with none of that inferior "Indio" blood at all. When people who had known her and her husband for years began to laugh at her claims, she moved to Santa Fe to live with her sister. Contact between mother and daughter now consisted almost entirely of Christmas and birthday cards.

Esperanza walked over and hugged him.

"You're home early, *Mi Carino.*"

"Not to stay, *querida*. I'm just here to change into my hunting boots."

She stepped back, the smile disappearing.

"I don't like the sound of that. Don't tell me you're chasing bad guys across the desert again."

"No. No bad guys this time.

I've got to find Chemehuevi Joe."

Esperanza frowned.

"The last time you were with Joe, someone tried to shoot you."

"Not this time. I promise."

"Why do you have to find Joe?"

"A wild dog bit Willy Gibson earlier this morning. A big dog. Part of a pack."

22

"Oh, that poor man. As if his life weren't hard enough."

"It was a nasty bite, but that's not the worst part. If we can't find that dog, Willy will have to have rabies shots."

"*Dios mios*. Those hurt. After he gets the first one, you'll have to lock him up or you'll never find him for the rest of the series."

"I think we sometimes underestimate Willy. I don't think he's afraid of pain. I just watched Doc Hayden clean the bite, disinfect it with iodine and stitch it up. Willy never made a sound.

But I certainly don't want to have him go through the agony of those shots. That's why I've got to find Joe. We're going to track the dogs. I'm a decent tracker, but nothing like him. I'd never be able to track the pack over what may be rocky ground. Only Joe can do that."

Horse took Esperanza into his arms for another hug and then turned and went into the bedroom. He came out in his stocking feet, carrying his hunting boots. He walked out to the back porch and sat down on the steps to put them on. Esperanza came out and sat beside him, draping her arm over his shoulders and leaning against him.

"Joe lives way back in the hills off the highway, doesn't he?"

"Yes. No roads to his place. That's the way he likes it."

"Are you going to ride Canyon?"

"No. Take longer to hitch up the trailer, get him in and out and then saddled up than it will for me to drive out there and walk it. Besides, it's a great day for a hike."

Esperanza laughed.

"Something tells me there's paperwork on your desk!"

"Caught me! But what a great excuse."

Horse stood up and started around the house. Esperanza came with him. He stopped beside his cruiser and looked out at the Black Mountains to the east and the Needles down the Colorado River to the south.

"I never get tired of looking at this."

They hugged again.

"You have water?"

"Canteen in the trunk."

Horse got in his unit and backed down the driveway to the place where he had created a turnout. Before he pulled in to turn around, he looked back to the house. The woman he loved was standing in the driveway, waving at him. It made him smile.

He waved back, drove down the dirt road and turned right onto Highway 95. When he passed five mile road, he keyed his mike twice.

"Dispatch."

"Fred, I'm just about to turn up the hill toward the Southern Cal Gas compressor station. When I get over Monument Pass, I'll be out of radio range. Hand any emergencies to Andy. Over."

"Roger. Anything else?"

"That's it. I'm clear."

CHAPTER 2

FINDING CHEMEHUEVI JOE

As Horse climbed through the Pass, he saw coyote gourd on both sides of the road. The bitter melons were yellow this time of year, but the leaves on the vines were still green. The bulk of Whale Mountain loomed on the south, and the dwindling foothills of the southernmost tip of the Sacramento Mountains lay to the northwest. As he left the pass, the highway made a long, sweeping left and headed directly south. There was no traffic on the road. The air coming through the vents was cold and seemed to carry a hint of rain, although the blue sky was cloudless from horizon to horizon. Creosote, white bursage, bayonet yucca and brittlebush lined the road beyond the shoulders. The spiky dried stems of last spring's flowers rose above the bluish-gray leaves of the brittlebush.

The road straightened. Horse could see the outline of the Stepladder Mountains to the southwest. The Chemehuevi Mountains rose on the east. Mountains where Wyatt Earp and his wife Josephine "Sadie" Earp had prospected for gold and silver while spending their winters in a small cottage in Vidal, California, throughout the 1920s. Mountains the Chemehuevi had roamed for centuries before the Spanish, then the Mexicans and then the Earps showed up, but named, as so many places in the United States are named, for something that is no longer there. Because only one Chemehuevi still lived in those mountains: the elusive, solitary and self-sufficient Joe Medrano.

Near Snaggletooth Mountain, Horse turned off the highway onto the barely discernible hint of a dirt road straggling off to the west. When his Ford Interceptor was shielded from view by travelers on the highway, he shut off the engine. He got out and locked his shotgun in the trunk. He could hear the manifolds of the cooling engine pinging in the cold air. He walked back the way he had driven, his canteen bumping against his left hip, his holstered .357 riding below his right. He reached Highway 95 and crossed it, then set off to the east.

It was indeed a beautiful day for a walk through the desert hills. The sky was azure overhead, and a soft, cool breeze out of the west followed him like a friendly phantom. When he was well away from the highway, the wonderful, calming stillness of the land where the Mojave and Colorado Deserts bled into each other closed in all around him.

Three quarters of an hour later, he arrived at a fork in the wash. The Red Rock Falls trail ran off to the northeast, and Trampas Wash cut southeast. He struck off through the rock, gravel-and-sand-filled Trampas Wash that would take him near Joe Medrano's place on the side of the mountains, just shy of the tallest peak high above the Colorado River and Lake Havasu. There were no footprints in the wash. The only sounds were the steady crunch of his boots in the gravel, the occasional "*cha cha cha cha*" of a cactus wren and the slow, squeaky notes from a male phainopepla, avid consumer of mistletoe berries and distant cousin of the northern mockingbird. The song morphed into descending, melodic trills and ended in a final rising note. The bird seemed to be keeping Horse company. As its inky form flitted through the wash ahead of him, he could see the white spots under its wings when it flared to land on a shrub.

Despite the coolness of the late fall day, as he moved farther to the southwest and the land began to rise, Horse started to sweat. He stopped and removed his hat and mopped his forehead with his bandana. He tied the bandana around his head, put his hat back on, and took a long drink of the well water in his canteen. Then he set off again. The wash became narrower and the sides steeper. Rocks and medium sized boulders crowded the bottom and made the going more difficult, as did the catclaw acacia, known locally as "wait-a-minute bush".

The Chemehuevi Mountains are an unusual, horseshoe shaped range. The open-ended, west to east trending sides of the horseshoe cradle a broad, handsome canyon on the east side of the mountains that slopes down to Devil's Elbow on the Colorado River below Topock. Horse was climbing toward the west-facing back of the horseshoe. When he reached the point where the rotted, eroded granite and volcanic rock loomed above him, he turned to the south and began to climb out of the steep-sided wash.

When he topped out, he was more winded than he expected to be. He resolved to get back to running the foothills of the Sacramento Mountains a few evenings each week. As he sat down on a rock to catch his breath, he caught the glint of a jet high above him in the vast, overarching emptiness of blue sky. Probably a passenger plane making its way along the highway in the sky from Los Angeles to Phoenix. As he shaded his eyes and stared at it, the sound of its engine caught up with the speeding plane: a reminder of the modern world reaching the ears of a man sitting on a hillside as ancient as forever.

Horse turned away from the jet and took in the broad view to the west. The sun had passed its zenith and was beginning to tilt. The barely-visible, tiny remaining sliver of the old moon was just about to drop below the Old Woman Mountains in the distance. Beyond them and farther to the north, Horse could see the Granite Mountains. He turned his head to look southwest beyond the Stepladders. He loved this desert country. Almost as much as his love for Esperanza, this rugged landscape completed his life.

As he sat on the rock, high above Trampas, Horse realized his life was so good that it scared him sometimes. There had been many times in Korea when he thought he would be killed before the sun went down. But he had survived somehow, while so many of the guys in his unit hadn't. Now he wondered how one man could be so lucky in a world filled with sickness, hunger, pain, injustice and unhappiness.

He knew better than to think of his life as a reward for any dues he might have paid. There were men whose lives had been much harder who had paid much more. Good men whose lives were forfeit in Korea. And men like Willy Gibson who returned home from war terribly injured. Horse didn't want to get complacent in his happiness. Someone might decide to more equitably balance the books. He took one more drink from his canteen and got to his feet and resumed his climb.

Thirty minutes later, he could see Joe Medrano's turquoise door farther up the hill. The last time he had seen that door, Harvey Vickers was in a prone position up there trying to kill Horse and Deputy Chesney with a .30-06 stolen from Joe's place. In response, Horse and Andy had set out to flank and triangulate the fugitive. Horse wanted to bring Vickers in. He had hoped not to have to kill or wound the man, but that was looking like the most likely outcome. While they were taking fire as they leapfrogged up the hill, tough, wiry and deadly Joe Medrano, armed with nothing more than a skinning knife, had circled silently behind the man, put the knife to his throat and disarmed him.

As Horse crested the small rise twenty five yards in front of Joe's oddly-shaped, scrap lumber home, he stopped and called out.

"Joe! It's Horse. You around?"

When his voice echoed off the mountainside, the cactus wrens ceased their calls. All he could hear was his own breathing and the wind blowing up the hill behind him.

He started walking again, the sounds of his boots louder in the new stillness. As he drew closer, he saw that Joe's door was ajar. A hasp and eye that hadn't been there the previous year had been screwed into the door and doorjamb. A padlock dangled from the eye. Horse rapped on the heavy door, and it slowly swung against the jamb. He could have pulled the door open and looked inside, but that didn't feel right. Instead, he lowered himself to the ground and leaned back against the wall next to the door. It wasn't long before the bird calls resumed on the mountainside.

He looked out over the terrain below him. High above the desert floor, two golden eagles soared effortlessly, riding a thermal. Suddenly, one of them folded its wings and plummeted toward earth. In a few moments, it was out of sight. The other eagle began to descend in lazy circles. The first one must have hit a rabbit or some other animal because it wasn't long before buzzards were spiraling, hoping the eagles would leave something behind. Even as he watched, more of the big birds showed up.

Where had they come from? Horse had not seen a single buzzard in the sky during his hike. They must have been high in the sky, their incredible vision scissoring the desert into strips like military intelligence specialists going over reconnaissance photos with magnifying glasses. Now they were above the eagles, their dihedral wings outstretched, the fingerlike tips of their outer primaries making small, incremental adjustments to the breeze as they watched patiently what was happening far below.

Because he had been up since before dawn, as he relaxed his eyes grew heavy. When he let them slide closed, he could see the red of the sun against his eyelids. He tilted his Stetson forward. He could smell sweat from the hatband. He listened to the world around him as he waited. Time passed as he relaxed against the wall, thinking of earth and rock and sky. When he realized the wrens had stopped calling again, he opened his eyes and pushed his Stetson back. Joe Medrano was in front of him, sitting flat on his heels, his elbows draped over his knees.

"Hello, Joe. Last time I opened my eyes to find you next to me you had taken my gun."

"Nighttime. Afraid you'd wake up, shoot me."

"How'd you know I wasn't sleeping just now?"

"Breathing different.

Haven't seen you since you brought my rifle back."

"I came out because I need your help with something."

"Okay."

Horse explained what had happened to Willy earlier in the day and about the dogs and why he had to find the big one.

"Willy okay?"

"Yes."

"Good. Like Willy. Doesn't talk much."

"I like him too, and I don't want him to have to get those shots. I need your help to track those dogs. I can't do it."

"Killing pets on the edge of that wash?"

"That's right. We pulled the reports. Lots of cats and small dogs missing. We know coyotes sometimes get one or two, but this is more than that."

Joe nodded.

"Domestic dogs turned loose, gone wild. Can't hunt like cats. Cats don't forget how to hunt."

"That's what I think. They'll keep coming back to the edge of town."

"Have to."

"For now, they're just after pets. But what if young kids go out in the wash to play? The dogs might go after them."

"Might."

"Can you track them?"

"Sure."

"When?"

"Tomorrow morning.

Come in. Have to get some stuff."

He rose to his feet in one fluid, effortless motion and pulled the door open.

Horse got up and followed Joe inside. He had never been in Joe's place before. There was a fire ring just inside the door. The ceiling above the ring was made of woven ocotillo to allow smoke to escape. He stepped around the ring and entered a room Joe had excavated out of the mountainside. There were two large containers of water and three covered, clay bowls on a handmade table. The solid rock above the table had been blackened by soot from oil lamps. There was one chair in front of the table. Against the back wall was an army surplus cot covered by a Navajo blanket. There was no pillow. Next to the cot were two big oil lamps with tall chimneys, the kind that used to swing with the motion of freight trains inside cabooses back in the days of steam engines.

Above the cot was a rifle rack made of wooden dowels set into a varnished piece of two by six. The rack was attached to the wall by bolts drilled into the solid rock. Resting on the dowels was a scoped rifle with an engraved and knurled stock. A hand-tooled leather sling was attached to the stock.

Horse walked over to take a closer look at the beautiful blanket. He had never seen one quite like it. While he was admiring it, he noticed a small photograph lying in the center. It was a picture of a Japanese woman. A picture he had seen before. A picture he thought he may have once held in his hands.

He wished he hadn't seen it.

He turned and walked back to the door to wait for Joe.

Joe walked to the table. He filled a small canteen from one of the of the water containers.

"Jerky?"

"Thanks. Didn't have time for lunch today."

"Venison or jackrabbit?"

"Venison, thanks.

So, you got your burro deer this fall."

"Scope you had put on my rifle? Couldn't miss."

Joe took the covers off two of the bowls. He handed several pieces of jerky from one of the bowls to Horse. He put more pieces into a leather pouch slung over his shoulder.

The two men went outside. Joe closed the door and locked the padlock in place

"Never used to lock this place before Vickers stole my gun. Still makes me mad."

They set off down the steep mountainside, Horse chewing a piece of jerky.

A half hour later, they were in Trampas wash. Ocotillo and barrel cactus lined the hills above the wash. The sun was not far above the horizon. The distant mountains were beginning to turn shades of purple and slate-blue. The air was chilled.

"Joe, I'm going to ask you some questions. You don't have to answer them if you don't want to."

"Okay."

"There was a picture on your cot."

"Japanese woman."

"I've seen it before. Mind telling me where you got it?"

"From guys don't need it anymore."

"Do you know where the girl in the picture is?"

"Gone."

"Know where?"

"Nope."

"Will she be coming back?"

"Nope."

"Reason I ask, two men came to Smoke Tree looking for her. Mafia guys. Killers. Had that picture."

"Didn't work out for them."

"Do you know where they are?"

"Know they won't be back."

"Want to tell me what happened to them?"

"Nope."

"Let me ask you this. Did the woman in the picture have something that belonged to those Mafia people?"

"Did."

"Knowing these guys, I assume it was money."

"Was."

"She still have it?"

"Last I knew."

The two men continued down the wash. It was broader now. The boulders had given way to desert willow and here and there a smoke tree.

They walked quite a bit farther before Horse spoke again.

"Heard you were doing some work for John Stonebridge up at the Box S last summer."

"That's right."

"Does John know where those two guys are?"

"Nope."

"Does John know where the woman is?"

"Nope."

"Did he ever?"

"Should've. Was living in his house."

They walked on in the remaining sunlight.

"Joe, any chance you were in Albuquerque last summer?"

"Was."

"I'm asking because this mob guy who runs the Serengeti Casino in Vegas keeps calling me. Says the car those two were driving turned up in the parking lot at the airport in Albuquerque last August, but nobody there saw the guys, and now nobody can find them."

"Why call you?"

"Because I arrested them on a 'carrying-concealed-without-a-permit' charge. That's the day I saw the picture. I had them in my jail for a while before they got bailed out. And by the way, that means not only are those Vegas people out whatever the girl had, they're also out the bail money they put up to get the guys out of jail. They didn't show up for their court date.

Those people in Vegas are heavy hitters, Joe. And they're pissed."

They walked for another quarter mile, the soft wind dying when the sun dropped behind the horizon.

"Mind telling me where you went after you left Albuquerque?"

"Big Res a few days."

"Visiting?"

"Woman up there I knew once, long ago."

"She have a name?"

"Used to call her Turquoise Girl."

Horse thought about that for a while.

"Turquoise like your door?"

Joe didn't answer, but Horse thought for a minute he had seen a smile flicker across Joe Medrano's face. But it might have been a trick of the fading light.

When they got back to Horse's unit, it was completely dark and windless. There was no moon, but the night sky was spangled with stars. They got in the car and headed for Smoke Tree.

"Where's Willy?"

"He's staying at the place Lucinda Morales had out at the dump."

"Like to talk to him about the dogs."

"Tomorrow?"

"Now be better."

Dropping out of Monument Pass, Horse pulled his mike off the hook and keyed it twice.

"Dispatch."

"Back in range. Anything come up Andy couldn't handle? Over."

"No emergencies. Over."

"I'm clear."

Horse turned off the highway and drove up the dirt road to the county landfill. He pulled up beside the little shack next to the road He left the engine running and the headlights on when he got out of the car. Joe got out and walked into the light. In a few minutes, Willy pushed open the door and looked outside.

"Orse!" he said.

"Willy."

"Zhoe!"

"Willy."

"Willy, Joe wants to talk to you about those dogs."

"Oh ay."

Joe turned to Horse.

"Meet you out at the rodeo grounds at sunrise."

"Why don't you come home and stay at our place? Esperanza would be glad to see you."

"Things to do."

Horse had learned there was no point in arguing with Joe Medrano. He just remained silent and then did whatever he had decided to do before you argued with him. Horse got back in his unit and turned around.

As his headlights swept over the two men, Joe was handing Willy a piece of jerky.

Chapter 3

HORSE AND JOE ON THE TRAIL

The following morning as the sun cleared the rim of the Black Mountains, Horse pulled off Highway 66 and drove up the sandy road to the rodeo grounds. When he pulled in behind the bleachers and got out, a voice not much louder than a whisper called down from above.

"Morning."

He looked up at the landing at the top of the steps that led to the announcing booth. As he walked toward the steps, he noticed dripping blood that had pooled on the ground below the landing. Bluebottle flies were all over the blood.

He hurried up the stairs.

Joe was squatting on his heels at the top of the landing. He was petting the head of a huge dog that was stretched out on the planks beside him.

The dog was dead.

"What happened?"

"Talked to Willy. Walked down here before first light. False dawn, dogs came down the wash."

"Where were you?"

"Bottom of the stairs, shirt wrapped around my left arm. Piece of jerky in my pocket. Knife out. Ran up the stairs. Big one here came after me. Others didn't. I got to the top first, turned around. Jumped for me. Got my arm in front of him. Hit it hard. Almost knocked me down."

35

Joe paused.

"Cut his throat."

It was the most words in a row Horse had ever heard from Joe Medrano.

He was bare-chested in the morning chill. His flannel shirt was hanging from the railing above the landing. His Levi's were splattered with blood.

He continued to pet the dog's head.

"Someone real mean to this dog. Look."

Horse stepped closer. There were scars all over the dog's ears and on its muzzle and around its eyes.

"Dog was whipped with a chain. Lots of times."

"Looks like it."

"Should be shot."

"You okay?"

"Yes."

"Where are the other dogs?"

"Whined and circled. Yelled at them. Didn't know what to do without the big one. Ran up the wash."

"You knew you were going to do this right after I told you about what happened to Willy, didn't you."

"Mostly. Wanted to talk to Willy first. Find out why this dog chased him."

"Lord, I never thought to ask him that. What did you learn?"

"Had a Slim Jim. Dog smelled it. Dog was starving. Other dogs not bold enough to go after a human. Not yet."

"Hell, Joe. I should have been up here with a rifle."

Joe shook his head

"Knew they'd come in bad light. Move too fast to track with a scope in this close. Might have missed with iron sights, or just wounded him. Dog would have suffered. My way, dead before he hit the boards."

"What if it hadn't worked? You could've been badly hurt."

Joe shrugged.

"Fair fight. Dog had a chance."

Horse leaned back against the railing

"Man, that's a big dog."

"Yeah."

"Some kind of mix."

"Some German shepherd, some bull mastiff, some boxer maybe. Getting skinny, though. Been full strength, might have turned out different."

"How big were the other dogs?"

"Medium. Mixes."

"Well, thanks to you the urgent part is already done. We have the dog we need for testing. Do you want to track those other dogs another time?"

"No. Do it today."

"Okay. I've got a body bag in the trunk. Be the first time I ever put a dog in one.

Then again, this dog is as big as some people."

Fifteen minutes later, they had zipped the animal up inside the bag and carried it to the cruiser. Horse estimated the dog weighed more than a hundred pounds. The sun was higher in the desert sky as they lifted it into the trunk. Joe had wiped the blood off his torso and put his shirt on.

"Gotta get this big fellow over to the vet."

They drove to Horace Creighton's veterinary office. It wasn't open yet. Horace and his wife lived in a small house behind the clinic. Horse walked around and knocked on the door.

Celine Creighton opened the door.

"Sorry to bother you so early, Mrs. Creighton, but I have to see Horace. Is he available?"

"He is. I'll get him. Come on in."

"I've got someone in the car with me. We'll wait out front."

In a few minutes, Horace Creighton came around the corner. A tall, heavy man with kind, blue eyes and sandy hair, he was dressed in his usual outfit of khaki pants and shirt.

"Mornin', Horse."

"Morning, Horace.

Horace, this is Joe Medrano."

"Joe," said Horace.

Joe nodded his head.

"What do you need?"

"I've got a dog we need to have sent to the lab in San Bernardino for testing. Need to make sure it didn't have rabies."

While Horace opened the door to the clinic and turned on the lights, Horse and Joe got the body bag out of the trunk and carried it inside.

The vet had them remove the dog from the bag and put it on the table. While they did that, Horse explained why testing for rabies was urgent. Horace said he would remove the head and have it on the way to San Bernardino before the day was over.

"Will they report the results to you?"

"Sure. I've worked with them before."

"Please call me as soon as you know anything."

"Will do."

"And send the bill to my office. Thanks again for taking care of this. I really want to avoid those shots for Willy."

"Anytime, Horse."

Five minutes later they were back on Broadway.

"Joe, you want to get some breakfast before we start?"

"Best go. Sun angle good for tracking something moving west. Shadows tell oldest from newest."

"What do you mean?"

"Edges higher on newer tracks. Makes shadows longer. Wind hasn't blown the ridges off. Will soon. Much later, no difference."

When they reached the rodeo grounds, Horse and Joe set off into the broad mouth of the sand-and-gravel-filled wash. This was classic low desert. The wash and the hillsides above it were dominated by widely spaced creosote interspersed with white bursage, some match weed, and an occasional cheesebush. Here and there a solitary gravel ghost appeared, unimpressive without the white flowers that gave the plant its name when the blossoms seemed to float above the ground in early spring. The occasional whiptail lizard skittered over the sand in front of the two men as they moved.

There were homes atop the high escarpment on the south side of the wash. Many of the residents had used the hillside as a dump. All kinds of things were strewn down the hill. The heavier objects, like old hot water heaters and discarded appliances, had tumbled all the way to the bottom and been partially buried by flash floods. Other junk, like bottles, cans, sacks of garbage, and scraps of lumber and discarded garden hoses, rested at various levels, creating a cascading *bajada* of trash. Horse saw a push mower that had been shoved down the hill and only made it a third of the way down but somehow remained upright. It looked like it was trying to mow a swath through the rocks and sand on the steep hillside. Some of the people had chosen not to litter. The bare hillsides below their properties attested to that fact. There were not as many of those.

Horse knew there was a similar escarpment above a different gully not too far from this one. The back yards of the houses on top of that one perched above the wash paralleling Jordan Street. Many of those owners had tossed the same kinds of trash from their back yards. When he was a rookie deputy, Horse had gone door to door trying to mobilize the neighbors to clean up the mess that was clearly visible from Jordan Street. Most of his efforts had met with blank stares or outright refusals. The owners who had not littered the hillside were all in favor of a joint effort. The ones who had tossed their discards saw no problem with the junk and had no interest in cleaning it up.

The owner who had dumped the most trash was a freight conductor on the Santa Fe.

"When I sit in my back yard, I can't see that stuff on the side of the hill," he told Horse.

"That's true," said Horse. "But people driving down Jordan Street hill can."

"If it bothers them, they should damn well clean it up."

And he had slammed the door in Horse's face.

Horse and Joe moved at a steady pace. Joe had no problem picking up the tracks. It was obvious the dogs had travelled through the wash many times. Horse and Joe were well over halfway to Eagle Pass when the tracks veered out of the wash and up the side of a low hill. Horse was amazed Joe had noticed the change in direction. Horse had missed it completely.

On top of the hill they found a stretch of desert pavement, a broad swath of stones so tightly compacted that no plants of any kind grew among them. A pavement that ancient Roman legions shod in sandals and carrying daggers and short swords could have double-timed across without breaking either stride or formation.

Their pace slowed to a crawl. Tracking was much harder now. Joe often stopped, sometimes lying on his stomach to detect the smallest of signs. After one such stop he stood up and turned to Joe.

"Hard to track over rocks. Dogs hadn't come and gone this way lots of times, couldn't follow them."

A half hour later, Joe stopped and smiled.

"Easy now. Know where they're headed. Dogs just didn't go straight there."

"I wonder why."

"Came this far south 'cause no cactus grows in these rocks. Coyotes can run in cactus, never pick up a thorn. Not dogs. They get stuck. Feet get infected. No cactus in the wash either, but had to get out of the wash to get home."

"So, where's home?"

"Not far."

They set off at a brisk pace to the northwest. The terrain began to get steeper. It was filled with rock that had eroded and tumbled down the mountains over millions of years as water and gravity and wind had combined to eat away at the Sacramentos. Some of the larger rocks were coated with desert varnish. The white bursage that had been interspaced between the creosote gradually gave way to pink barrel cactus, bayonet yucca and stands of teddy bear cholla. Mojave spiny hopsage and Mojave indigo began to appear, brown and grayish green and hardly noticeable without their showy spring flowers.

Joe stopped and pointed farther up the hill.

"Where the dogs went."

Horse tried to make out what Joe was pointing toward. He couldn't.

"Your eyes are a lot better than mine, Joe. I don't see anything but desert where you're pointing. But I do know the only place out that way belongs to Caleb Clovis. You think these are his dogs?"

"Likely."

"So why do you think they're roaming around?"

Joe shrugged.

"Went somewhere, left no food. Be like him."

"You think he's the person who hurt that big dog."

Joe nodded. "Mean man."

"You're right about that."

They set off again, side by side. As they walked, Horse told Joe what he knew about Caleb.

"Back in '55, I was working the night shift when the dispatcher called me back to the station. When I got there, Eunice Clovis was sitting on the bench. She had walked across the desert in the middle of a cold winter night wearing nothing but slippers and a torn bathrobe. Her feet were chewed up something awful.

But her feet were the least of her injuries. Caleb had beat her up real bad. I took her to the hospital. The doc put seventeen stitches in her face and taped up her ribs. She had lost a couple teeth, and the doc was afraid she might lose an eye.

And she was shaking. At first I thought it was shock, but then I realized she was terrified. When the doctor asked about the scars on her back, she wouldn't answer. I don't think I've ever felt sorrier for a human being."

"Caleb go to jail?"

"Nope. Doc kept Eunice in the hospital overnight for observation. Had a concussion. We picked her up in the morning and took her back to the station, but she wouldn't press charges.

Caleb showed up a few hours later to report her missing. When he came in the door, Eunice got up and walked out to the truck. Sergeant Chesterfield tried to put the fear of God in Caleb, but Caleb just laughed at him.

Stuck a dirty finger in his face and said, 'What God has joined together, let no man put asunder, bub'."

Steve was about six months short of retirement. He told me later he thought seriously about shooting the bastard. But he tamped it down to save his pension. Caleb walked out the door and drove off with Eunice beside him."

"Too bad."

"That Caleb didn't go to jail or that Steve didn't shoot him?"

"The second."

"About a year later, when Caleb and Eunice were in town one Saturday, they went to the Palms. Caleb was drinking heavy and Eunice started trying to get him to go home. Said she was afraid he'd get too drunk to drive.

He wouldn't stop drinking, so she stood up to leave. Said, "I'm not riding with you. I'll walk home." Caleb got up and knocked her down. She got up and ran out the door with him after her.

Do you know Mac, the guy who owns the Palms?"

"Don't go those places."

"He's a retired gunnery sergeant with no use for a man who would hit a woman. He went out the door after Caleb. Eunice had crawled under the truck to get away. Caleb had hold of her ankle and was trying to pull her out. A bunch of guys were out there watching him, doing nothing.

Mac lit into Caleb and beat him up and down Front Street. Those who saw it said they were afraid Mac was going to kill him. Caleb managed to break loose, and he ran. Mac caught up with him down the street past the old hotel under the colonnade there. Got Caleb up against one of those green, iron poles and was just hammering him. Took five guys to pull him off.

When they had hold of Mac, Caleb wiped the blood off his face and said, 'I know you think you done somethin' here, you ignorant jarhead. But that woman's coming home with me, and when we get there, I'm gonna hit her twice for every time you hit me.'

When Caleb got back to the truck, Eunice was sitting inside staring straight ahead. They drove off."

As Horse and Joe topped the next rise, Horse could see some kind of a building on the edge of the distant *bajada*. To its north were grayish-green salt cedars. He could also make out buzzards circling in the sky.

"Uh oh. That doesn't look good."

"On the roof, too."

"Good grief, Joe, I can barely make out some kind of low building and buzzards in the sky.

"Good eyes. Father had them too."

A half hour later, they were nearing an odd structure and the group of trees. There was a truck parked out front. As they walked closer, Horse began picking up the unmistakable odor of something dead.

He looked at Joe.

"Yeah. Smell it."

"Have you seen the dogs yet?"

"Behind the place."

They drew abreast of the truck. It was an old Studebaker. There were two fifty-five-gallon drums chained in the back. Horse rapped on one of the drums. It was empty. Horse looked through the driver side window. The keys were in the ignition. Trash on the passenger side of the seat had spilled over onto the floor. A lot of the trash appeared to be empty liquor bottles and beer cans. Because of the odor of death hanging in the air, he decided it would not be wise to open the door. If there had been foul play, he might want to try to lift prints from the door handles or the steering wheel.

They walked on. Three dogs came boiling out from behind the house and ran toward them, barking and snarling. Horse drew his revolver and fired once into the air. The dogs made an abrupt left turn and circled back behind the house. The vultures that had been sitting on the roof lifted off in a black cloud, pinions creaking as they lumbered into the air.

Horse stopped and took in the primitive building. It reminded him of the huts of impoverished farmers he had seen in the Korean countryside. On the south side, there was a wall a little more than six feet high made of unpainted cinder block. The top row of blocks had been mortared in place on edge so the open ends faced sideways. A long two by six had been jammed into the opening on the block closest to the front of the house. It angled downward to meet a low wall made of stacked railroad ties that formed the north side of the glorified lean-to.

Two by fours of diminishing lengths had been cemented into the ground and nailed to the sloping two by six. Overlapping pieces of plywood, drywall, particle board, beaver board and cardboard had been fastened to the two by fours, sometimes with nails, sometimes with screws, making the completed wall look like a patchwork quilt.

A roof of corrugated metal followed the angle formed by more two by sixes as they sloped down to where they were nailed into the railroad ties. Rocks and old tires kept the desert winds from blowing the roof away.

A piece of plywood had been crudely attached by gate hinges to the two by four closest to the cinder blocks. The other side was fastened by a hook and eye arrangement of the type usually used on screen doors. There was a cabinet-style pull below the hook.

This close to the building, the odor of decay was much stronger.

Horse shouted, "Hello. Anybody home?"

He knocked on the crude door. There was no response. He went around back and knocked there with the same result. He tugged on the pull screwed into the door.

The door was apparently locked from the inside.

Horse went back around to the front. He got his pocketknife and used the blade to pop the hook from the eye. Then he wedged the blade into the seam between the door and a two by four and pulled it open without touching it. The smell of death flooded out of the door. Both men had smelled that odor many times: Joe in the South Pacific in World War Two and Horse in Korea. They stepped back a few yards.

The buzzards circled impatiently not far above them, entranced by the smell.

Horse moved forward and looked inside. Two bodies were sprawled on the dirt floor in the middle of the single room. The people had been dead a long time. One of the bodies was clad in a dress.

He stepped back again.

"Most probably Caleb and Eunice.

I'm going to have to go inside for a while. It would be best if you stayed out here. Don't want to create confusion about any clues might be in there."

Joe nodded. He took off the red bandana he was wearing around his head and handed it to Horse.

44

"Bad in there."

"Thanks."

Horse tied the bandana over his nose and mouth.

Ten minutes later, he came outside. He took off the bandana and handed it to Joe.

"They've both been shot to death. Couldn't find a gun."

Who would want to shoot these two? Caleb I could understand. Felt like shooting him myself a few times. But Eunice? And this couldn't have been a robbery. Hell, these people didn't have anything."

"Had a son."

"Clarke. Clarke Clovis. Successful musician now. Don't know how he managed to do it, coming out of this place."

"Where is he?"

"Lonnie Jenkins, the band teacher at Smoke Tree High, got him a scholarship to some fancy music school back in '56. He plays in jazz clubs all over the West Coast now. Guy can flat play a trumpet."

"Heard him. Practiced in the hills."

"Something strange here. The front door was hooked from the outside. The back door wouldn't open either. I checked it while I was in there. It was hooked from the inside.

Might take a while to figure this one out."

Horse pushed the door closed with his boot and used his knife to re-set the hook in the eyebolt. They turned and walked away from the lean-to. Before they had gone twenty yards, the buzzards were landing on the roof again.

As they walked back toward Eagle Pass Wash, Horse thought about the son who had grown up in the shack where Caleb and Eunice now lay dead. He thought about how difficult life must have been for a young boy living in such grinding poverty and seeing his mother constantly abused by his father.

Horse wondered if Clarke had also been a target of his father's anger.

Death on a Desert Hillside

CHAPTER 4

HELP FROM INSIDE

It was late afternoon by the time the two men got back to the rodeo grounds. Joe looked like he could walk another fifty miles. Horse thought he was maybe good for another two hundred yards. They got into Horse's unit and drove to the substation. When they got there, Horse asked Joe to come in with him. Joe didn't look happy about it, but he followed Horse inside to his office.

Horse got on the phone to San Bernardino while Joe wandered around the office. Horse was put through to Captain Pete Hardesty. The Captain was the detective who monitored all the active homicide investigations in the county.

"Pete Hardesty here."

"Carlos Caballo, Captain. I've got a situation out here, and I'd appreciate your help."

"Sure, Carlos. What's going on."

"A double homicide in a remote area."

"Everything out your way is remote."

"Yessir, it is.

The victims were an older guy and his wife. Lived pretty far out of town down a dirt road. Looked like they'd been dead two weeks or so. Both been shot multiple times."

"Lieutenant, it's well within your authority as station commander to handle the investigation on your own with your own people."

"I know it is, but I wanted to check with you and see if you think we should have a detective from your office out here."

"Okay, tell me everything you know about the case so far."

Horse related the events that led to the discovery of the crime. He went over the condition of the bodies and the fact that he hadn't found the murder weapon. He also explained about the door being hooked shut from the outside and the back door being secured from the inside.

When he was done, Captain Hardesty was quiet for a moment.

"You know everybody out that way. Can you think of any reason anyone would want to kill these people?"

"The man was a real S.O.B., but I can't imagine anyone wanting to kill his wife. And I sure don't think robbery was a motive. Caleb and Eunice were dirt poor."

"As you well know, these things are usually about money or sex or family. Any family members?"

"They have a son. Didn't exactly have a happy childhood. Left home to go to school. Has a career as a musician in the Los Angeles area."

"I know you're planning to check him out."

"Yessir. Soon as I can find him."

"Horse, no one knows the Eastern Mojave like you do. If you can't come up with a motive, nobody I send out there will be able to. The detectives working out of this office are used to city streets. Probably get lost if you turned them loose on the desert.

But I can sure see why this case is bothering you."

"There's too much that doesn't make sense. At first I thought it was some kind of a murder/suicide. But I couldn't find the murder weapon. So it's obvious someone killed them and left. And then there are those two locked doors.

Now, why would someone do that? I mean, you're in a panic and running away, you don't stop to latch the door. And if you're not in a panic and you're thinking about covering up the crime, you leave the door wide open. Between the coyotes and the buzzards, in a few days those bodies would have been dismembered and scattered all over the desert. Wouldn't be enough left to autopsy. I would think the killer would want that.

But latching that door protected the evidence."

Captain Hardesty was silent for so long Horse thought the connection had been broken.

"Are you still there, sir?"

"I'm checking my schedule. Give me a second."

Horse heard the sound of the receiver being set aside. While he waited, he spoke to Joe.

"Sorry to keep you waiting so long."

Joe shrugged

"Your job."

Captain Hardesty came back on the line.

"You know, Horse, I think I can shuffle a few things and take a ride. Haven't been to the far east end of the county in a while."

"That's great, Captain. I'd appreciate your expertise on this. And Esperanza and I would be glad to have you stay at our place."

"Much as I'd like to take you up on that, I'm going to have to do an out and back in one day. That's all the longer I can be gone. I'll be there early in the morning. Meet you at your office. Say about eight?"

"Looking forward to it, Captain."

"The county will pay the local mortuary to drive the bodies to San Bernardino for autopsy."

"I'll notify them we'll be delivering the bodies and have them ready to get them on the road.

I'm putting a man out there overnight, and I'll have the deputy coroner go out there with us in the morning."

"Until morning, then."

When Horse hung up, he noticed Joe had stopped wandering and come to rest in a chair.

"The guy who oversees almost all the homicide investigations in the county is coming out tomorrow."

"A friend?"

"He is. Pete Hardesty played a big part in getting me hired.

49

I've got to make another call, Joe."

"No hurry."

Horse pushed the button on his intercom.

"Fred, get me the Askew Funeral Home. Buzz me when you've got them."

"Yessir."

Horse pulled out a legal pad and was making notes when Fred let him know the mortuary was on the line. Horse made the arrangements for transport the next day and gave an estimate of what time the bodies would be delivered.

When he was finished, he buzzed the dispatcher again.

"Fred, find me a deputy who would like some overtime. Someone who's coming in for the swing shift and doesn't mind pulling a double would be good. Have him bring a sleeping bag. Tell him he's going to spend his shift and the graveyard shift at the crime scene where Caleb and Eunice Clovis were murdered."

"You got it, Lieutenant."

"And find someone scheduled for the graveyard who wants to come in early and work patrol for the swing and then his own shift."

"I'll take care of it."

While Horse was working, Joe had left the chair and begun circling the office again.

Horse got to his feet.

"I appreciate you patience, and I want to thank you for all your help. I never would've been able to follow those dogs across that desert pavement. No way."

"Anytime."

"The least San Bernardino County can do is buy you dinner. How long since you've had a big steak?"

"Venison or beef?"

Horse smiled.

"Good point. Beef."

"Few years. Place have pie?"

50

"It does."

"Peach, maybe?"

"Sometimes. And they always have a mean apple."

"Apple works."

Horse started for the door and then stopped.

"Oh Lord, forgot the most important call of all. I'd better tell Esperanza I won't be home for dinner."

The hint of a smile crossed Joe's face.

"Better."

Horse called Esperanza and let her know Joe had found the dog that bit Willy.

"We tracked the other dogs to the Clovis place. Caleb and Eunice were inside. They had been murdered."

"That's terrible."

"Tell you all about it when I get home."

He explained he was taking Joe out for a steak to thank him for his help.

"You actually talked Joe Medrano into going to a restaurant?"

"Mentioned there might be peach pie there."

Esperanza laughed.

"I can see how that might do it."

"After Joe and I eat, I'm going to drive a deputy out to the place to keep watch overnight. Probably not necessary, but best to do things by the book. Pete Hardesty's coming out in the morning to have a look-see."

"You be careful out there. *Tú eres el amor de mi vida, ya sabes.*"

"*Y tu a mi.*"

He said goodbye. He and Joe walked out of his office and stopped at the dispatcher's desk.

"Fred, this is Joe Medrano."

"Pleased to meet you Mr. Medrano."

Joe nodded

51

"When you find a deputy, have him come in soonest and get the pickup ready to go. Have him make sure it's full of gas.

Joe and I are going for a bite to eat, so I'll be off the air for a while. If we have a real emergency, call me at Bob's Broiler."

As the two men drove through town, the peculiar light of the late autumn desert twilight was leaking out of the sky. The melancholy fall light mixed with the lights of businesses lining 66 and the unbroken stream of oncoming headlights to create a patina reminiscent of an impressionist painting.

On the north end of Smoke Tree, they turned in at Bob's Broiler. While it was the fanciest and most expensive restaurant in town, it still had a dirt parking lot. They sat in the cruiser for a few minutes, letting the dust settle before they got out.

The restaurant had white table cloths that were actually changed after only two or three uses, plus linen napkins and crystal water glasses. It was where people from Smoke tree celebrated special occasions like anniversaries and where high school boys took their dates on prom night.

In deference to the high standards of the place, Horse took off his Stetson before the hostess led them to a table in the back corner. At five o'clock, the dining room was not yet full, but Horse and Joe turned the few heads that were there: Horse with his uniform and sidearm and Joe with his blood-encrusted Levi's, long, black hair and red bandana. Conversations stopped and didn't start up again until Horse and Joe were seated. They ordered their steaks and sat without speaking until their food came. Both men were comfortable with the long silence.

When they finished their steaks, the waitress delivered the disappointing news: there was no peach pie. Joe had to settle for apple with ice cream for dessert. He must have liked it because he ordered a second piece. When he was finished, they had a final cup of coffee.

All the tables were full by the time they left, and the dining room fell silent again as Horse and Joe threaded their way through the tables. Many of the customers nodded to Horse, but he saw no indication any of them knew Joe Medrano. He wondered what they would think if they knew Joe had somehow managed to eliminate two button men from the Mafia.

Night had fallen when they drove back through town. Horse stopped at the market and bought eight cans of dog food and a cheap can opener and then continued on to the substation. Stuart Atkins was already there. He climbed out of the department truck to meet them. He shielded his eyes until Horse cut his headlights. Stuart continued to fan dust out of his face with his Stetson as the two men got out of Horse's unit and walked up to him.

"Evening, Lieutenant."

"Evening, Stuart. This is Joe Medrano. He tracked the dogs that have been attacking pets along the wash on the northwest edge of town. He also killed the big dog that bit Willy Gibson yesterday."

"Shot it?"

"No. Killed it with a knife."

Stuart put out his hand.

"Pleased to meet you, Mr. Medrano."

Joe touched the deputy's hand briefly.

"Same."

"I'll be ready to go in a while. I'm going to run Joe out to his place."

"Rather walk," said Joe. "Honor a spirit."

"You sure? That's a long walk this time of night."

"Same as day."

Horse laughed.

"Got me there.

And Joe? Thanks again."

"Sure. Still owe you for that gun."

"No you don't, Joe. You squared that long before I brought it to you."

Joe nodded and turned away from the two men, heading south into the desert night. Within moments the darkness had swallowed him.

Horse and Stuart walked to the pickup.

"I'll drive. A little tricky finding the road we need."

They drove back into town and then turned off Broadway and climbed to the top of Jordan Street hill. They drove through the town's only subdivisions and turned left on Desert and right on Monte Vista. A few of the houses had Christmas trees in the windows and Christmas lights edging the roofs. They turned left onto the last street on the west side of town. When Edge

Street ended, Horse drove the pickup over the berm and onto the dirt road that led to Eagle Pass.

Three quarters of the way to the pass, he turned onto a rough track that paralleled the foothills of the Sacramentos. With the truck in compound low, they ground along in and out of drainages for a long time until their headlights revealed the old green Studebaker pickup.

When Horse stopped the truck, the dogs came out from behind the house as they had earlier in the day. Horse drew his gun and put it in his left hand. He stuck his arm out the window and fired a round. As before, the dogs wheeled as one and ran back behind the house.

He backed the pickup and turned it around.

"That was just to let them know who's boss. There's dog food and a can opener in that sack. Open a couple of cans and you'll have friends for life. They look like they're starving.

There's a sandy wash back down the road a ways. Be a good place for your sleeping bag tonight. No reason to sleep on a bunch of rocks."

Stuart pulled the door open and climbed out, holding his heavy coat and the sack of dog food. He got his sleeping bag and canteen out of the bed of the truck and dropped them on the ground.

"Enjoy the stars, Stuart. Keep your eyes open as long as you can. If anybody comes out here, they'll come in a vehicle. I don't think anybody's going to walk over this desert in the night. You'll get too tired to stay awake from time to time. When that happens, take a short nap and then get back on watch. Almost zero chance anyone will show up, but I don't want anybody disturbing this place before I get back in the morning with Captain Hardesty. Expect us around nine or so."

"The Captain's coming to Smoke Tree?"

"Yes. So look sharp when he shows up."

"Yessir."

"See you tomorrow."

Stuart stepped away from the truck, and Horse drove off into a windless chilly night under a sky filled with countless stars.

When he got back to town, he keyed his mic twice.

"Dispatch."

"I'm headed for the barn, Merle. Any reason I need to stop by? Over."

"Nossir. All pretty quiet. Over."

"I'm clear."

When Horse got home, Esperanza met him on the porch with a hug and a kiss. He left his boots on the porch and padded into the living room in his stocking feet. He hung his Stetson and his gun on the hat rack. He was glad to see Esperanza had a fire in the fireplace.

He sat down on the couch and told her all about his day, from the time he met Joe at the rodeo grounds to when he dropped Stuart near the crime scene.

"Well, that's good news for Willy.

But Joe felt bad about killing the dog?"

"Sure seemed to. Wouldn't let me take him home. Said he wanted to walk and honor a spirit. I guess he was talking about the dog."

They sat silently for a while.

"I've been thinking about Caleb and Eunice Clovis ever since you called. I can't imagine who would want to kill them. It couldn't have been a robbery. They didn't have anything."

"You're right, *querida*. But it's like Pete Hardesty said. It's got something to do with money or family."

"You don't think Clarke had anything to do with this, do you?"

"No. I can't imagine him hurting Eunice. But I'm going to have to find him."

"How are you going to do that?"

"After I learn what I can out at that shack tomorrow, I'll call Lonnie Jenkins. If Clarke has stayed in touch with anyone in Smoke Tree, it'll be Lonnie."

While they were talking, fatigue washed over Horse like a breaking wave. He stretched his legs out and leaned back on the couch. He was soon asleep. Esperanza sat beside him looking into the fire and listening to his deep, slow breathing for a long time. She was glad he was home and safe. She didn't want to wake him, but she knew he'd be stiff and sore in the morning if he didn't get into bed.

She got up and tugged on his hand.

"Come on, soldier. Be reveille before you know it."

CHAPTER 5

LIFE CHANGES

Andy Chesney would later marvel at how something seemingly unimportant could bump a person's life onto a completely different path. Andy's life changed because Deputy Stuart Atkins had his eye on a boat.

Stuart's neighbor was selling a 1958 Arkansas Traveler fourteen-foot glass runabout with a Scott Atwater Super Scott motor at a sweet price. Plenty of horsepower for water skiing but good for fishing too. So,when the dispatcher called and offered him some overtime, Stuart jumped at the chance. Getting paid overtime for sitting on a desert hillside under a starry sky didn't sound like a bad deal, even if there were a couple of dead bodies nearby.

And because Stuart wouldn't be working his own shift, Andy, who was working graveyards that week, agreed to work a double and pick up some overtime of his own. The extra money would be nice, and it wasn't as if he had anything else to do. His social life was not exactly on fire.

Deep into the first half of his double, Andy was patrolling the north end of River Road out near the Nevada State Line. The Castillo Ranch, which straddled the California/Nevada border on the river bottom, had been losing steers. Someone had been driving the dirt roads out there at night looking for cattle. When they found a steer, they would spotlight it, shoot it and gut it, and then hack it into quarters and drive off with it in their pickup. Horse wanted the guys doing it caught before Juan Carlos, the ranch foreman, came across them first and scattered them all over the river bottom with his old Winchester pump. Or even worse, got shot himself. There was plenty of potential for a bad incident.

On the dirt road that paralleled the Colorado, Andy pulled off near the old scout camp and parked next to a stand of ancient salt cedars. He killed his lights and rolled down his window so he could listen for vehicle noises or rifle shots.

It was cold in the river bottom. The air coming in through his window was damp and musty and tinged with the odd smell that came off tamarisk trees: not a resinous scent like the pine trees they resembled, but a dusty, ancient and acidic odor. He lifted his heavyweight sheriff's department jacket off the seat next to him and stepped outside to put it on. He zipped it up and walked across the road to the steep bank above the river. There was no moon, but the sky was filled from horizon to horizon with stars shining so brightly they were reflected in the dark waters of the Colorado.

Andy stared into the inky darkness on the other side of the river. There was not a man-made light to be seen anywhere between the Arizona bank of the river and the distant mountains. He squatted on his heels and listened to the surge and gurgle of the water out in the channel as he thought about his future.

He was coming to the end of his second year with the sheriff's department. He was no longer a rookie. The Smoke Tree Substation had not been his first choice of duty stations coming out of the sheriff's academy. A graduate of Fontana High School, he had hoped to stay in the San Bernardino Valley, or maybe go to Big Bear if he had to leave. But he had been assigned to Smoke Tree, and when you are new in the department, you go where they send you, even if it was your last choice.

He had to admit there were times when the Mojave Desert wasn't bad. From October to December and from April to early June, the place had its moments. But the terrible heat of summer and the awful winds of winter could wipe away the memories of those times. And there was something else. The pool of single women his age was very small. It seemed the girls in Smoke Tree either married young or blew town once they graduated from high school.

But now he had enough time in to apply for a transfer before the wind began to howl out of the north hard enough to strip the paint off a house. He liked working for Lieutenant Caballo. He considered the man a straight shooter, and he had learned a lot from him. But in spite of his admiration for his boss, he had made up his mind to submit the paperwork in hopes he could be back in the San Bernardino Valley in 1962.

Andy walked back to his unit and climbed in and turned on his personal radio. When he worked graveyards, he carried the small Phillips transistor. When things got slow, or he was taking a break, he listened to the little radio. He kept it on low so it wouldn't drown out any calls coming in from dispatch. He usually had it tuned to KOMA out of Oklahoma City because he liked rock and roll. But sometimes he tried to pick up country and western out of Albuquerque or Denver because the music reminded him of his dad, a man who brought his taste for country music with him when he moved his family from Alabama to California.

At ten o'clock, he changed the station from KOMA to KOB Albuquerque to pick up the hourly news from ABC. Ever since the "duck and cover" drills he experienced in elementary school after the Russians got the atomic bomb in late 1949, Andy had been increasingly concerned about what was happening in faraway places. He was obsessed with world news as a child because it seemed to him the world grew more ominous every day.

As Andy got older, his fears had peaked each year as the Christmas holidays approached. He became convinced the Russians would launch a sneak attack on the United States at Christmastime. After all, could there be a better time to catch a Christian nation by surprise than when it was celebrating the birth of the Prince of Peace? He had ended his prayers between Thanksgiving and Christmas by begging God not to let the Russians attack over Christmas. He had known it was an irrational fear, and he shared it with no one. But even as an adult, the fear still haunted him.

When the East Germans built the wall between East and West Berlin at the end of the summer of 1961, Andy was convinced it had bumped the risk of nuclear war up another notch. That concern was reinforced in late October when an argument between an East German border guard and an American official led to a sixteen hour faceoff between American and Soviet tanks at Checkpoint Charlie in Berlin. And then, on the very last day of October, the Russians detonated the most powerful hydrogen bomb in history.

So when the lead news story out of KOB that night centered on the largest escape from East Berlin since the wall had gone up, Andy could feel his fear escalating again. The story explained that a train engineer had put his wife, four children and seventeen friends on his train. Then he ran the train past the border guards at Albrechtshof station and on to freedom in West Berlin. While Andy was glad for the people who had made it to freedom, he hoped the escape wouldn't make the Russians do something foolish with their new bomb.

When the news ended, he turned off the radio and let the deep silence surround him. There was always a melancholy to river bottom nights that spoke to centuries of stillness. That melancholy was more pronounced on fall and winter nights. He was submerged far down in his own thoughts when his department radio burst into life.

"Problem on River Road. Anyone out that way? Over."

The sound startled him so much he fumbled his mic and scrambled to pick it up off the floor.

"Chesney. I'm probably closest. I'll take it. Over."

"See the woman at 1337 River Road. Possible prowler or peeper. Over."

"On the way. Chesney clear."

Glad to have something to do that might drag him out of his anxious state, Andy cranked his unit to life. A huge cloud of river bottom silt geysered into the air as his wheels struggled to gain purchase in the soft dirt. He cranked the wheel and slid onto the hard pan. He kicked his headlights to high beam and lit his light bar. There was probably no one within miles, but you never knew.

Ten minutes later, after blasting over a lot of badly washboarded sections and power sliding through a series of sandy turns, he hit the straight stretch that led out of the river bottom. He blew past the Warren Ranch, pursued by a towering cloud of dust. He was moving over seventy miles an hour and the needle on his speedometer was still climbing when he bounced onto the hardball at the bottom of Paiute Wash. He pushed the pedal to the floor and added his siren to the mix to warn anybody above as he started the steep climb out of the wash.

He kept the car at full throttle as he flew over the top of the hill, and his speedometer touched eighty as he fought his way through the curves on the narrow two-lane blacktop that cut through the desert. Mailboxes began to appear along the road. His brights picked up some reflective numbers that let him know the house would be on the west side of the road.

Coming up fast on the driveway that should lead to the house, he slammed on the brakes. He saw *1337* on a mailbox on the south side of the driveway. He cranked the wheel hard to the right and started to skid. The back end of his unit broke free and took out the mailbox and its wooden post before he could straighten out. As he fishtailed through the dirt, his headlights picked up a figure breaking cover from the rusted-out cars and old appliances that had been discarded twenty five or thirty yards from the house. The hefty figure, maybe five nine or five ten and around two hundred pounds, bolted over the side of the hill into the gully below. Andy caught the flash of a white face under a black or navy blue watch cap before it turned away and the figure disappeared, swallowed into the shadowy depths of the arroyo on the moonless night.

His inclination was to give chase, but his first responsibility was to check on the person who had made the call and be sure she was okay. As his unit slid to a stop, he registered multi-colored Christmas lights outlining a small window near the door. He turned off the siren but left the light bar blinking as he hustled out of the car and through the dust cloud that had boiled up under his wheels.

He banged on the door with the butt of his four-cell flashlight.

"Sheriff's Department."

A visibly shaken woman pulled the door open. He registered red hair, green eyes and a spray of freckles.

"Thank God."

"Are you all right?"

"Yes, I was just…"

"Did the person you reported get into your house?"

"No, but…"

"I saw someone running as I drove up. Lock your door and wait inside."

The woman did not hesitate. She closed the door, and he heard a dead bolt slide into place.

He returned to his unit, killed the headlights and light bar, and unlocked his shotgun. He shut down the engine and pocketed the keys. He moved away from the house toward the gully, sweeping the ground in front of him with the broad beam of the flashlight. It didn't take him long to find the place where the stocky man had clambered down the side of the hill. When the widely-spaced, deep prints hit bottom, he could see marks where the man had lost his balance and fallen in the soft sand before getting up and running west up the wash.

By the widely spaced divots, Andy could tell the man had been running hard. He broke into a jog and followed. It was soon obvious the person he was following had too much of a head start. Also, he didn't want to leave the frightened woman alone in the desert night, wondering what was going on outside her house.

He walked back to where he had entered the wash, climbed up the steep side and went to his car. He reached inside, got the mic and keyed it twice.

"Dispatch."

"Chesney. I'm at the residence. When I pulled up, I saw someone run into a gully next to the house. Got a look at him before he disappeared over the side, but by the time I checked on the woman and got over to the gully, he was long gone. Over."

"Is the woman okay? Over."

"She says the guy didn't get in the house.

Listen, the man ran west. I know there's a dirt road up that way that comes out on 66. He may have parked a vehicle up there. Do we have another unit close by? Over."

"Steve Harlan is just coming out of South Pass. Over."

"Ask him if he knows where the road I'm talking about comes out. If he does, have him pull off onto the shoulder near there and watch. We're looking for a white male, five nine or five ten, stocky build. Dark clothes. Wearing a watch cap. We might get lucky and catch the guy trying to get on the highway. Over."

"Wilco."

"Chesney, clear."

Andy secured the shotgun in its holder and re-locked the car. He walked to the woman's house and knocked on the door.

"Deputy Chesney, ma'am."

The door was opened quickly.

"Hello. I'm Christine Gehardy"

"Is it okay if I come in, or would you rather come out and sit in my car while I write this up?"

"Oh, where are my manners? You'll have to excuse me. I'm a little flustered.

Please, come in."

She pulled the door open and stepped aside so Andy could enter.

He was greeted by the smell of cinnamon and vanilla as he walked into a very Spartan living room. There were green asphalt tiles on the floor and yellowed Celotex tiles on the ceiling. There was a blonde coffee table in front of an early-American-style couch that sat against the far wall. The cushions were covered with a green-checked gingham fabric, and the arms were bare wood. The only other pieces of furniture in the room were an easy chair of the same style and an end table against the south wall. There was no television set in the room, but there was a small, plastic radio next to a reading lamp on the end table. There was a Christmas tree near the easy chair. The tree was decorated with red lights and silver balls.

The north wall of the house was dominated by two bookcases made of concrete blocks painted green and supporting shelves of unfinished pine. Both cases were crammed with books.

"Would you like a cup of coffee, deputy?"

"Yes ma'am. That would be great."

Christine walked down a narrow hallway on the other side of the couch and turned into another room. Andy could hear her opening and closing cupboards. He walked over to the closest bookcase and looked at some of the titles on the collection of paperbacks. *Catcher in the Rye*, *Grapes of Wrath*, *The Great Gatsby*, *The Sound and the Fury*, and *A Farewell to Arms* were all books he recognized.

He had never heard of *Cry, the Beloved Country* by someone named Alan Paton, *The Stranger* by Albert Camus, *Goodbye, Columbus* by Phillip Roth or *A Separate Peace* by John Knowles. The only hardback book on the shelf was called *Catch-22*. It aroused his curiosity. Catch twenty two what? He was tempted to pick it up and leaf through it, but he thought it would be rude to do that without the woman's permission. But clearly, this was a woman who liked to read.

Christine came back down the short hallway.

"The percolator's plugged in. Would you like to talk to me in here or in the kitchen?"

"I prefer the kitchen. Easier to write at a table."

When Christine led him into the small room, he could see a rack of date and nut cinnamon pinwheels cooling on top of the stove.

"So, that's what smells so good. My mom used to make those at Christmas."

"I'm sure mine aren't as good as hers, but you're going to find out in a minute because you're getting a couple with your coffee."

"That's very kind of you."

The kitchen table had chrome legs and a red, Formica top. The chairs matched the table. Andy sat down on one side. He put his clipboard on the table and pulled a pen out of his shirt pocket.

Christine sat down across from him.

"So, Christine. Could you spell your last name for me?"

"G-E-H-A-R-D-Y."

"And 1337 was the address on the mailbox I just knocked over at the bottom of your driveway. My apologies for that."

"It's all right. I'm glad you were in such a hurry to get here."

"Mrs. Gehardy, in case you didn't catch my name, I'm Deputy Chesney."

"It's 'miss', deputy."

"Got it. Okay, tell me what happened."

"I was walking down the hall from my bedroom and I turned into the kitchen without switching on the light.

That's when I saw a face in the window."

"Can you describe it?"

"It was a man. I could only see his head and shoulders, but I think he was pretty big. The light wasn't good enough to see the color of his eyes. He was wearing a knit cap of some kind, so I couldn't see his hair."

"What color was the cap?"

"I couldn't really tell."

"What happened next?"

"I screamed. Loudly."

Andy noted the use of the adverb.

"And what did he do?"

"His face disappeared, but I couldn't hear any footsteps running away. It's real quiet out here. I didn't have my radio on, and I'm a long way from the road. If he'd run, I would've heard him."

"What did you do after he disappeared?"

"I got my butcher knife out of the drawer and went around and checked all the doors and windows to be sure they were locked."

"And were they?"

"Yes."

"Then what?"

"I called your office. I know I'm outside the city limits here, so I didn't call the Smoke Tree Police. Then I stood in the hallway and waited for someone to get here. I thought if I stood in the hallway, I could hear anyone who was trying to break in. It seemed like I stood there forever. I was standing there nearly paralyzed with fear when I heard your car coming up the driveway. I went to the window and peeked through the curtain. I was very happy to see your lights.

Then you came to the door and told me to stay inside."

Andy looked up.

"You know, you handled yourself very well. You made a plan and stuck to it."

"Thank you. I'm still trembling.

I think the coffee's done, and I could sure use a cup."

Christine got up and went to the kitchen counter. She filled two mugs with coffee and brought them to the table. Her hand was shaking when she set Andy's mug in front of him, and some of the coffee spilled. She returned to the counter, put pinwheels on a plate, brought them to the table, and sat down again.

They both sipped some coffee and Andy bit into a pinwheel.

"Hey, this is great! Just like mom's."

"Thank you. I'm glad you like it. Please, have as many as you want. I have dozens in the refrigerator.

Did you see the man when you went looking for him?"

"I found the place where he had run down the hill into the gully and then ran west up the wash. I followed him a little way, but he had a big head start."

He drank some more coffee.

"Miss Gehardy, is this the first time you've been bothered by a prowler?"

Christine did not answer immediately. It seemed to Andy she was struggling to frame her answer.

"I'm not sure how to put this. I don't want you to think I'm some crazy lady living out here on the edge of town."

She paused.

"Ever since about Halloween, I've been having this eerie feeling someone is watching me."

"Can you explain what you mean by 'eerie feeling'?"

"I can't do much better than that. Sometimes I just get kind of spooked."

"Aside from that feeling, can you think of anything odd that has happened? An event of some kind?"

"One night last week, about ten o'clock, I was sitting at the table grading papers when I heard water running somewhere in the house. At first I thought maybe the toilet was leaking or something. But I checked all through the house and couldn't find anything. I decided it might be outside. I turned on the porch light and went out front. Water was running out of the hose. The faucet was turned all the way open."

"And you're sure you didn't just forget that you had it on?"

"Oh, no. And like I said, it just started to run all at once."

"That's a common ploy used to lure someone out of their house."

"I didn't know that."

"Well, other than cops and robbers, not many people do. If it happens again, don't go outside. Don't even open your door. Call the office, and we'll get someone out here."

"Just call in and say the water's running?"

"That's right. Refer to the conversation we're having. Tell the dispatcher Deputy Chesney told you to call if something like that happened again.

Anything else you can recall that I should put in this report?"

"No, I think that's pretty much all of it."

"Okay. I'm going to make another recommendation. You should get rid of all that junk out there by the side of the house. And trim those salt cedars. Cut off any branches that are lower than about four feet from the ground. Things like those low branches and that pile of junk make it too easy for someone to sneak up on your house without being seen."

"I don't own this house. I just rent it."

"Then call your landlord and tell him the sheriff's department has recommended doing those things for your safety."

"All right, I'll do that tomorrow."

"One more thing. You said you were grading papers when you heard the water come on. Are you a teacher?"

"Yes. I teach at Rio Vista Elementary."

"I'm going to ask you a question that requires some speculation on your part. Is there anyone at work who makes you feel uncomfortable?"

"Uncomfortable how?"

"Unwanted advances. Off color or suggestive remarks. Or even staring at you in a way that seems inappropriate?"

"No, nothing like that. My colleagues are wonderful. In fact, the only person who has ever made me uncomfortable was the person who interviewed me for the job last summer."

"And who was that?"

Christine laughed.

"The superintendent, Dr. Symington."

Andy started to make a note.

"No, please! Don't write this down, but he looked at me like I was a specimen on a slide under a microscope. Or an insect he had found on the bottom of his shoe. Very cold and dismissive. But after I was hired and went to

67

work for the district, I found out he makes everyone feel that way. It turns out he's some sort of genius who doesn't relate to people very well."

"But you don't think he was looking at you in a, how should I say this, a sexual manner?"

She laughed again.

"I've never been looked at in a less sexual manner in my life."

"Okay, but other than that odd experience, nothing else at work?"

"Nothing."

Andy stood up.

"When I type this up at the end of my shift, I'll mention I've told you to call the station if the water suddenly gets turned on outside in the middle of the night.

I'm pulling a double tonight, so I'll be on until tomorrow morning. I'll cruise by a few times between now and sunup. If I come up your driveway, I'll hit my light bar so you'll know it's me and not a bad guy."

"Thank you. That makes me feel better."

Andy picked up his Stetson and headed for the door. Christine followed him.

"Thanks for the coffee and the great pinwheels, Miss Gehardy."

"You're welcome, Deputy Chesney. And please, it's Chris."

Andy put on his hat and pulled the door open. He turned before he went outside.

"And Chris? I'm Andy."

The last thing he saw before he closed the door was her smile.

When he got back in his unit, he drove down the driveway but paused before he pulled onto River Road. He keyed his mic.

"Dispatch."

"Merle, did the deputy coming down South Pass know the road I was talking about? Over."

"He did. He pulled over and sat there for a while. Said the only thing he saw come up that road was an STPD unit. Over."

"Wonder what a Smoke Tree patrol car was doing outside the city limits. Over."

"I can switch to their frequency and ask their dispatcher to check. Over."

"Don't do it on the air. Call on the telephone. I've got a funny feeling about this. Over."

"Roger. Anything else? Over."

"No. Thanks Merle. I'm clear."

Just after midnight, Andy drove to the 66 Truck Stop Café. While he ate dinner, he thought about the girl with the red hair and green eyes.

"Schoolmarm," he said out loud.

He liked the sound of the word. It made him smile.

Three times between midnight and first light, he drove to her house. Each time, he went up the driveway and hit his light bar. On the final pass, he saw the curtains behind the front window part. Chris peeked out the window and gave him a wave. He flashed his high beams in response.

When that happened, in spite of the double shift, he felt better than he had in a long time.

Chapter 6

A STRANGE WAY TO LIVE, A STRANGE WAY TO DIE

Horse was up and outside long before daybreak. He stood on the back of their property and watched the stars slide down and blink out behind the Sacramento Mountains. When they could no longer be seen, he walked to the corral and fed Canyon and Mariposa. Then he walked the entire property in the crisp air of a windless morning. Esperanza saw him in the dim, gray light of the false dawn as he returned to the house. He was wearing a pair of paint-stained, olive-drab fatigue pants and a flannel shirt she had tried to get rid of many times, only to have him rescue it from the trash. He was wearing his hunting boots.

She put breakfast burritos, salsa and black coffee on a tray and carried everything out to the table on the veranda.

"You dressing casual today?"

"Have to go out and work the place Caleb and Eunice died. Don't want to ruin a uniform."

"Are you going to let me throw out that shirt when you get back?"

"Sure am. These pants too."

Wrapped in blankets, they ate breakfast and watched the Black Mountains materialize from the darkness, first as vague outlines and then in more detail. By the time they had finished their third mug of coffee, the sun was just about to climb above the horizon. When it rose, the air warmed and the southwest breeze came to life. The yellow leaves on the cottonwoods north of the house began to dance. A pair of ravens appeared, riding the first thermals of the new day.

Horse kissed Esperanza goodbye. Then he went off to start a day he knew he wasn't going to enjoy. A dust devil spun across the dirt road in front of the truck as he drove toward the highway. When he got to 95, he turned south and drove to the county landfill. Horse stopped in front of the makeshift cinder block structure. He got out and leaned against the truck and waited for Willy to come outside. When he did, Horse told him about Joe killing the big dog so it could be sent in for testing.

"You settling in here okay?"

Willy smiled. Only his lips formed the smile while the rest of his face remained immobile.

"Ice!"

"I'm glad you like it. Would you like to stay here or go back to the rodeo grounds now that the big dog is gone?"

"Ere."

"Okay."

He unbuttoned his shirt pocket and pulled out some business cards.

"If anybody asks you why you're staying here, or gives you any kind of grief about it, give them one of my cards. Tell them to call me."

Willy smiled again and touched his only thumb to his forehead in a kind of salute.

Horse got back in the truck. When he got to his office, he picked up the phone and called the deputy coroner, Dusty Spires. Spires was a heating and air conditioning contractor who wove his duties around his business life. Business usually came first. The phone rang for a long time before someone picked up.

"Spires Heating and Air."

"Horse here, Dusty."

"I take it you're not calling about your heater."

"Nope. We've got two dead bodies."

"Where?"

"Foothills of the Sacramentos. Caleb and Eunice Clovis."

"Don't know them."

"Then you've missed your chance."

72

"What happened?"

"I think we have a homicide."

"Okay. Tell me how to get there. I'll meet you."

"You'll never find the place by yourself. Captain Hardesty is on his way out here from San Bernardino. Due to arrive about eight. If you drive out to the station, you can either ride with us or follow us out."

"I'll follow you."

"Then come in your pickup. Your car won't get over the desert we have to cross."

"Be right out."

Horse hung up and walked into the outer office. As he usually did, he checked the overnight log on the dispatcher's desk. He stood reading until something caught his eye.

"Merle, tell me about this incident Andy responded on last night."

Merle took him through the sequence of events.

"So, Andy asked you to call STPD on the phone and not on their radio frequency?"

"Yessir. Said he had a funny feeling about a black and white being out there."

"And what did you find out?"

"Their dispatcher said they had no on-duty unit anywhere near the area."

"How about off-duty? Did the dispatcher say anyone off duty had called anything in?"

"Sorry, I didn't think to ask."

"That's all right. It was just a thought."

Horse went into his office and dialed the STPD number.

"Smoke Tree Police Department."

"Lieutenant Caballo, sheriff's department. Is Chief Rettenmeir in?"

"Hold on. I'll let him know you're on the line."

After a few moments of silence, Horse heard a click.

"Rettenmeir."

"Mornin' Chief. Horse here. Got a question for you."

"Okay."

"Do some of your guys take their units home at night?"

"Sometimes. I think it makes neighborhoods safer when there's a black and white in a driveway."

"How about last night?"

There was a pause.

"Why do you ask?"

"One of my deputies responded to a prowler/peeper call out on River Road. As he pulled in, he saw a male running away from the house. He told the resident to stay inside and lock the door and then went after the guy, but the suspect was gone. My deputy went back to his unit and asked our dispatcher to have any of our units in that area keep an eye out for a possible vehicle on that old dirt road that runs west into Highway 66.

The deputy who responded saw a black and white pull off the dirt road onto the highway and head for town. Later in the evening, when my deputy had our dispatcher call yours to ask about a unit in the area, your guy said you didn't have anything out that way."

"What are you saying here, Lieutenant?"

"Not saying anything. I'm asking for assistance. If there was an off-duty guy with a unit out that way last night, maybe he saw something that would help us."

There was a silence.

"I'll ask my guys."

"I'd appreciate that, Chief. Can you tell me who had units at home last night?"

The chief raised his voice.

"I said I'd ask. How about you run your own damned department and let me run mine."

Horse found himself listening to a dial tone.

Horse was no fan of the Smoke Tree Police Department. Most of the officers had been let go by other departments for various infractions, most involving excessive violence or possible corruption. But he had never before had any kind of a personal problem with the chief, so he was surprised by Rettenmeir's angry response.

He hung up and walked out to the dispatcher's desk. He leaned over the microphone and pushed the transmit button.

"Come in, Andy."

"Andy here. Over."

"Will you be working your regular swing shift today? Over."

"I will. Over."

"Okay. I want to talk to you when you come in this afternoon.

I'm clear."

Horse went to the supply room and got two body bags and carried them out to the pickup. He was back at the dispatcher's desk when Captain Hardesty walked in with some folded clothing under his arm.

Horse stood up and extended his hand.

"Captain."

"Lieutenant.

We're going to be working together all day. All this 'lieutenant' and 'captain' stuff is going to get old. It's Pete, okay?"

"Sure. And everybody out here calls me Horse."

"Right. We've heard that."

"Well, the truck's ready and the deputy coroner is on his way."

"The guy know what he's doing?"

"He's seen a lot of dead bodies, but I don't think he's any kind of an investigator."

"Okay. Got a place where I can change out of my uniform into these civvies?"

"Sure. Use my office. There are some hangers in the closet you can use for your uniform."

Fred, the morning dispatcher, had taken over the front desk when the captain came out wearing Levi's and a gray sweat shirt. He had his weapon in a holster clipped to his belt.

Horse went and got his gun belt and hat off the rack in his office. When he came out, he made introductions.

"Fred, this is Captain Hardesty. He's coming with me out to the Clovis place. Captain Hardesty, Fred is our day dispatcher. He does a great job for us."

Fred got to his feet.

"Heard a lot about you, sir."

The two men shook hands.

"Hope it was good."

"One hundred percent."

"Fred, I'll be out there for quite a while. Route everything through the patrol sergeant. I'll catch up when I get back."

"Got it."

The two men walked out the door.

"Pete, I brought you a canteen of good water from my well. None of this Smoke Tree alkali soup."

"Bless you. I certainly remember Smoke Tree water.

Let me get my kit out of my car."

As Horse was walking to the department pickup, Dusty Spires pulled into the lot and got out of his pickup.

"Horse."

"Dusty."

"So, you think we have a homicide?"

"Looks like."

Before he could explain, Captain Hardesty walked over carrying what looked like a large tool box.

"Captain Hardesty, Deputy Coroner Dusty Spires.

Dusty, this is the department's expert on homicides."

"Nice to finally meet you, Mr. Spires. I've certainly seen your name and signature on a lot of documents."

"Pleased to meet you too, Captain."

"Follow me out, Dusty. We're going to take Eagle Pass Road from where the pavement dead ends at Edge Street."

As they drove through Smoke Tree, Horse told Captain Hardesty about the case in more detail than he had the day before, beginning with meeting Andy and Willy alongside 66 on Monday and ending with leaving Stuart Atkins out on the hillside the previous night.

"So, you found these dead bodies because you tracked the dogs?"

"That's right."

"How in the world did this Joe Medrano guy track a bunch of dogs over the desert?"

"That's a good question. I couldn't have done it. Joe is unusual. Not to mention resourceful and self-reliant. And I've never known a man more likely to be underestimated."

Horse stopped at the end of Edge Street and waited for Dusty to catch up. When he saw the deputy coroner in his rearview mirror, he drove up over the berm and onto Eagle Pass Road. As they drove west into the desert, Captain Hardesty scanned the landscape.

"I've got to get out this way more often. It's nice to be in a place where everybody's not crammed together."

"Come out for the weekend sometime. Bring Wilma, too. Esperanza and I would really like you to stay at our place."

"Wouldn't want to impose."

"No imposition at all, Pete.

Quail season's almost worn out up in the Providence, but we could amuse the chukkars by chasing them up and down the hills."

"I'm still trying to recover from the last time. I seem to recall we climbed up out of Wild Horse Canyon all the way to the top of the mesa just in time to see those shifty devils fly off across the valley to the next hillside. But I still wouldn't mind having a good hike out that way."

"Just let me know when you can make it."

The morning sun was heating up the inside of the truck as it rattled along the badly washboarded road. Horse rolled down his window. After a few miles, he turned onto the primitive track that ran directly north, parallel to the Sacramento Mountains. He dropped the truck into compound low and they ground in and out of gully after gully as they drove across the wine-goblet shaped *bajadas* spilling their contents down the hillsides.

Finally, he dropped into the sand and gravel wash where he had suggested Stuart set up camp. When he climbed the other side, the Clovis place was below them. They could see Stuart sitting on a rock next to the old Studebaker truck. The dogs that had barked at Horse and Joe so fiercely the day before came out of the aethel trees on the north side of the house and trotted toward them. They showed no signs of aggression. Once they had a good look at the truck, they wandered over and sat on the ground near Stuart.

Horse thought it was amazing what a few cans of dog food could do.

He rolled up his window as they came to a stop so the cab wouldn't fill up with dust. Stuart got up and waited for the cloud to settle. Then he walked toward them, the dogs trailing behind single file. When Horse and Captain Hardesty got out of the truck, the dogs shied away and formed a skirmish line behind their new hero.

"You look like Little Bo Peep and her sheep."

"Yeah. These dogs have taken a shine to me."

"And your can opener."

"That too."

"Stuart, this is Captain Hardesty. Captain, Deputy Stuart Atkins."

The two men shook hands.

"Good morning, Deputy. I remember when you graduated from the academy. Pretty high up, as I recall."

Stuart smiled.

"I'm surprised you remember, sir. Good to see you again."

"How was your night, Stuart?"

"I was dazzled by stars and sung to by two different packs of coyotes. Other than that, nothing happened until sunup. Then the buzzards came back and landed on the roof. I shied a rock or two at them and they just looked at me. When I let off a couple rounds, they got airborne.

Now they're just floating around up there, giving me the creeps."

The three men craned their necks and looked into the clear sky. Thirty or forty buzzards were making lazy arcs as they floated on the thermals.

"Keeping the desert clean, Stuart. Nature's garbage men."

Dusty Spires, who had been lagging behind during the drive so he wouldn't have to eat Horse's dust, pulled in and parked. He got out and joined them.

"Mornin', Stuart."

"Dusty."

Captain Hardesty walked back to the department truck and lifted out the large tool box containing his equipment.

The four men walked to the lean-to together. The odor of death was strong. They stopped in front of the crude door Horse had re-latched the previous afternoon.

"Don't know if you can get a print off the door or the hook, but I unlatched and latched it with my knife blade."

"Could get lucky. I'll try."

Captain Hardesty set his tool box on the ground and opened it.

"How many of us are going in?"

"Just you and me and Dusty.

Stuart, I need you to stay out here and make sure those dogs don't get into the place while we're working."

Stuart nodded and walked away. The dogs turned and followed him.

Captain Hardesty handed out rubber gloves.

"This'll just take a minute, and then we can go inside. Bear with me here."

He got dusting material and a brush out of the box. He quickly dusted the door around the hook and the door handle and then the handle itself. He lifted some partial prints with tape and attached them to cards. He pulled a pen out of his shirt pocket and labeled the cards.

"Okay. Nothing great, but might come in handy. We'll see."

He put the cards in the box and closed the lid.

Horse popped the hook out of the eye and pulled the door open. The smell intensified.

The captain picked up the box and led the three men inside. He put it on the ground as they surveyed the room and the two desiccated bodies on the dirt floor.

There were no windows. The bodies were next to a card table and three cheap, mismatched folding chairs in the middle of the room. One of the chairs had overturned. The other two were still upright, but one of them was at an angle to the table. There was an oil lamp on the table that had not been disturbed by what had taken place. Horse was surprised it had not fallen over.

There was a wood-burning stove against the south wall. A large black skillet sat on top. Next to the stove was a galvanized sink. A drainpipe leading from the sink exited through unfinished plywood to the desert outside. An empty porcelain bucket sat on the dirt floor. Angled into the corner created where the south wall of descending height met the low north wall made of railroad ties were two army cots. Dirty blankets and pillows without pillowcases were piled on each one.

"When I came in yesterday, I looked at the bodies to confirm they were Caleb and Eunice. Then I made one circle of the room looking for a gun. I thought maybe we had a murder/suicide.

When I was sure we didn't, I checked to see if the back door was hooked from the inside. It was.

I left everything just as you see it."

"My God," said Dusty, "somebody shot these poor people all to pieces."

"My guess," said Captain Hardesty "is they were both shot once to put them down and then finished off when they were on the ground."

"I agree. I think Caleb there was trying to stand up when he was hit. It looks like the missus was still sitting in that overturned chair when she got it, and she went over backward."

They walked closer to the bodies.

"It must have been a rifle or a large caliber handgun. The bullets that didn't stay in the bodies should be in the ground underneath them."

"Might be some in the walls too if those first rounds went all the way through."

The deputy coroner walked closer and leaned down over each body in turn.

80

"I'd say ten days to maybe two weeks. The bodies are well past the 'bloat' stage, so all the fluids have leaked out, but that's just my uneducated guess."

"I think you're very close," said Captain Hardesty. "If we find centipedes and millipedes beneath the bodies, that will mean bones are exposed and they've shown up to work on them. That would be two weeks. If there aren't under them yet, it'll be closer to ten days."

"Well, as I'm just a deputy coroner, my report will show I declared them deceased as of now. The Medical Examiner will have to determine the cause of death and give you a professional estimate of when they died."

"So, Dusty," said Horse. "I take it you agree we've got a murder on our hands."

"Sure do.

And now, gentlemen, I'll leave you to it. This humble metal bender has to get back to work. I hope I can forget what these people looked like before I go to sleep tonight."

He turned and walked outside. The two lawmen followed him, glad to be temporarily away from the smell of death.

"Deputy Coroner Spires, does this mean you're not going to help us get those two into the body bags."

"That's definitely what it means. And good luck with it. At this stage, it's going to be hard to keep skin from sloughing off and limbs from coming loose. I'm glad to say I won't be here to share that experience."

He walked to his truck.

"I'll write my report as soon as I get back and send it off to San Bernardino.

Pleased to meet you, Captain."

"Likewise, Deputy Coroner."

As Dusty started his truck, Horse and Captain Hardesty walked back toward the lean-to. Stuart called out to ask if they needed his help.

"Not yet, Stuart. The Captain's going to gather some evidence. We'll call you when he's finished. Just keep those dogs away from the door."

"Will do."

Horse noticed some of the buzzards had settled on the roof again. He drew his revolver and fired into the air. The buzzards lurched laconically into flight. The dogs ran off into the desert. Stuart walked off in the direction the dogs had taken.

Horse and Captain Hardesty went back into the gloomy shack with its stench of death and decay.

"Before we do anything else, I'm going to get some photos. I'll send them to you when I get them developed."

He walked to his box and got out a 35mm camera with a flash attachment, several rolls of film, and a clip board that held a pad of graph paper. Standing just inside the door, he made a plot on the graph paper of the immediate area around the bodies. Then he walked around the corpses in a clockwise direction taking photos. He paused after each shot to note on the graph paper the number of the photo and where he was standing when he took it.

When he was finished photographing the bodies, he returned to the place he had started the series. He labeled a new piece of graph paper and proceeded to photograph the rest of the room. He moved in the same clockwise fashion he had moved the first time. He had used three rolls of film before he put the camera and the graph paper diagrams in the box.

He pulled fingerprint powder, a brush, adhesive tape, and fingerprint cards out of the box.

"I'll be dusting for prints in here, but I'm not going to try to get prints off the corpses. I'm afraid the skin will slough off. I'll let the medical examiner get the prints when he does the autopsy. He's a heck of a lot better at that kind of thing than I am."

He moved around the room, dusting likely surfaces and lifting prints and putting them on the cards. He labeled each card.

"You know, Horse, there are newer materials for lifting prints than this old fashioned carbon black, but I still think it's the best. Can't beat the contrasts."

When he was finished, he put the cards in a separate compartment in the box.

"Okay. Now let's have a look around and see if this room tells us a story. That oil lamp is first. If it's out of oil, it may mean the killer came at night and left the lamp burning when he went away."

He moved to the card table and picked up the carbon black-smeared lamp.

There was no fuel. He turned to Horse.

"Doesn't mean it couldn't have been empty already, but it seems to point to something that was done at night."

As the captain spoke, a gust of wind blew the door closed. With the only light in the windowless room coming in through the cracks in the makeshift walls, it was suddenly very dim. Horse had a sudden, irrational vision of Caleb and Eunice lurching to life. He moved quickly to the door.

He pushed against the door. It didn't open. He pushed harder.

Captain Hardesty had turned to watch him.

"Is it stuck?"

"Doesn't fit snug enough to get stuck. It must be latched."

"Maybe Stuart latched it to keep the dogs out."

"I don't think so.

Stuart! Yo, Stuart!"

There was no response.

"Must still be out rounding up his dogs. Let's go see what happened."

Captain Hardesty and Horse went out the back door. They walked around to the front of the lean-to and looked at the door.

It was latched. Stuart was nowhere in sight.

Horse stepped up and flicked the hook out of the eyebolt. It fell to the side. He started re-latching it and flicking it open and counting the number of times he did it. On the fourteenth count, the hook remained balanced in an upright position on the eyebolt. He pulled the door open. The hook remained upright. He gave the open door a push, and he and Hardesty watched as it swung toward the building. When it hit, the hook fell into the eyebolt and re-latched the door.

"I'll be damned," said the captain. "The killer didn't mean to leave the door latched. He left it open, sure that coyotes and vultures and mice and all other kinds of creatures would scatter pieces of the bodies all over the landscape. If the door had stayed open, that's exactly what would've happened. The killer wasn't very lucky."

83

"Luckier than Eunice and Caleb."

"That's true. And if those dogs hadn't come to town hunting for pets and garbage, this scene might not have been discovered for months."

"Here's how I think it happened," said Horse. "When the killer came, that door was closed but not latched. The hook was balanced upright on the eyebolt. He eased the door open and walked in, and the door stayed open. Caleb and Eunice were sitting at the table. Caleb started to get up, and the killer shot him. When he turned the gun on Eunice, she was still sitting. Then he walked closer and shot them several more time as they lay on the ground. When he was done, he went out the door and never looked back."

"But you'd think those dogs would've come after him when he approached the place."

"Unless they knew him."

"So, you'll be looking for someone who was out here often enough to get to know the dogs well. And if you find him, we can compare his prints to the ones we just lifted inside."

"That's probably the best we'll be able to do. I can't imagine there was a witness to this."

"Well, enough fresh air for now. Back inside."

Horse picked up a rock and propped the door open. Captain Hardesty went inside as Horse went around back and propped that door open too. When he poked his head inside, visibility was better.

He decided to survey the area around the back door.

The first thing he noticed was a big stack of mesquite wood cut in stove lengths. Next to the stack was a fifty-five-gallon drum with a pump sticking out of the top. Horse rapped the drum. It was almost empty. That explained the empty drums chained in the back of the Studebaker. Caleb had been about to make a run for more water.

Next to the drum stood a wood-burning stove. It was smaller than the one inside. There was another stack of mesquite wood next to it. Horse turned and looked at the back of the crude building. A large washtub was hanging from a hook screwed into one of the pieces of lumber that made up the back wall.

Horse walked out from behind the house to the stand of salt cedars that stood off to the north. There was a primitive clothesline suspended between two of the trees. A cloth bag filled with clothespins hung from the line.

It looked as if Eunice had boiled water on the stove and poured it into the washtub to do the laundry. Then she wrung the clothes out by hand and hung them between the aethel trees. He thought about doing that on a cold and windy winter day.

On the other side of the trees, he saw something metal on the ground. He walked over to investigate. It took him a minute to understand what he was seeing. When he did, he shook his head and decided to be sure he showed it to Captain Hardesty and Stuart before they drove back to Smoke Tree.

He went back inside the building. Captain Hardesty had the lid up on a cooler he had dusted for prints earlier. The lid was covered with carbon black. Inside the cooler, rotting pieces of sandwich meat and moldy cheese floated in a foot of water.

"Guess someone went to town with this ice chest from time to time."

He pointed to the crude shelves nailed to the wall.

"Lots of rice and beans, too. Probably most of their diet. Looks like mice have torn into the packages. Mice tore open the flour bags and the containers of oatmeal, too. Might have been some potatoes, but if there were they're gone."

Horse walked over for a closer look. There were jars of mustard and catsup and cans of sardines. The lowest shelf held a collection of different colored plastic dishes along with four plastic drinking glasses, three coffee mugs, a few mismatched pieces of flatware, and a can of Maxwell House coffee.

"Horse, this next part is not going to be pleasant. We have to get these corpses into the body bags. We'd better get Stuart to help us."

They walked outside and sucked in fresh air for a few minutes. Stuart was leaning up against the old Studebaker. The dogs were sitting in a semi-circle in front of him.

"See you rounded up your fan club."

"Yessir. They ran off a ways."

"We're going to need your help inside."

Stuart walked over. The dogs followed him but sat down as they got closer to Horse.

The captain handed Stuart a pair of rubber gloves. The three took a few deep breaths of good air and went inside and got to work.

It took almost an hour to get all the parts of each corpse into its own bag. As the men lifted the bodies, centipedes and millipedes and several scorpions skittered out from under them where they had been feasting. Skin and hair sloughed off. Caleb's right arm and Eunice's left foot detached as the men worked to maneuver the bodies into the bags. Halfway through the operation, Horse spotted one of the dogs trying to edge into the room. He clapped his rubber-gloved hands. It bolted, making whimpering noises.

When they were finished, they zipped up the bags and carried the sad cargo one bag at a time to the pickup. They lifted each one carefully over the dropped tailgate and into the bed. Stuart climbed up and pulled each bag closer to the cab so the tailgate would close.

While they were loading the bodies, the buzzards had settled on the roof and on the ground around the open door. As Horse approached, the ones on the roof stayed in place, but the birds on the ground lifted into the air. When he looked inside, three of the vultures were already walking over the ground where the bodies had been. As soon as they saw Horse, the birds, so graceful in flight but so ungainly on the ground, hopped awkwardly out the back door, hissing and grunting as they moved.

Captain Hardesty entered the room as the birds went out. Stuart was glad to stay outside with the dogs. Horse walked over to the shelf and picked up spoons and forks. He and the captain set to work digging in the stained dirt. It wasn't long before they found the bullets beneath where the heads of the two victims had been. Passing through the skulls had caused both *coup de grace* bullets to mushroom. The one that had passed through Eunice was about an inch below the surface. The one that had gone through Caleb had not penetrated the ground.

"Looks like a .38," said Horse.

Captain Hardesty put each bullet in its own plastic container. The containers looked like large, pill bottles. He labeled each bottle.

"Enough there for ballistics?"

"Plenty, if we ever find the weapon."

They went back to work and found more bullets beneath where Caleb and Eunice had died. The ones that had gone through the torsos were in better condition.

"Should we check the walls?"

"Yes. If nothing else, we may be able to find out if they all came from the same gun."

They found one bullet partially lodged in a piece of particle board on the wall behind where Caleb's body had fallen, and one lying on the ground three feet to the right of that one.

"I think this one went through the woman. It confirms that she was sitting down when she was shot. My guess is the bullet hit the ground on a downward angle as it passed through her and didn't have enough energy to lodge in the wall after it ricocheted. It just dropped to the ground. In spite of hitting the dirt, it's in the best shape of any of the bullets we've recovered so far."

He put the bullet in the container marked "Eunice" and walked slowly back toward where she had been sitting. After a few steps, he stopped and knelt down.

"Here's where it hit the ground."

Horse walked over and looked at the impact divot.

Captain Hardesty rose and walked back to his box. He put the containers inside.

"Based on the damage to the bodies, I think the medical examiner is going to find more rounds when he does the autopsies. And that's going to show that the killer reloaded and fired again. If it was a revolver, the hammer would have been sitting on an empty chamber. That means only five rounds."

"And a lot more rounds than that were used here."

"There was a lot of hate in this room."

"Or contempt. Or both."

Hardesty stripped off his rubber gloves and got his graph paper out of the box. He marked on the paper where each of the bullets had been found. He put the paper in the box and closed it up.

Horse latched the back door. Then he and Captain Hardesty walked out the front, glad to be finished with their gruesome chore. Horse moved the rock away and closed the door.

"When Joe Medrano and I came out here yesterday, I peeked inside that old Studebaker, but I didn't touch anything. Because of the smell, I was already thinking something bad had happened."

The captain and Horse walked over beside the truck. Stuart followed. The dogs followed Stuart at a distance but kept a wary eye on Horse. Captain Hardesty put his box on the ground and opened it up again.

"Let me see if I can pick up some prints from the door handles or inside the cab. If nothing else, we can use them for elimination purposes."

He dusted both doors, the steering wheel, the interior handles and the dashboard. He also dusted a few of the liquor bottles and beer cans. He picked up a few useable prints, but they all seemed to be from the same person. When he was finishing the passenger side, he called Horse over.

"Found something interesting buried beneath all this trash. First, let me see if I can lift any prints off it."

Horse walked around the truck and watched as the Captain worked on a boxy, yellow device. When he was finished, he turned to Horse.

"Is it what I think it is?"

"Geiger counter. After that fellow struck it rich over in Utah, everybody suddenly became a uranium prospector. Not as much interest now, but we had people crawling all over the desert with these things for a few years."

Horse picked up the device and carried it to the department pickup, getting his hands dusted with carbon black in the process. He put it in the bed of the truck with the bodies. Captain Hardesty stored his box in the cab.

"Before we leave, let me show you both something over this way."

Horse set off toward the salt cedar trees. Captain Hardesty and Stuart followed him. The dogs trailed behind. When Horse got past the trees, he stopped. He turned and pointed at something lying on the ground.

"When I came outside and saw that, it took me a minute to realize what it was."

"Looks like an upside down truck bed."

"Look closer. There are two holes cut in the bed. See them?"

"Yes."

"Next to them there's a thick catalogue of some kind. Sears Roebuck would be my guess."

"Oh, Lord. Don't tell me!"

"Portable privy. When the slit trench under the holes fills up, you hitch a rope or chain to that hook there and drag it where you've dug a new trench. Then you dump some lime in the old trench and cover it with dirt. Those trees there provide privacy, and Sears or Monkey Ward or J.C. Penny provides the toilet paper at no charge. And two holes there, one for momma and one for pop."

"Now I've seen it all."

"Not quite yet. Walk over here with me."

Horse moved north to the edge of a gully. The three men stood on the hill looking down at an incredible amount of trash.

"My God. How long have these people lived out here?"

"I'm not sure."

"It looks like every bit of garbage they ever had went into this gully."

"Knowing Caleb, he just threw everything out the back door. Eunice probably hauled it over here and dumped it down the hill so she wouldn't have to look at it or walk around it every time she came outside."

The men turned away. As they walked back to the truck, followed by the dogs, Stuart spoke up.

"Lieutenant, what's going to become of these animals?"

"I don't know. I don't think the pound will come out here to pick them up."

"Do you think they'll take them if I bring them in?"

"Sure. But if someone doesn't adopt them, they'll be put down."

"Well, hell, I'll take one of them myself. Kind of taken to that lop-eared one. Maybe they can find a home for the others."

"Could be. That's real good of you, Stuart. After we finish with what we have to do, you can bring the truck back out and round them up."

The three men crowded into the truck, Stuart in the middle. The dogs watched them as they drove away.

As soon as they reached town, Horse drove directly to the Askew Mortuary. It didn't seem right to leave the bodies in the back of the truck a minute longer than necessary. He thought Eunice especially had suffered enough indignity, in life as well as in death.

89

The owner of the funeral home and one of his sons helped the men unload the bodies and get them into the hearse for the long drive to San Bernardino. Captain Hardesty gave very specific instructions about where the bodies should be delivered.

"I'm going to be heading to San Bernardino myself. In fact, I may get there before you do. If I do, I'll be at the morgue to meet you. I'd like to talk to the medical examiner before he goes to work. If you get there first, tell him I told you to have him wait until I arrive."

They got back in the truck.

"That's an unusual name: 'Askew.' I don't think I've ever heard it before."

"Well, I can tell you it leads to a lot of bad jokes. The most common one is, "Askew don't ask you. He just takes you.""

When they pulled into the parking lot at the substation, Stuart headed for his POV. Horse walked with Captain Hardesty to his car where the captain collected a plastic trash bag.

"For my civvies. Don't want to smell those clothes all the way home. I'll be on the road as soon as I get a quick shower and change back into my uniform."

"Fred will scare you up a clean towel. I'm going home to shower. After working with those bodies, I feel like I'll never get clean again."

"I know what you mean."

"Pete, you'll probably be on the road before I get back. I want to thank you for taking the time to drive all the way out here today."

"Glad to help. And I'm glad you figured out why the door was latched."

"It may be that Caleb's laziness may help us catch his killer. If Caleb hadn't been too shiftless to pick up a pair of pliers or a screwdriver and give that eye bolt one more quarter turn, the door wouldn't have latched."

"I was thinking about that while we were driving back to town. I was also thinking that maybe someone who thinks his tracks have been covered will get a little careless. Who knows. 'For the want of a nail a shoe was lost', and all that."

"Thanks again for the help. I'll keep you up to date on anything we find. This case is as much yours as it is mine now."

"I'll let know what the autopsy turns up, and I'll send you the photos."

The two men shook hands.

Horse went out and got in the department pickup. He drove out of the parking lot and turned south on Highway 95. He and Esperanza had no neighbors, so Horse went into the tack house when he got home and stripped down to his underwear. He walked gingerly across the dirt toward the house in his bare feet, watching carefully for patches of puncture weed.

"Nice outfit, Senor Caballo," said Esperanza when he came in the back door.

"*Hola, querida,*" he said as he blew her a kiss. "Don't hug me until I get a shower. I left my clothes in the tack room. I'll burn them when I get home tonight."

He stayed in the shower a long time. He scrubbed himself over and over and washed his hair three times. He didn't get out until all the hot water was gone.

After he dried off, he put on a clean uniform. As he walked down the hall in his stocking feet carrying his half boots, he picked up the smell of cinnamon. When he went into the kitchen there was a ham sandwich, potato salad and a cup of coffee at the table.

"You're the best, *querida.*"

Esperanza sat and talked with him as he ate his late lunch. They talked of everyday things and did not mention the horrible job Horse had been doing all day. As they spoke, he could feel the tension leaving his neck and shoulders.

After he had another cup of coffee and a *churro* sprinkled with powdered sugar for desert, he kissed Esperanza goodbye and went out to the truck. The cab still held the smell of death. He rolled down both windows and popped the vent wings to air out the interior as he drove.

Back at the office, he turned the truck over to Stuart Atkins so he could go round up the dogs. He was checking his messages when the deputies working the swing shift began to arrive. He walked to his door and called to Fred.

"When Andy comes in, remind him I want to see him."

He was at his desk updating his notes on the case when Andy tapped on his half-open door.

"Afternoon, Andy. Come in and sit down and tell me all about this call you took last night out on River Road."

Andy moved to the chair in front of Horse's desk.

Andy related the events of the previous night, including his call to Merle about the black and white another deputy had seen getting on 66.

"So, you did get a brief look at the guy as you drove up."

"Yessir. Not a real good one, but I did pick up a few things."

"Give me what you've got."

"White guy. Five foot ten or so. Maybe one ninety, two hundred. I wasn't close enough to see eye color, and I couldn't see his hair because he was wearing a cap."

"How about clothing, other than the cap?"

"Levi's, maybe. Dark jacket zipped all the way up. Boots."

"What kind? Hiking, cowboy, military?"

"Hiking or military, I would say."

"That's pretty good for a glance.

Andy, when I got in this morning, I called Chief Rettenmeir. Asked him if he still lets people take units home. He said he does. Said he would ask if anyone had been in one of the units out that way last night. And then things got strange."

"How's that, sir?"

"When I asked him who had taken cars home, he got real defensive. If I had to guess, I'd say he's not really in control of things over there. But I've suspected that for some time."

"So have I."

"For now, keep this under your hat. Don't want these departments at each either other any more than they already are. I'm sharing my concerns with you because you're directly involved with this incident."

"Yessir. Got it."

"Good. And take care out there tonight."

"Will do, sir.

Anything more on the Clovis thing?"

"Captain Hardesty, Dusty Spires and I were out there for quite a while today. Definitely a homicide. Both people shot multiple times."

"Any ideas?"

"Not yet. Generally when this kind of thing happens it's money or family. Caleb and Eunice sure didn't have any money. The only family I know of is their son Clarke. He was in L.A. somewhere, last I heard. I don't make him for this, but I'm going to get hold of him. I'll see if he won't drive out here. If he won't and doesn't have a good reason not to, I might have to have him picked up and held until I can drive in there."

"I guess I never knew this Clarke."

"Left out of here before you came.

That reminds me. You're coming up on two years here. I remember when we worked that case out in the Chemehuevi Mountains together last year you told me you wanted to get back to the city. And you've never said anything about changing your mind.

You've got enough seniority now to make a move. I'd like you to stay in Smoke Tree. You've turned out to be a real good deputy with a knack for this work. But if you've got your heart set on leaving, I'll give you a strong recommendation.

Any thoughts you care to share with me on what you might do?"

"Well, sir, I'm not entirely sure yet. But I'll let you know when I make a decision."

"All right, Andy. Talk to you tomorrow."

Horse was puzzled when the deputy left. Andy had always been so adamant about getting out of Smoke Tree as soon as he could.

At seven o'clock that evening, Horse dialed the phone number for Lonnie Jenkins.

"Hello."

"Lonnie, Carlos Caballo calling. Please pardon me for disturbing your evening."

"No problem, Horse. Just waiting for Wagon Train to come on. What's on your mind?"

93

"I'm trying to track down one of your former students."

"Which one?"

"Clarke Clovis."

"Far and away the best musician I ever worked with. In fact, the best musician I have ever known. An incredibly talented trumpet player."

"You know, I still remember that group you had. The one that played local dances."

"The Blue Notes. That was quite a crew. Coach Dean Lucas on drums or rhythm guitar, our English teacher Al Sorrento on clarinet, Clarke on trumpet and me on saxophone. And if the place had a piano, Chandler Franks, the choir teacher, would come along and add another dimension.

We had some fun nights and made some good music."

"I remember you guys played all the swing-era stuff: Benny Goodman, Artie Shaw, Tommy Dorsey. Esperanza and I love that music. We have fond memories of the dances when you played on Saturday nights at the Elks club.

Tell me, how did you come across Clarke in the first place?"

"When he was just starting junior high, I took the high school dance band over to the multi-purpose room and put on a little concert for the incoming seventh graders. When the show was over, I asked anyone who might be interested in joining the junior high band program to stay behind. Clarke was one of the kids who stayed. I let the ones who were interested walk onto the bandstand and talk to the high school students and ask questions about their instruments.

Clarke headed straight to the trumpet section. No hesitation. He knew immediately what he wanted to play."

"How long before you knew he was something special?"

"Not much more than a month. He was in the band class I put on for the kids two days a week. I taught them some of the basic music skills. If they showed a real interest, I would let them take an instrument home so they could practice.

By the time first semester ended, he was light years ahead of everybody. When he started the eighth grade, I put him in the high school band. Only junior high kid I ever did that with. By the time we put on the Christmas concert for the community, he was first chair. I was afraid that would ruffle a few feathers, but the guy he bumped knew Clarke was better. Clarke just took off from there and never looked back.

I started giving him private lessons."

"Caleb Clovis didn't strike me as the kind of man would pay for music lessons for his son."

Lonnie laughed.

"He certainly wasn't. I never saw a father so determined his son wouldn't succeed. He did everything he could to keep his boy from progressing. Wouldn't even let him play the horn in the house. Clarke told me he had to walk out into the hills and get far enough away that Caleb couldn't hear him. Had to hide his trumpet out there, too.

In fact, the first horn he had, Caleb found it out in the desert. Smashed it against the rocks until it was beyond repair. The only thing Clarke could salvage was the mouthpiece."

"That must have been sad for him."

"Broke his heart. But you know, in the long run it turned out to be a good thing."

"How's that?"

"Clarke was a sophomore in high school when that happened. He was already playing with our group at dances in Smoke Tree and Kingman and Twentynine Palms. Anyway, the guys in the group took up a collection and bought him a really good horn: a Conn 6B Victor. My, he could make that trumpet sing! It wasn't very long before he was the attraction. Sometimes when he launched into a solo, people stopped dancing and just listened. In my opinion he was already better than Harry James by the time he left high school.

Did you know about his scholarship?"

"That would have been around 1956?"

"That's right. I took him for auditions at the Thornton School at U.S.C., the Colburn Conservancy in L.A., Chapman University and the University of Redlands. He was a knockout everywhere. People couldn't believe someone that young could be that good. In the end, he had his choice.

He went to the Thornton School. A full ride. Had to work on campus for pocket money because his dad wouldn't contribute a cent. Hell, Caleb tried to stop him from going. But Clarke was eighteen by then.

On the weekends he began to prowl the jazz spots in L.A. and Hollywood. By the time he was a junior, he was sitting in a few places, and then a few more. It wasn't long before he had a reputation. He didn't finish school. Just went to work playing clubs and playing as a sessions musician in recording studios."

"How long since you've seen him?"

"Jean and I went to hear him play at the Lighthouse Café in Hermosa Beach in 1959. Saw him and Chet Baker on succeeding nights, and I'll tell you, it was hard to say who was better. He's that good."

"Do you know where he lives now?"

"Hollywood."

"Does he ever come back to visit?"

"As far as I know, he hasn't been back to Smoke Tree since the day Jean and I put him on the Super Chief and gave him money for a taxi from Union Station to U.S.C."

"Not even for the holidays?"

"Nope. At least I don't think so. I think if he'd ever come back he would've given me a call. I mean, in a way, Jean and I were a second family to him. We bought him clothes for when he played with the Blue Notes and kept them here at the house.

He wrote to us and called from time to time, but I'm pretty sure he never came back."

"Do you have a phone number for him? It's really important I get hold of him."

"Do you want to tell me why you're trying to find him?"

"I can't until I've talked to him."

"Okay. Hang on and I'll get it for you."

Horse heard the sound of the receiver being set aside. He could hear news in the background. It sounded like the Huntley-Brinkley report.

In a few moments, Lonnie was back on the line. He gave Horse a number with a Los Angeles area code.

"Thank you, Lonnie."

"You're welcome."

Horse hung up and sat thinking about what Lonnie had told him. Just because Lonnie said Clarke had never been back to Smoke Tree didn't mean he hadn't. It had been his experience that people did all kinds of things that people close to them knew nothing about.

He dialed the Los Angeles area code and the number Lonnie had looked up. It only rang twice before it was picked up.

"Hello."

"Is this Clarke Clovis?"

"Speaking."

"Clarke, this is Lieutenant Caballo of the San Bernardino County Sheriff's Department. I'm calling from Smoke Tree. Clarke, there's just no easy way to say this. Your mother and father have been murdered. My apologies for breaking it to you over the phone like this."

"Murdered?"

There was a momentary silence.

"Who killed them?"

"We don't know."

"Can you tell me what happened?"

"They were shot. Both of them."

"Where did this happen?"

"At your home."

Clarke's voice broke.

"So, mother died in the Godforsaken dump she had to live in all those years," he said.

Horse could tell he was crying.

"She deserved better than that. Just for putting up with Caleb she deserved better than that."

There was silence as Clarke struggled to get himself under control.

"But why would anybody kill them? It can't have been robbery. They didn't have anything. Never did. If you added up the value of everything they ever owned it wouldn't come to, to…"

He sputtered to a halt

"Clarke, do you need a minute? Do you want me to call you back in a half hour so you can absorb this?"

"No, no. I'm okay. Sorry, but I don't know what to do."

"Arrangements have to be made. Can you come out here so we can take care of that and talk in person?"

Horse heard Clarke take a deep breath.

"Okay. Okay. I can do that. I'll drive out in the morning."

"That will be fine. What time can you be here?"

"I'll leave around five. Be there around eleven or so."

"Do you know where the substation is?"

"Sure.

You know, Lieutenant, I haven't been in Smoke Tree since I left high school. I know it's not that far from where I live, but in a many ways it's farther than Chicago or San Francisco or New York."

"Well, this is a sad occasion, but I'm sure there are a lot of people here who'll be glad to see you."

"Mr. and Mrs. Jenkins, and the guys I played with in the Blue Notes, sure. But I was a nothing and a nobody to my classmates. Never had a friend my own age."

There was deep bitterness in his voice, and Horse was reminded again of how difficult Clarke's childhood must have been.

"Speaking of Lonnie, I got your phone number from him. He wanted to know why I had to talk to you, but I couldn't tell him before I talked to you."

"I understand."

"I was thinking, when you've had some time to collect yourself, you might give him a call. He's probably worried about why I had to get hold of you."

"Sure. Of course I'll call him."

"Once again, Clarke, I'm sorry I had to give you this news over the phone. And thank you for agreeing to come out. Drive carefully."

"I'll see you tomorrow, Lieutenant."

"Goodnight, Clarke."

When Horse hung up, he reviewed his conversation with Clarke Clovis. He hadn't sounded like a man with something to hide. And he had sounded genuinely surprised to hear his parents had been murdered

Horse stayed at the office a little longer, adding his conversations with Lonnie and Clarke to the case notes. When he turned out his lights and walked into the outer office, Merle was doing yesterday's crossword puzzle in the Los Angeles Examiner.

"All quiet out there?"

"Mostly. Had to dispatch a unit to Cadiz Summit. Otherwise, everything's okay."

"What's going on a Cadiz?"

"Apparently some drunk is causing a problem at the café. The owner requested help."

"All right. Good night, Merle."

"Night, Lieutenant."

Chapter 7

CHRISTMAS ON THE DESERT

In his dream, the frozen bodies lay sprawled in unnatural positions along the shoulder of the road and in the ditches lining each side. The fighting had been so fierce, Horse was afraid he wouldn't live long enough to ever get to a warm place.

As his unit moved down the road, feet dragging in exhaustion, equipment clanking, one of the corpses suddenly sat up and spoke.

"You there, boy! You caught that sonofabitch shot me?"

Horse fell out of line and walked to the desiccated, rag-wrapped body.

"I don't know who shot you, Caleb."

"Well, you'd damn well better find out. And it's Mr. Clovis to you, wetback. That sorry-ass badge you wear don't mean you don't have to show respect to your betters."

Horse ignored the insult.

"Who was it, Caleb. Who shot you?"

The corpse smiled a disgusting, cunning smile full of rotting teeth.

"Well now, that's for me to know and you to find out, beaner. Think I'm going to do your job for you after you tried to get between me and my Eunice?"

Caleb lurched to his feet.

"Say, where is that sorry bitch?"

"Eunice is dead too."

"Good. Never did want no one touching her after I was gone."

Caleb turned to take in his surroundings. When he turned his head back to look at Horse, it tilted at a precarious angle and came to rest against his shoulders. The eyes that stared at Horse were now vertically aligned.

Caleb took a step toward Horse. When he did, his head detached from his body and hit the frozen ground. It bounced and then rolled. It came to rest against Horse's boot. The hate-filled eyes stared up at him in consternation.

Caleb's body, now headless, folded in on itself in slow motion and fell to the ground.

The head spoke to Horse.

"Say, wetback, just where in the hell are we?"

"Korea, Caleb. This is Korea."

"Be damned. Never knowed it was so cold."

Caleb's eyes closed with an audible click.

Horse stood staring down at the closed eyes, but Caleb did not speak again. Nor did his eyes open.

Horse turned away, stepped back into line and joined the weary marchers.

As he did, a mixture of rain and sleet began to tumble out of the sky. Horse could hear it striking his steel pot. He unshouldered his pack and rummaged through it, looking for his poncho. He couldn't find it. He was getting wetter by the minute. He knew he could die of hypothermia if he got soaked through.

Maybe someone else had a spare. He tried to call out to the soldiers stumbling past him. At first he couldn't even get his mouth to work. Finally, he managed to force open his lips slightly and croak, "poncho."

No one heard him. He began to panic.

"Poncho," he tried to shout, but his throat was constricted and his voice came out as nothing more than a muffled moan. He tried again and again without success.

Someone was calling his name.

The frozen field, the corpse-littered road, the rain and sleet and the leaden sky faded away as he rose toward consciousness like a man struggling to rise from the bottom of a well.

"Carlos! Wake up! You're having a bad dream."

He opened his eyes.

Esperanza was kissing his face.

"I was?"

"Shhh! It's all right. It was just a dream. It's okay now."

Horse rolled onto his side and wrapped his arms around Esperanza. She scooted closer to him. He was shaking. He still felt like he was freezing.

"I was back..."

"I know *mi carino*. I know. But you're here with me now."

"Thank you for waking me up. I was in Korea, and there was rain and sleet..."

He stopped talking.

"*Escucha, escucha*, Esperanza."

They lay quietly, wrapped in each other's arms.

"I hear it," she whispered. "It's raining."

Horse shook the remaining wisps of the dream out of his head and swung his feet onto the floor.

"I know these dreams. If I go back to sleep now, I'll be pulled back into it before morning. I'm going to get up for a while. You go back to sleep."

"I've got a better idea. Let's go look at the Christmas lights on Broadway. They'll be beautiful in the rain. They'll push that nasty dream out of your head.

I'll make some hot chocolate to take along."

Horse leaned back on the bed and kissed her cheek.

"Ah, *querida*, you always know just what to do."

They got up and got dressed. Esperanza went into the kitchen to heat the milk for the hot chocolate. Horse got the old Stanley thermos out of the cupboard. All the while they listened to the soft sound of the rain on the rock roof.

Rain was rare in Smoke Tree. Less than four inches fell in a normal year, and almost all of that came in February and March. Although there were sometimes flash floods in August, they were usually from rain that fell far off in the mountains and rushed without warning down Paiute Wash under a cloudless sky.

A sudden, heavy rain sometimes hit the town itself in summer, but that was a rare occurrence.

But not as rare as rain in December. While rainclouds would sometimes appear on the distant, western horizon, struggling to reach Smoke Tree, they hardly ever did.

When they walked outside, the perfume of the damp desert night filled the air. The creosote all around them gave off a sweet smell it had at no other time. The rain had subsided to a soft drizzle. It was now more like a steady drip than a rainstorm. They stood on the veranda for a while, taking it in. The cloud ceiling was very low, and they could see a faint trace of lights of Smoke Tree on the undersides of the clouds to the north.

Horse unlocked the passenger door of his Ford Interceptor. Esperanza got in with the thermos and two mugs. Horse handed her a Navajo blanket, one of their favorites. He went around to the other side and climbed in. When the big engine rumbled to life, the department radio blinked on. Horse adjusted the volume to a soft hiss. He and Esperanza rolled slowly down the long, dirt road to Highway 95. There were no cars on 95. That was not unusual in the overnight hours. But when they reached the stop sign where 95 merged with 66, traffic was moving steadily in both directions.

Highway 66 never slept. They merged into the flow.

The Christmas lights above the road began where 66 turned north and became Broadway, Smoke Tree's main street. Horse drove slowly through town. The engine in the patrol car was muted at slow speed, and they could hear the sibilant whisper of the wide, high-performance tires hissing on the blacktop that glistened in the light, steady rain. The multi-colored lights overhead were reflected in the blacktop outside their windows behind the cone of their headlights. "Vacancy" signs blinked from the only two motels on Broadway. All the restaurants were closed. Only one service station was open.

The overhead lights ended where Smoke Tree's only traffic signal blinked yellow as they approached the point where 66 swung east off of Broadway and passed by the Santa Fe depot before turning north again.

"Which way, Espy? On down Broadway or follow 66 all the way through town?"

"Let's turn around and do Broadway again. The lights are so pretty. Then we can come back this way and go up Jordan Street Hill and see if anyone still has their decorations lit this time of night."

Horse went across the intersection and pulled into the parking lot at the Bank of America. He shut off the engine.

"How about some of that hot chocolate?"

Esperanza unscrewed the stainless steel top and handed him the thermos. He twisted out the big cork and filled the mugs Esperanza held out to him. They sat silently, sipping cocoa and watching the traffic slow for the curve. Traffic was light, and sometimes the intersection was empty for a minute or more. When that happened, the Greyhound station sign was reflected in the street beneath the blinking traffic light that added its own orange smudge to the blacktop. Their windshield gradually beaded with moisture, putting a halo around the lights outside and making Horse and Esperanza feel comfortably isolated in their own world.

When their mugs were empty, they saved the rest of the chocolate in the thermos for later. Horse pulled out onto the street and set off south down Broadway. They made another pass through town, then turned back the way they had come, enjoying the lights and the gentle rain.

"*Que linda,*" said Esperanza.

"It is, isn't it? I'm glad we never moved away."

"Me too. This is home. I don't ever want to leave."

The radio barked when somebody keyed a mic.

"Dispatch."

"Andy here. Going for beans. Over."

"Roger. Is it quiet out there? Over."

"Quiet as the grave since I settled everybody down out at Cadiz. I'm clear."

Horse shuddered, suddenly remembering the sound Caleb's eyes had made as they clicked shut at Horse's feet in his dream. He willed the image away. Not the kind of thing he needed to be thinking about.

They continued across the intersection when they came back to the Broadway/66 split. Horse drove north several blocks before turning west up Jordan Street. They climbed the hill to the projects and drove the three parallel streets of shabby, low-cost, rental housing. Almost every house had at least one string of Christmas lights visible.

They drove out of the projects, back onto Jordan Street, and on up the hill where they idled slowly through the streets of Smoke Tree's only two subdivisions, both built in the 1950s. Except for "The Heights" where Smoke Tree's very few well-to-do families lived, these were the most expensive houses in town. A few houses still had Christmas lights on, but most of them were dark.

When they had driven all the streets, they drove back to Jordan Street and turned down the hill.

"Did you notice, *querida*?"

"Yes. The most lights in the poorest neighborhood."

"Let's drive to the part of town where we were kids and see if it's true over there. I never really thought about that kind of thing when we were young. Did you?"

"*A veces.*"

Horse took Jordan Street across Broadway and east to where it dead-ended into Highway 66. He waited for a break in the traffic and then turned left. After a few blocks, he turned right off 66 and took the underpass beneath the Santa Fe tracks.

As soon as they passed Smoke Tree Hardware and Building Supply, a mismatched collection of small houses began to line both sides of Garces Street. They drove each of the north/south streets: Hidalgo, Valencia, Otero and Zapata. Then they drove the east/west streets: El Paso, Alameda and La Paz. Almost every house in the close-knit neighborhood was illuminated by Christmas lights

"Just like the projects."

"Just like."

Horse slowed to a crawl at the corner of Valencia and El Paso to see if his mother was awake. Her windows were dark, but the strings of green and red lights he attached to the eaves and overhangs of the little house for her every December were shining brightly.

"I think your mama went to bed."

"Probably before nine."

"I wish she'd come and live with us."

Horse shook his head.

"It doesn't matter how many times we invite her. She's not going to come. She wants to stay in the house where she and Papa lived when they were young."

Horse drove back to Garces and took it east all the way to the washboarded dike road that paralleled the Colorado River at the east edge of town. He drove slowly south. There was not a single light visible anywhere across the river. He stayed on the dike until it merged with a dirt road that had come across the bridge from the Arizona side of the river. He stayed on that road as it turned west to the bay and buildings that were the property of the Bureau of Reclamation and its endless, river-dredging operations. He continued on past the Bureau complex until the road went over the Santa Fe Railroad tracks at an unmarked crossing. He pulled onto 66 again and then turned left into the parking lot of the Flying "A" station. The station was closed, but the sign was on. By the light from the sign, Horse could see someone had painted holly, small Christmas trees and Frosty the Snowman on the station window.

The simple decorations made him smile.

He shut down the cruiser, and he and Esperanza listened to the light rain through the partially open windows as they drank the last of the cinnamon-flavored hot chocolate.

When he started the engine again, Esperanza touched his arm.

"Let's go through the downtown just one more time. It's so peaceful tonight."

"Okay."

They joined the traffic and drove into town again. They were on Broadway approaching Zion Street when Horse saw someone standing in the rain on the corner, arms spread wide and face upturned.

"Is that Willy?"

"Looks like."

Horse turned onto Zion and rolled down his window.

"Evening, Willy."

Willy lowered his head. He stepped off the curb and walked over.

"Ainin, Orse."

"Yes, it is, Willy."

"Ain in Ecemer!"

"Yes. Pretty rare."

Willy ducked his bare head and looked into the car.

He smiled.

"Miss Eseranza!"

"Hello, Willy."

"Amos Rismas, Miss Eseranza."

"It sure is. Be Christmas pretty soon."

"Aray."

"Yes, hooray."

"No. Rismas aray."

Horse turned to Esperanza and translated.

"Christmas parade."

"Oh, I'm sorry. Sure, Christmas parade this Saturday."

"Willy, I should have the results about that big dog tomorrow. I'll come out and see you when I get them."

"Oay."

"Would you like us to drive you home?"

"Oh, no."

Willy bobbed his head and lifted his hand as if he were doffing an imaginary hat.

"Ni, Miss Eseranza."

"Night, Willy."

"Ni, Orse."

Willy walked back to the sidewalk. They watched for a few moments as he headed for Front Street, waving his damaged hands as he carried on a conversation with himself.

As Horse and Esperanza drove home, the tempo of the rain increased. They were back in bed by two in the morning. Horse lay listening to the rain for a long time before he fell asleep.

He did not dream again.

Chapter 8

THE SURVIVING SON

In spite of the hours of sleep he had missed, Horse was up at 5:30. When he walked outside, the clearing, black sky was filled with stars curled in their westward spiral. Canyon and Mariposa began to nicker and shuffle in their corral in anticipation of breakfast.

He and Esperanza were on the veranda drinking coffee when the light began to come into the sky. As they watched, the remaining clouds from the rain of the night before drifted up the flanks of the Black Mountains. They reached the top as the sunrise drew closer, the rays streaking the rising clouds red, magenta and orange. Just before the red ball lifted, the clouds were suddenly shot through with streaks of gold and silver. A moment later, the sun cleared the Black Mountains. When it did, the last of the clouds disintegrated into faint multi-colored wisps. There would be no rain this morning for Kingman or Peach Springs or Seligman. The sky left behind was a huge bowl of cornflower blue so clear that Horse and Esperanza could see a dusting of snow on the Hualapai Mountains over eighty miles to the southeast.

After breakfast, Horse walked out to inspect Esperanza's garden in the full light of day. Years before, she had established the garden next to the corral with its ready source of fertilizer. The squash and beans were ready to pick, as were the broccoli and cabbage. The previous night's cold snap had finished the tomatoes, but they had been just about done anyway. The few that remained on the almost leafless vines were all they were going to get.

Gardening on the Mojave was a challenge. No vegetables could be grown in the heat of the desert summers. But with careful timing, it was possible to take advantage of two growing seasons each year. The first involved planting in late February and harvesting in early May. The second season started in late September and sometimes lasted until early December. Everything Horse tried to grow promptly died, so he limited himself to maintaining the compost pile and hauling load after load of soil from the Colorado River bottom to mix into the plot for Esperanza, who was a wonder at coaxing life from the harsh conditions.

Horse walked over to look at the three pomegranate trees on the north side of the garden. The fruits would be ready for picking by Christmas. That meant lots of pomegranate jelly for the coming year. The leaves had completed their seasonal change from green to orange and were beginning to fall. The trees looked like holiday decorations, filled as they were with a crop of red fruits.

Horse returned to the house for one more cup of coffee before going to work. When he drove down the dirt road toward Highway 95, the sun was already well up in a Mayan-blue sky completely devoid of clouds. The thirsty desert had swallowed every single drop of the overnight rain. It was as though it had never fallen. Dust billowed behind his unit.

He stopped at the front desk to talk with Merle and review the overnight log. Other than Andy driving out to Cadiz Summit Café and making it clear to a drunk at the café that he was on the verge of spending the night in jail in Smoke Tree, it had been a quiet night.

Horse was in his office catching up on his poster board and reviewing his notes when his intercom buzzed.

He walked to the door and stuck his head out.

"Yes, Fred?"

"A man named Dixon on the line. Says he's calling from Blythe. Says he'll only talk to you."

"Okay, I've got it."

He walked back to his desk. He picked up the phone as he sat down.

"Lieutenant Caballo speaking."

"What the hell kind of a outfit you runnin' up there?"

"Sir, I have no idea what you're talking about."

"This here is Wright Dixon. I own property out on River Road."

"Go on."

"Had me a call from my renter yesterday night. Told me one of your deputies said she should tell me to get rid of a bunch of junk beside the house and trim them salt cedars."

"Yessir. He talked to me about the situation out there. Deputy Andy Chesney responded to a prowler/peeper call at your property. When he drove up, someone was hiding in all the junk piled up near the house. He couldn't go after the guy until he made sure your tenant was okay."

Dixon interrupted.

"So?"

"Deputy Chesney talked to the young lady when he came back from trying unsuccessfully to run down the suspect on foot. She was very shaken. She said she thought someone might have been prowling around the place a couple of other times."

"Oh, horse puckey! Damned hysterical female. Probably her time of the month."

"Well, Mr. Dixon, Deputy Chesney doesn't have a 'time of the month', and he definitely saw the prowler."

"And that makes it all right for him to tell my renter to tell me to haul trash and trim trees?"

"That was his recommendation."

"Just where the Sam Hill does your boy get off interfering in my private business?"

"He was doing his job. Your tenant is a vulnerable woman living in an isolated place. She has enough security problems just being there, let alone dealing with a custom-made hiding place for some pervert. My deputy made the right recommendation. In fact, I'm glad you called so I can tell you personally to get that trash out of there and trim those trees, Mr. Dixon."

"I'll do no such a damn thing. And you can't make me."

"But I can tell you it's the right thing to do and hope you'll have the sense to do it."

"Well, I don't aim to. That silly woman can just move."

The line went dead.

It was the second time in two days someone had hung up on Horse.

He got up and opened his door.

"Fred, has Andy come in off shift yet?"

"No, Lieutenant."

"When he does, send him in."

"Will do."

Ten minutes later, Andy Chesney was sitting in front of Horse's desk. Horse recounted his conversation with Wright Dixon.

"Thanks, Lieutenant, for sticking up for me."

"Sure. Mr. Wright was wrong.

Anyway, I wanted to let you know he's probably not going to do anything about the problem. And if we started issuing citations about junk on properties in unincorporated areas, that's about all we'd ever have time to do."

"Understood, sir.

Can I ask you something?"

"Of course."

"Would it be improper for an off-duty deputy to help a young woman haul some stuff away and trim some trees?"

Horse smiled.

"No, certainly not. But this is the first I've heard about this being a young woman. Your report didn't mention her age."

"Well, yessir. She is. A young woman, that is."

"Any chance this young woman is also pretty?"

Color rose to Andy's face.

"Real good chance, Lieutenant."

"Just wondered.

Now, go on home and get some rest. You're going to have to keep your strength up. I suspect you're going to be lifting some big, bulky items into the bed of your pickup this weekend."

"Yessir."

Horse was plowing through the paperwork that had lain fallow on his desk since Monday morning when Fred opened his door.

"Horace Creighton on the line for you, Lieutenant."

"Got it, Fred."

Horse picked up his phone.

"Good morning, Horace."

"Good morning, Lieutenant. Good news! The lab in San Bernardino says the big dog wasn't rabid."

"That's a relief. Thanks for calling."

When Horse hung up, he picked up his gun and hat and walked out of his office.

"Be out for a bit, Fred. Need to deliver some good news to Willy Gibson."

"No shots for Willy?"

"That's right.

And I'm expecting a visitor. If he shows up, tell him I'll be right back."

Horse drove to the landfill. He pulled up outside the building where Willy was living and knocked on the door. Willy broke into a smile when he opened the door.

"Orse!"

"Morning, Willy."

"Ome in."

Horse stepped inside.

The small room was immaculate. The dirt floor had been swept clean. The bed was made and clean. Dishes were stacked on a small table. Willy's duffel bag, a galvanized bucket half full of water and a folding chair were the only other items in the room. Willy had hauled out all the junk Lucinda had accumulated over many years.

"I came out to tell you the good news. The dog that bit you didn't have rabies. You won't have to get those shots."

"An oo!"

"You're welcome. Came out as soon as I heard. I didn't want you worrying."

Willy smiled at his friend. His kind, gray eyes seemed to gleam in the dim light.

"Gotta go. Have to meet someone at my office."

Horse walked outside and got in his car. As he drove away, he could see Willy in the rear view mirror waving goodbye with both damaged hands.

When Horse got back to the substation, Fred handed him a message slip. Captain Hardesty wanted Horse to get back to him as soon as possible. Horse hurried into his office and made the call.

"Hardesty."

"Morning, Captain. Lieutenant Caballo."

"Morning Horse. Got some results for you from the autopsy."

Horse got his case notes and picked up a pen.

"Ready."

"The medical examiner pulled two more rounds out of each body. I walked them over to ballistics and they tell me all the rounds came from the same gun. .38 caliber. Everything points to a single shooter.

And your coroner made a pretty darn good guess about how long the bodies had been in the shack. The official estimate puts the murder in the Thanksgiving holiday window."

"That gives us something more definite to go on."

"Next, the ME managed to get partial prints from the skin remaining on the fingers of the victims. They match up with the prints I lifted inside the shack and off the pickup. But those prints don't match the partial from the door and a couple of other complete prints from inside the place."

"So, whoever shot Caleb and Eunice had probably been in the shack before."

"Right. Just as we thought, it looks like the killer opened the door and walked in shooting."

"So it's not likely he stuck around to put fingerprints all over the place afterward."

"Unless he was looking for something."

116

Horse thought a moment.

"You know, Captain, I just can't imagine there was anything of value to be found."

"So, since theft probably isn't the motive, we're back to family. Have you been able to track down the son?"

"Talked to him on the phone last night. He's driving out from L.A. this morning. Should be here any time."

"Any chance he'll voluntarily provide a fingerprint?"

"I think he will."

"Okay. I'll photograph the unknown prints. I'll hand them to the conductor on the Super Chief this afternoon with instructions to leave them for you at the dispatcher's office at the depot."

"Okay. Train should be in around nine. I'll pick them up.

Captain, if Clarke gives us a print and it's different from the ones you're sending, we'll be one step closer to crossing him off the probable list."

"If we eliminate him, where does the investigation go?"

"I'm hoping my talk with Clarke will lead somewhere."

"Okay. In the meantime, I'll put the photos I took in the mail to you for your file."

"That reminds me. What about the crime scene? Do you want to keep it closed up?"

"For now. Do you think the son will want to see it?"

"I don't know."

"Well, if he does, go ahead and take him out, but don't let him touch anything.

Any other thoughts about the case?"

"One more thing. That Geiger counter we took out of the shack is sitting in my office. Something about it bothers me. I don't know much about those things, but I do remember coming across a guy using one down in the Devil's Elbow area near The Needles. The one he was carrying looked a lot more sophisticated than this one."

"Is there someone out there you can ask about it?"

"Not that I know of. But there are a couple of places in Vegas that started selling them after the whole 'get rich quick with uranium' thing took off. I'm going to run up there with this one and get an opinion. Like you said, it's either family or money. Uranium isn't money, but it has value. It may be a long shot, but maybe there's something there."

"Let me know what you find out, or if there's anything I can do to help."

"Will do, Captain. And thanks again."

"Anytime, Lieutenant. Anytime."

When Horse hung up, he added the new information to the poster board. Then he reluctantly started back to work on his pile of paperwork.

It was almost noon when Fred knocked on his door.

"Your visitor is here."

"Step inside for a minute, Fred."

Fred approached his desk.

"I'm going to ask Clarke to allow us to fingerprint him. Have everything ready in case he consents."

"Will do."

"Send him in."

Fred walked out of the office. A moment later, there was a young man in the doorway. He was over average height and very thin. He had deep-set, dark eyes and black hair that curled down over his forehead. There were traces of acne on his cheeks. He reminded Horse of a taller version of a young Frank Sinatra.

Horse stood up.

"Clarke, I'm Lieutenant Caballo. Come in and have a seat."

Clarke sat down and looked directly at Horse. Horse took that as a good sign.

"Let me start by saying how sorry I am about what happened to your mother and father."

"When I talked to you last night, Lieutenant, you didn't tell me when they were murdered. And I was so shook up, I didn't ask."

"As nearly as we can tell, around Thanksgiving."

"And you just now learned about it?"

"That's right. The day before yesterday."

"Who found them?"

Horse decided not to try to explain yet about Joe Medrano and tracking the dogs across the desert.

"I did."

"Then how do you know when they were killed?"

"Autopsies were done by the Medical Examiner in San Bernardino."

"Is Mother's body there now?"

"Yes. The county will return both bodies to the Askew funeral home here in Smoke Tree."

"Just Mother, Lieutenant. I want to bury her at Desertview."

"And Caleb?"

"I don't care what they do with him."

"Clarke, it's clear you didn't like your father…"

"'Didn't like' hardly covers it, so let's not beat around the bush. I hated Caleb. He was heartless and cruel and evil. When I was little, I had this fantasy he wasn't really my father. That my real father would show up some day and rescue my mother and me."

"You told me on the phone that you hadn't been back to Smoke Tree since you left soon after high school. Not even for holidays?"

"Not for any reason. This is the first time I've been back since September of 1956."

"Okay, I understand you hated Caleb, but didn't you want to visit your mother?"

"She told me never to come back."

"Why would she do that?"

"Let me explain. Thanks to Mr. Jenkins, I got a scholarship to the Thornton School at USC."

"Yes, he told me about that. He told me you were so good you had your choice of top-notch schools."

"When I turned sixteen, I had started working in the summer and after school. Caleb took every cent I earned. I started as a box boy at Milner's Market, and when I was eighteen, Mr. Milner gave me a full-time job as a checker. It paid a lot more money, but no matter how much I made, Caleb took it all."

"When did you turn eighteen?"

"In July of '56."

"If you were making more money by then, why didn't you just move out?"

"What do you know, Lieutenant, about how Caleb treated my mother?"

"I know of two bad incidents."

"But you didn't do anything, did you?"

"Your mother wouldn't press charges. Legally, there was nothing we could do."

"Caleb's the reason I didn't move out. He told me that every time I didn't come home with my paycheck, he would whip my mother."

"Wait a minute. When you say 'whip', you mean beat her, right?"

"No, Lieutenant. I mean whip her. He whipped her with a leather belt. That's why she told me to leave and never come back. She said if I left town he might whip her a few more times, but he'd stop once he knew I was never coming back. She wanted me to get away so I could have a better life.

I told her I'd come back for her when I was done with school and making a living, but she told me she wouldn't leave Caleb. She said no matter where she went, he would come after her, and it would be even worse for her.

I tried to convince her L.A. was so big, he'd never find her there. It didn't matter. She was too afraid, too defeated."

There were tears on his face. He wiped them off and continued.

"I know she's in heaven. If there's justice in God's universe, anyone who suffered like she did has to be. You know, Lieutenant, I had Mr. Sorrento for English at Smoke Tree High. One of the books he had us read was *Walden Pond*. You ever read that?"

"Can't say I have. But that's Thoreau, right?"

"That's right. He wrote in that book, 'The mass of men lead lives of quiet desperation'.

I remember thinking that was only half right. If he thought men led lives of quiet desperation, he should have studied women. There's nothing that turns desperation to despair like helplessness. And my mother was helpless. She was a prisoner of Caleb's violence and her own fear."

He paused to regain his composure.

"I hope to God it didn't take her a long time to die."

"I don't think so, Clarke. From what we could piece together at the scene, I think she died almost instantly."

"Caleb too?"

"Yes."

"That's too bad. I was hoping the rat bastard had suffered. I guess I'll just have to settle for him burning in hell."

Both men sat with their own thoughts for a moment.

"Clarke, there's something I have to ask you to do."

"What's that?"

"We lifted a lot of prints inside the shack. They were almost all from Caleb and your mother. But there were a few prints that didn't match theirs."

"Who did they belong to?"

"We don't know. But I want you to allow us to fingerprint you."

"You mean you think I did this?"

"We have to eliminate you as a suspect. Copies of the unidentified prints we took at the scene are coming out on the train this evening. I can compare your prints with those. If there's no match, we can pretty much cross you off the list."

"Pretty much?"

"Investigations don't end until the killer is found."

Clarke sat silently a moment.

"Okay, I'll do it."

"Good. Come with me."

They went into the outer office, and Horse took the prints. After Clarke cleaned the ink from his fingers, they returned to Horse's office.

"Thank you again, Clarke.

Now, did Caleb or your mother have any living relatives that you know of?"

"As far as I know, Mother never had any contact with her family."

"Where did she grow up?"

"On a farm in Livingston County, Missouri, not too far outside Chillicothe. Her father was a sharecropper, just like Caleb's father."

"Is her family still there?"

"I have no idea."

"What was your mother's maiden name?"

"Smythe. That's S M Y T H E."

"How about Caleb's family."

"His mother and father are dead."

"Any brothers or sisters?"

"One older brother."

"What's his name?"

Clarke thought for a moment.

"Tyler. Tyler Clovis."

"Did you ever meet him?"

"No. Best I know, he never came out here."

"When did Caleb and your mother come to Smoke Tree?"

"Mother told me they came west in 1935. This is where they ended up."

"Why Smoke Tree?"

Clark laughed a bitter laugh.

"Mother said Caleb promised he would take her to California if she eloped with him. When they crossed the river from Arizona, he said this was all the California she was going to get. Said he didn't have enough money to go any farther anyway."

"So how did Caleb buy the land."

"What land?"

"Where your place is."

"He didn't."

"Did someone give it to him in trade for something?"

"Nope. They just went far enough from town that Caleb thought no one would notice and squatted there."

"Why that particular place?"

"Because it's completely worthless. Caleb said no one would care. And he was right. No one ever said a word."

"So, the land belongs to the Bureau of Land Management?"

"I don't know."

"Well, they own all that land out that way."

"Then I guess it belongs to them. They're welcome to it"

"I can drive you out there if you want."

"I never want to see that place again."

"What about the dogs?"

"Dogs?"

"They had four dogs on the property."

Clarke shook his head.

"When I was a kid, I wanted a puppy so bad! Caleb wouldn't allow it. Said he wasn't spending money to feed a dog. Said it cost enough to feed me. I guess they got dogs after I left."

"Do you know how Caleb and your mother made ends meet when you were growing up?"

"Mother worked as a fry cook different places. Wherever she worked, Caleb worked washing dishes. If you hired her, you got him too."

"I see."

"But then Caleb would get fired, usually for being drunk at work. And if he got fired, he wouldn't let mother keep working there. Said he didn't trust her to be around other men when he wasn't there."

"What did they do for money when Caleb got fired and cost your mother her job, too?"

Clarke shrugged.

"This and that. Washed cars down at the Mobil station in the summer. Did clean up jobs around town and hauled stuff away with the old Studebaker.

But I can tell he did two things without fail. Drink up their money and beat Mother."

"And you? Did he beat you, Clarke?"

"Not much. The occasional backhand if I got too close to him. But he mostly ignored me, unless he wanted my paycheck when I got older. He stomped me pretty good a couple of times when I wouldn't give it up. When I got big enough to hold my own, that's when he beat my mother instead if I wouldn't hand over the money."

"One more question."

Horse got up and took the Geiger counter off the shelf in his office. He put it on the desk.

"I found this in his pickup."

"What is it?"

"It's a Geiger counter. Did you ever know Caleb to go prospecting for uranium?"

"Caleb? Prospecting? That would involve walking. Maybe even up and down hills. It would be like work. No, I don't think anyone ever caught Caleb doing any extra work."

"Clarke, thank you for driving out her and meeting with me. I really appreciate your cooperation.

How long will you be in Smoke Tree?"

"I called Mr. Jenkins after I talked to you last night. I'm going to stay with them tonight. I'll go by the funeral home in the morning and make arrangements for mother before I drive home. I'm playing at a club in Hollywood tomorrow night."

"When are you heading to the Jenkins' place?"

"We planned to meet after school, but I've got a little surprise for Mr. Jenkins. I'm sure concert band still meets last period. At least it did the whole time I was in school. I'm going to drop by with my horn. Play a little for the kids. Maybe I can inspire one of them like Mr. Jenkins inspired me."

"He'll like that. And the kids will too."

Since you don't have to be there for a while, I'd like to buy you lunch and hear about what you're doing now. Unless you'd rather not."

"No, Lieutenant, that sounds fine."

Horse strapped on his gun and picked up his Stetson. He and Clarke walked into the outer office.

"Going to lunch, Fred. Any emergencies, call the Bluebird Café. I'll be there with Clarke."

"You got it, boss."

When they went outside together, Horse saw a black '58 Thunderbird parked next to his cruiser.

"You want to ride with me?"

"No, I'll meet you at the café. I can drive up to the school from there after lunch."

A short time later, Horse and Clarke both parked on Broadway and walked to the Bluebird. When they went inside, the lone waitress called out, "Anywhere you want, Lieutenant."

They took a booth by the window and pulled the menus out from behind the napkin dispenser.

In a few minutes, the waitress came over with a coffee pot and two mugs.

"Coffee?"

They both nodded. She filled their cups.

"I'll give you a minute to decide."

After they studied the menu, the two men sat sipping their coffee and watching the steady stream of traffic outside the window on Route 66 until the waitress returned with her order pad.

"What'll it be, gentlemen?"

125

"What do you recommend, Robyn?"

The waitress looked at Clarke closely.

"Do I know you?"

"I was in your class at Smoke Tree High."

"Really?" She studied him a moment longer.

"Sorry, I don't remember."

"Clarke, Robyn. Clarke Clovis."

"Boy, I'm drawing a blank here."

"That's okay."

Robyn took their orders, walked behind the counter and hooked them on the wheel.

"I was wondering, Clarke. How did you get back and forth to school all those years? There were no school buses out your way."

"Until third grade, Caleb took me in the truck."

"And after that?"

"When I started fourth grade, Caleb said I was big enough to walk. So I did. Down the hills from our place, then across the big wash and up that steep cliff on the other side. Three miles in all."

"That long walk for a child.

You went to Rio Vista Elementary?"

"Right. And then Smoke Tree Junior High. That's when something good happened, and my life changed forever."

"Lonnie Jenkins?"

"That's right, Lonnie Jenkins. I owe him a lot."

"Lonnie told me Caleb didn't like you playing the trumpet."

"Hated it. Probably because I loved it. I had to practice out in the hills. Hide my trumpet out there too. He found it one time and destroyed it."

"Lonnie told me about that. And Joe Medrano told me about you practicing out in the hills. Said he used to hear you out there."

"Who?"

"Joe Medrano."

126

"So that was his name. Sometimes when I was practicing, I got the feeling maybe someone was watching me. And then once I caught a glimpse of some guy."

"Joe must've meant for you to see him. People only see Joe if he wants to be seen."

Robyn came back with their orders. As she put the plates in front of them, she glanced at Clarke several times, trying to place him.

When she walked away, Horse spoke again.

"Do you mind if I ask you about something else?"

"Go ahead."

"No electricity out your way. Or water either, right?"

"Right. No electricity. The only water we had was what Caleb hauled. And God help you if you wasted water on unimportant things like taking more than two baths a month. That's the reason the kids in elementary school called me 'stinky'.

When I got to junior high and high school, I loved P. E. class because I got to shower five days a week."

"How'd you do your school work?"

"By oil lamp when I was in elementary. But only after Caleb passed out. He'd smack me if he caught me with a book. Said he didn't want me getting above myself. Said an 'F' had always been good enough for him, and it should be good enough for me.

In junior high I stayed after school and studied in the library. Meant I ended up walking home across the desert after dark. And the same in high school until I started working after school. Then I just went anywhere there was light after I got off work."

"How were your grades?"

"Good. I was especially good in math."

"But you say Caleb didn't want you to get higher than an "F". Wasn't there trouble when your report cards came?"

"Never happened. No mail service out there."

"And parent-teacher conferences?"

Clarke almost choked on his coffee.

127

"You've got to be kidding, Lieutenant!"

"So, no electricity, no running water. That meant no swamp cooler. How in the world did you manage to sleep on those hot summer nights?"

"We slept outside. On cots. Mother would fill the washtub with water. You would soak your sheets, then get on the cot and cover yourself. That would make it cool enough to get to sleep until the sheet dried out and the heat woke you up.

Then you did the whole thing again."

"How about cooking? I saw that wood stove in the shack,"

"Mother only cooked on it in winter. Summers she used the smaller stove out back. Had lots of meals with sand in them.

All in all, not a great life."

"Doesn't sound like it."

"You know, sometimes when I was starting out as a musician, I'd travel with some band playing small town gigs. We always stayed in the cheapest motels we could find. The other guys would gripe about the accommodations. I'd remember Smoke Tree and smile."

"How's life treating you now?"

"Real good, Lieutenant."

"Lonnie says you play in jazz clubs."

Clarke nodded.

"Up and down the coast. And sometimes in Chicago or New York. I also get lots of work as a studio musician on recordings. I've got a good reputation, and music is what I love. I can hardly believe I get paid for it."

"Based on that good looking car, it looks like you get paid well."

"I do. More than I ever thought I'd make."

"I don't see a ring on your finger, so I'm guessing you're not married."

"No, I'm not."

"Girlfriend?"

"No one special. One thing about being a professional musician: you're on the road more than you're home. Doesn't lend itself to anything steady."

Horse nodded.

128

"So, I guess the movies are wrong. In the movies, women are always chasing after the musicians. Especially the drummer and the trumpet player."

Clarke smiled.

"Well, there's a bit of truth in that. I mean, there are always girls around."

"You know Clarke, I remember hearing you play when you were young."

"With the Blue Notes?"

"That's right. My wife and I used to dance to your music. You already had a special sound."

"Thanks."

"I think you're quite a success story in spite of everything you had to overcome. I'm real happy for you. I hope your career just keeps getting better."

Robyn came back by and refilled their coffee cups.

"Thanks, Robyn."

"You're welcome, Lieutenant."

She turned and walked away and then suddenly turned back.

"I've got it! You're that boy that used to play the trumpet real good in the band."

Clarke smiled.

"That's me."

"You ever do any more of that trumpet stuff after high school?"

"A little. You ever do any more of that cheerleading stuff?"

Robyn didn't answer. She wasn't sure whether she'd been insulted or not.

After Horse paid the bill, they walked outside.

"Clarke, if you don't mind, I'd like to be at the cemetery when you lay your mother to rest."

"Thank you, Lieutenant. I appreciate that. I'll let you know when that's going to happen."

Horse handed Clarke one of his business cards.

129

"If you think of anything at all that might help us find the killer, please call."

Clarke put the card in his wallet.

"I will."

"If I don't see you again before you leave, safe journey."

Horse watched Clarke get in his car and drive away.

On the way back to his office, Horse sorted through his impressions of the young man. The difficulties he had endured growing up had marked him and maybe made it hard for him to really connect with other people. Perhaps it was more than time on the road that kept him from having a serious girlfriend.

There was definitely an edge to Clarke, and Horse thought he could see why jazz, with its frenetic, hyperkinetic energy and brittle, high-voltage overtones would appeal to him. It was the music of small, smoke-filled clubs, the antithesis of the wide openness of the desert. It was also the music of detachment and "cool," tamped-down emotions. And Clarke certainly seemed detached and purposely repressed.

Horse smiled at himself for indulging in pop psychology and reading too much into Clarke's choice of music. Maybe he should just admit he wasn't "hip" enough to understand jazz.

Late that evening, Horse pushed open the door of the cavernous Santa Fe Depot. His boot heels rang against the tile floor, but there was no one there to hear. The waiting room that had been so glorious in the heyday of train travel was shabby, dusty and empty. The high-backed benches sat unoccupied. The hanging chandeliers shone down on no one. The melancholy room echoed with the voices of those who had once filled it to capacity, just as they had filled the Harvey House that had been part of the depot long ago. That elegant place, with its apron-clad girls, linen tablecloths and polished silverware, now abandoned, had once been filled with the excitement of people taking lunch or dinner on a stop during what had been a transcontinental adventure.

The arrival/departure board behind the glass case above the tile wainscoting showed the Super Chief was running on time. It was a shame that there were no passengers waiting to get on.

Horse walked through the waiting room and out onto the cobblestone platform. A steel-wheeled baggage cart stood idle in front of the locked doors of the Railway Express Agency. He heard the train blow for the crossing where the rail line intersected the highway. The rails began to vibrate and sing their quivering, metallic song with the approach of so many tons of steel being pulled down the tracks by four thousand horsepower. Then he saw the headlight swing onto the final straight stretch toward the depot. It lit the tops of the rails to a silvery sheen. The train was coming so fast it was hard to believe it was going to stop in time. But the engineer hauled it down, brakes squealing and hydraulics pumping, into a gentle glide until it loomed in front of him, the huge diesel engines thrumming with enormous power.

As if it could hardly be bothered to stop.

As if it were impatient to get underway.

Underway to places where people actually clambered aboard with excited faces, lifting their luggage onto the racks at the end of the car. Not places like Kingman or Flagstaff or Winslow, but maybe Albuquerque. Yes, the engine seemed to rumble to itself, there will be passengers in Albuquerque. And if not in Albuquerque, then surely in Kansas City. There must be passengers in Kansas City!

As the massive engines idled, only three people got off. The conductor, Barry Wentworth, stepped out of the observation car. The engineer and the head brakeman climbed down from the cab. The engineer and brakeman that would take the train east climbed aboard. Barry and the replacement conductor nodded to each other as they passed. The replacement swung on board and gave the new engineer the highball.

The entire exchange of responsibility took less than two minutes. The gleaming, silver train was already straining into thunderous motion toward the next station when Horse met Barry halfway to the dispatcher's office.

"Evening, Barry."

"Evenin', Horse."

"Quiet night?"

"They're all quiet now."

Barry reached inside his uniform jacket and pulled out a small package.

"Captain Hardesty sends his regards."

He handed Horse the package.

"Thanks, Barry. We both appreciate it."

"Always glad to help."

Fifteen minutes later, Horse was back at the substation comparing the prints he had taken from Clarke with the prints in the photographs.

They were not the same.

Although it eliminated a simple solution to the murder, Horse was glad.

Chapter 9

ATOMIC TOM

Early Friday morning, Horse drove through Klinefelter on Highway 95 on his way north to Las Vegas. On the other side of the wide spot in the road with its amazing sweetwater spring and a decaying motor court, he crossed the Santa Fe tracks at Arrowhead Junction. On the other side of the rails he slowed to check on Hugh Stanton, the elderly owner of the old service station there. Mr. Stanton had suffered a stroke the previous June and nearly died. If young Aeden Snow hadn't glanced over as he was driving by and seen the old man lying in the dirt in front of the gas pumps, Mr. Stanton would probably not be alive this brisk, winter morning.

As he pulled off the highway, he saw Mr. Stanton sitting in his customary spot: a rocking chair beside the steps that led up to his enclosed porch. As Horse drove onto the dirt apron in front of the station, he slowed his speed to a crawl so he wouldn't cover the man with dust. He parked the cruiser and got out.

As he walked up, Hugh Stanton struggled to rise.

"Don't get up, Mr. Stanton. Just stopped by to say hello."

"Much obliged, Horse. Seems to take me longer and longer to get out of a chair these last few months."

Hugh Stanton was almost pathologically thin. His black eyes were buried in a face full of lines and creases. He was dressed in his usual outfit: gray, canvas pants, olive-green T-shirt, long-billed green cap and high-top boots. His only concession to the chilly weather was an unbuttoned flannel shirt over his T-shirt

133

"How have you been?"

"Good, Horse. Slow, but good. When I had me that stroke, the doc told me I might have trouble rememberin' things, but that's not been the case."

He laughed.

"Course, if it was, I wouldn't be able to recollect it, would I?"

Horse smiled.

"Mr. Stanton, you seem like your usual self to me."

"Well sir, still up in the dark to fix my coffee and toast so I can watch the sun rise over the Dead Mountains ever mornin'. That's a sure enough blessing."

Horse turned and looked toward the mountains. Both men studied the peaks.

"Say, Lieutenant, you ever hear from Aeden Snow?"

"Talked to his dad a while back. Said Ade's a little homesick and tired of the damp weather on the coast, but otherwise fine.

I guess college and football keep him busy."

"Good. Sure wish Johnny Quentin had gone with him."

"I do too. I never understood why Johnny joined the Army."

"And say, I hope things turned out okay for the young woman."

"Which young woman is that?"

"Oriental gal. Was with Ade when he come by the station on the Fourth of July."

Horse realized he was about to get another piece of a puzzle.

"Why would anything be wrong?"

"Like I told young Aeden when he stopped by the next week, I had some bad types come by here looking for her back in the early spring."

"Could you describe them for me?"

"Two of them. Big men. Nasty, mean lookin' fellas. Greased back, black hair. Both a them was packin' side arms inside their jackets. Come inside wavin' around a picture of a woman. Asked me if I'd ever seen her. I told them no. They seem inclined to argue about it. Told them even if I had I wouldn't tell them. Told them to leave out of my place. One of them didn't like that. Got real testy with me. I pulled that old sawed off, double barreled coach gun out from beneath the counter and thumbed back the hammers. Showed him where the cow ate the cabbage."

Horse couldn't help but smile. He would like to have seen that.

"Did they ever come back?"

"Nossir. But I did think I saw their big, black Chrysler just a-flyin' past around the time Aeden come by with that gal. I'm pretty sure she was the one in the picture. That's why I told him about it next time he stopped by."

"I know you keep a pretty close eye on the highway. Did you ever see their car go back by?"

"Well sir, it's a funny thing. I was out back pokin' around when I seen it take the cut off onto old 66 and head toward Goffs. Thought maybe they was lost."

"I have a feeling you don't have to worry about ever seeing them again."

"And the young woman?"

"Fine, as far as I know. She's not around here anymore, though."

"Well, I'm glad she's okay. Seemed a nice sort. I think young Aeden had took a shine to her."

They looked at the mountains a while longer.

"Well, Mr. Stanton, always a pleasure visiting with you.

I'd best be on my way."

"All right, Lieutenant. Thanks for stoppin' by to check on me, but you don't have to do that. I'm getting' way on in years, and one of these days my old ticker'll just stop. But it don't worry me none. I just hope I'm sittin' out here in my rocker when it happens. I'd like them mountains to be the last thing I see in this life so's I can remember them in the next."

"For my part, Mr. Stanton, I hope you live a long, long time. I'd miss stopping by to visit with you."

Horse turned and walked to his car.

He pulled onto 95 and continued north. In a few miles, he crossed into Nevada. As he drove, he put Mr. Stanton's information together with what he knew from arresting the two men in Smoke Tree and what Joe had told him earlier in the week. He doubted he would ever know all the details of the story. He had a feeling there had been more than money involved in the hunt for the young woman. He doubted there was a safe place for her anywhere in the country if the Mafia was still determined to find her.

There was no speed limit in Nevada, but because of the dips and curves, Horse held the cruiser to a steady sixty five miles an hour as he drove toward the former mining town of Searchlight. He passed through town and gradually picked up his speed.

When he came to the long, straight stretch that rose to the north, he could see for miles ahead. He took his Ford Interceptor up to a hundred and held it there until he saw the sun glinting off the windshield of a southbound vehicle on the upslope ahead of him. He slowed until the vehicle passed by. It was the only vehicle he had seen since leaving Arrowhead Junction.

The road began its long curve toward Railroad Pass. Horse pulled onto the shoulder and got out. He stood under the pale blue of a desert winter sky and looked to the south at the huge expanse of the Mojave Desert spread out below. It was a view he never tired of. Tens of thousands of square miles that contained perhaps six hundred people if everyone in Searchlight and all the cowboys in the Providence, New York and Ivanpah Mountains were at home.

Horse thought about the millions of years of change, sometimes infinitesimal, sometimes violent and sudden, spread out in layers below him. Oceans arriving and receding and then arriving again. Huge movements as the crust of the earth bent and folded and twisted and then folded again. Volcanoes erupting and leaving lava behind to be eroded away to nothing before more volcanic eruptions spread more lava. The violent history of the earth laid bare.

He saw the Newberry Mountains, known to the Mojave Indians as Avi Kwami, the sacred place where their creator, Mutavilya, called them together and gave them their clan names. And the place where Mutavilya's son, Mastamho, the savior of the Mojaves, stood with his giant stick and created the Colorado River, the river of life.

Beyond Avi Kwami, he could see the Sacramento Mountains west of Smoke Tree, and beyond them, far to the southeast, the Hualapais in Arizona, ancestral home of yet another tribe. The snow he and Esperanza had seen on the peaks of the Hualapais Thursday morning had melted away.

Horse stretched his back and flexed his knees as he enjoyed the cold air and the silent panorama. Reluctantly, he got back in his car and drove on.

Twenty minutes later, he pulled off Boulder Road outside Henderson, Nevada. He parked in front of the grandly named Atomic Tom's Uranium Prospecting Emporium. He hoisted the Geiger counter taken from Caleb's truck and went into the small shabby stucco building. There was a TV antenna sticking up above its flat roof.

The one room store was filled with prospecting equipment. Pointed-tip and chisel-tip rock hammers hung alongside crack hammers and hand mattocks. There were canvas rock sample bags and cloth-covered canteens in abundance. Everything in the place looked dusty, and the dust motes disturbed when Horse opened the door fluttered around the room in the light from the morning sun that filtered through the bare windows. The store smelled of dry desert – like shattered granite or andesite.

As Horse walked up, a man who looked like he was in his late fifties turned away from a topographic map he had been tacking to the wall behind a glass counter filled with rock specimens. There were so many maps they looked like wallpaper. The man was dressed in a faded khaki shirt and pants. He looked like he could use a shave. He smelled like he could use a shower.

"Are you Tom?"

"That's me. Tom Tierney."

"I'm Lieutenant Caballo of the San Bernardino County Sheriff's Department. I'm hoping you can satisfy my curiosity about something."

"Sure. Got nothing but time. Not exactly a rush on prospecting equipment lately."

Horse put the boxy, yellow device he was carrying on the counter.

"What can you tell me about this piece of equipment?"

The man glanced at it and shook his head.

"I can tell you it's a piece of junk. Back when uranium prospecting was booming, the company that built that thing started putting ads in newspapers and cheap magazines for them. They sold them through the mail.

They should have been arrested for fraud."

"Why's that?"

"Completely inaccurate. False readings galore. I never took one apart to see what made it click, but it wasn't uranium."

"How much did these sell for?"

137

"Twenty nine ninety nine. That right there should have told people something."

"How much does a good one cost?"

"Anywhere from a few hundred dollars to a thousand. And even good ones aren't really good for serious prospecting. They only work if the ore is above the ground or just below it."

"So what do you need to really prospect for uranium?"

"In my opinion, a spectrometer is best."

"What would one of those set you back?"

"A good spectrometer? Between five and ten thousand dollars. It's a real sensitive and accurate piece of equipment."

"So Geiger counters, even the good ones, only get the easy stuff?"

"That's right. Charlie Steen found the Mi Vida mine outside Moab, Utah, with one. Sold the rights to that mine for nine million dollars. Built him a quarter of a million dollar mansion on a hilltop outside of town. Heard he threw some hellacious parties up there.

Vernon Pick found the Hidden Splendor over by Hanksville, Utah, with one. Darn near died finding it. Got richer than Croesus. Unlike Charlie, got himself a long way away from the desert. Lives over in the Santa Cruz Mountains on the coast."

"And those stories started the boom?"

"Yep. Pretty soon the desert was crawling with amateurs. But the really big boys were already flying spectrometers around in helicopters. The little guys didn't stand much of a chance once that started. And then the Atomic Energy Commission drove the final stake into the little guys' hearts."

"How did they do that?"

"From 1949 to 1959, there was a guaranteed price for any find of a certain quality. But more importantly, there was a $10,000 bonus, payable immediately. That allowed some of the little guys to keep going. Without the bonus, most of them have called it quits.

And that's why I'm closing up shop here pretty soon."

"Can I pick your brain about something else?"

"As long as you don't pick it with one of those tools gathering dust on the wall."

"Say a guy goes out with one of these things and gets a false reading and thinks he's struck it rich. What does he do next?"

"Files a mining claim."

"And how do you do that?"

"First, you drive a big stick into the ground or make a big pile of rocks and stake your claim. Best to put your claim paper in something waterproof and nail it to the stick or bury it inside the rocks in a tin can. What you've got when you're done is called your claim monument."

"And then?"

"Pace off your claim. Pile rocks or drive stakes at all four corners around your monument."

"How big can the claim be?"

"No more than fifteen hundred feet long and six hundred feet wide."

"That's a pretty big chunk of dirt.

And that's it?"

"Not quite. You file a copy of the claim with the county recorders' office in the county where you staked the claim. In a few weeks, the county mails you a copy of the recorded claim. You mail that copy to the state headquarters of the Bureau of Land Management, and you're done."

"And you own the land?"

"Oh, no. Not yet. You have to have samples assayed. If the samples are high enough quality, then your claim is 'proved out'. When that happens, *then* you own the land."

"Thank you, Mr. Tierney. You've been really helpful."

"Now Lieutenant, I don't suppose you're going to go prospecting with that thing?"

"No, Tom, I'm not. But I think maybe someone else did."

Horse picked up the faulty equipment and stuck out his hand.

Tom shook his hand but seemed reluctant to have Horse leave. Horse suspected he might be the only person who would come into the shop that day.

"You know, Lieutenant, every time I see one of those things you have there, it reminds me of something that happened in the Depression. Up in the northern states and Canada they were having a real problem with potato bugs eating the crop. So a company started running ads in newspapers up that way for a guaranteed potato bug killer. Claimed it was so simple even a child could use it."

Horse had heard the story many times before, but the man had been very generous with his time, so Horse resigned himself to hearing it again.

"The ad claimed if you sent in $1.50, cash or money order only, you would get your guaranteed bug killer in the mail. And if you sent your money, your bug killer came.

Problem was, it was just two pieces of wood, each about the size of a playing card. Instructions came with it. Said to let the potato bug crawl onto one of the pieces of wood and then smash it with the other piece."

The man started to laugh so hard Horse was afraid he was going to choke.

"That's a good one, Mr. Tierney."

"Sold thousands of them before the post office shut them down."

He laughed again and shook his head.

"Anyway, Lieutenant, I know you have to be on your way."

"Thank you again, sir, for your help."

"And thank you for listening to a story you've probably heard before and being kind enough to pretend you hadn't."

Chapter 10

ANDY GOES CALLING

Andy Chesney got up at two o'clock Friday afternoon, brushed his teeth and took a long shower. He shaved and slapped on some of what his father always referred to as "foo foo water". He dressed in his very best Levi's and his pearl-snap-button shirt, the one with the pink and yellow cactus flowers embroidered across the shoulders.

By three, he was walking into the office at Rio Vista Elementary School. A secretary in a print dress looked up from her work over half-moon reading glasses as he stood at the counter.

"Can I help you, sir?"

"Yes ma'am. Is school out for the day?"

"Yes. The children are gone, but the staff is still here."

"I'm looking for one of the teachers. Christine Gehardy."

"And you are?"

"Andy Chesney, but Miss Gehardy knows me as Deputy Andy Chesney."

The woman smiled and pushed the glasses off her nose, letting them dangle from her neck from a silver chain.

"Ah, the knight who protects damsels in the night!"

"Well, I don't know about that."

"Since you're not in uniform, I'm assuming this is a social call?"

"Mostly, but with a little official follow-up thrown in."

The secretary pointed.

"If you go out the door and turn left and keep going down that corridor, you'll find room seven. I'm pretty sure Christine will be there."

Andy unconsciously raised two fingers to the Stetson he was not wearing.

"Thank you."

He went outside and walked down an empty corridor that echoed with the energy of recently departed children. There was something melancholy about the click of his boot heels on the cement absent their excited voices.

The door to room seven was closed. He hesitated. What was the protocol for a closed classroom door when there was no class in session? Was it like someone's home? Should he knock, or would that make Christine interrupt what she was doing to come and see who it was?

In the end, he rapped on the door, pulled it open and leaned his upper body inside.

Christine was at her desk. She looked up and smiled at him. He went the rest of the way into the room.

"Deputy Chesney. I almost didn't recognize you without the uniform."

"Good afternoon, Christine. I came by to talk to you about the situation at your place out on River Road."

"It's not good, I'm afraid. I called my landlord. He told me quite emphatically he wasn't going to remove the junk or trim the trees. He said I could move if I didn't like it."

"I know. My boss, Lieutenant Caballo, talked to him and got the same response. I don't think it's safe for you out there with those hiding places close to your house, so I'm offering to help you get rid of that junk and trim the trees. I can come out in my pickup tomorrow and start hauling stuff to the dump."

"What a generous offer! Thank you so much."

"I'm on the midnight shift again tonight. When I get off in the morning, I'll catch some sleep and then come out. Say about noon?"

"That would be fine. This will make me feel a lot better about living out there."

"I'll see you tomorrow, then. And I'll drive by a few times tonight to check on your place."

She smiled. Andy thought it was just about the prettiest smile he had ever seen.

He stood there, unsure of what to say next.

"Well, I'd best be going."

Andy turned and left, careful not to let the heavy door slam behind him.

After Andy was gone, Christine Gehardy sat in the quiet room and thought about how odd it was she was in Smoke Tree at all.

She grew up in western Pennsylvania and was the first in her family to go to college. When she graduated with her degree and her teaching credential, she started searching for a job near where she had been born and raised. She soon learned teaching opportunities were scarce in coal country because of the slow decline of the traditional mining industry. Automation underground and strip mining on the surface was trimming the work force and eroding wages. She looked all through June and July without success.

Christine knew California was booming. It was the fastest growing state in the union. The Los Angeles School District could hardly build schools fast enough. There was a huge demand for elementary school teachers. Several of her classmates had talked of going there because the jobs paid well compared to western Pennsylvania. Discouraged with her job prospects close to home, she started to think about leaving the place she had lived all her life. Because hers was a close knit family, she sat down and talked it over with her mother and father. They sadly agreed it might be best to look elsewhere.

She made a few phone calls and soon had an interview scheduled in Los Angeles in August.

She packed her car with everything she owned, which wasn't much. She drove west to Chicago where she picked up Route 66. As she drove farther west, she began to hear warnings against trying to cross the Mojave Desert in the heat of day. The conventional wisdom was to cross after sundown or well before dawn.

Since her 1950 Ford was not the most reliable car, she took the warnings seriously. She left Flagstaff one morning and got to Kingman about

143

noon. It was hot there, but not unbearably. After a quick lunch, she decided to drive on to Smoke Tree, spend the night there, and head across the Mojave very early the following morning.

She couldn't believe how fast the temperature rose when she left Kingman and drove through Yucca Flats and on down the hill. She stopped and opened all her windows, but that didn't help. It was like opening the door of a blast furnace. She had never, ever experienced that kind of heat.

She drove on through the blinding, white-hot glare to the valley floor below. When she crossed the bridge at Topock, she saw Colorado River for the first time. It was so blue. So appealing. She made the short drive to Smoke Tree with her car overheating badly and checked into the least expensive motel she could find to conserve funds. It was two 'clock in the afternoon. The *Pepsi* thermometer outside the motel office door stood at one hundred and eighteen.

She soon discovered why the room had been so cheap. The tiny window air conditioner was no match for the fierce heat. She sat in the room for a while, sweating and longing for the swimming hole near her home in Pennsylvania. And thinking about the beautiful blue river she had crossed.

Christine dug out the bathing suit she had planned to wear when she got to the Pacific Ocean. She left the air conditioner running full blast and went out and got in her car, practically getting second degree burns in the process. She drove until she saw a sign for Sunset Beach.

The Colorado was even colder than she had hoped. A lot colder. It felt wonderful. She stayed until after sundown. Between frequent dips in the fast-moving water, she sat on the beach, coated with Coppertone to keep from getting the sunburn of the century.

When the relentless sun slipped over the horizon, she drove back to town. When she went into her motel room, she discovered management had come in and turned the air conditioner on low. It was almost as hot inside as out. She turned it back to high and took a tepid shower before going out for something to eat. She found a place that sold five hamburgers for a dollar. She paid her dollar, plus a quarter for a frosty mug of root beer, and sat at a picnic table with her food. As she ate, she watched the cars stream by on 66 a few feet from where she was sitting.

Most of the cars were heading west.

"All these people," she thought, "heading for Los Angeles."

After she finished eating, she drove around town while she waited for her motel room to cool down. She saw kids laughing and playing outside, even though the temperature was still well over a hundred degrees. She drove by the two ball fields in town and saw games underway beneath lights surrounded by clouds of bugs. When she had seen most of the streets in town, she stopped at a little park on Palestine Street and sat on a swing, spinning around and listening to the silence and thinking.

For the first time, she thought hard about a question she had purposely avoided. What was small town girl from the Allegheny Mountains going to do in a big, noisy, crowded city like Los Angeles? Where would she live? How would she get to know people? Would she be safe? And just like that, she decided she wasn't going to L.A. She went back to her room, cranked up the air conditioner that had once again been turned to low, and slept well in spite of the heat.

She didn't get up early the next morning to start across the desert. She slept almost to check-out time instead. Then she went to the office and got the local phone book. She looked up the address for the school district office and asked the clerk for directions. She drove there on the off chance there might be a teaching job available in Smoke Tree. If it turned out there wasn't, she was going to backtrack to Kingman and then to Williams and then to Flagstaff. One of those places might have a job.

It turned out a job had just opened up. One of the teachers had discovered she was going to have a baby, and district policy prohibited women who would be "showing" from being in a classroom with young children. Christine interviewed with the Superintendent. By afternoon, she had been hired to teach at Rio Vista Elementary. She called the LAUSD and cancelled her interview.

In the tiny house she rented on River Road, with its inadequate swamp cooler, the heat of late August and early September had been a challenge. But by early October, the worst was over and fall was delightful. She began to enjoy the vast and open desert around her. She liked to look out the front window of her house at the Colorado River stretching out below in a broad panorama from the chalk cliffs on the north to The Needles in the south beneath a sky so deeply blue it was almost indigo.

And she liked Smoke Tree. There was certainly nothing fancy about it, but the plain, somewhat drab, blue collar town reminded her of home. People were friendly and unpretentious. They smiled at her in Milner's Market and at the bank and at the post office. They invited her to church. And the people she worked with made her feel welcome.

She loved the children in her fourth grade class. Mexican, white and Mojave Indian, their diversity was something she had never experienced in rural Pennsylvania where the population was ninety nine percent white.

As the Christmas holidays approached, she had to admit she was a little homesick for that special season in the hills and hollows and sulphurous creeks of the Appalachian Mountain Range of western Pennsylvania with the family gathered and the possibility of snow. But as she sat in her quiet and empty classroom, all in all she did not regret her decision to stay in Smoke Tree.

She had carved out a little niche for herself on the easternmost edge of the Golden State.

Chapter 11

EAST SIDE INCIDENT

Just after one a.m. Saturday morning, the phone on the bedside table woke Horse from a deep sleep.

"Yes."

"*Hijo*, there are a lot of men in the Alvarado's yard."

It was his mother. He was immediately wide awake.

"*Que esta pasando, Mama?*"

"I was asleep. Car doors slamming woke me, *y luego voces*. I got up and looked out the front window and saw some men in Arturo's yard. I walked outside. *Luego vinieron mas hombres.*

Arturo's windows were dark until one of the men started shouting. *Luego, sus luces se encendieron.*"

"What was the man shouting?"

"Send out Javier. But it sounded funny."

"Funny how?"

"He said the name the gringo way, not the Mexican way. Then he walked toward the *porche*. When he reached the *pasos*, Arturo came out the door carrying a baseball bat."

"Did Arturo say anything?"

"*Ya sabes, hijo mio, no oigo tan bien mas*, but something like, 'You're not welcome at my house in the dark of night'."

147

The man started up *los pasos*. Arturo lifted the bat and said, 'Take one more step and I'll bust your head open'. He said that real loud. *Le oi buena.*"

"What did the man do?"

"He backed down the steps and stood with the other men. One of those who came late had a bottle. The men passed it around. I don't think it was the first bottle they had, either. Arturo was standing on the porch staring at them. *Con su bate de beisbol.*

That's when I came inside to call you. I'm afraid they're trying to get *suficientemente valiente* to go up on the *porche.*"

"You did the right thing, mama. *Voy en camino.*"

He hung up.

"What is it, *novio*?"

"Some kind of problem across the street from Mama."

"Is Consuela all right?"

"I think so, but she wants me to come down."

His department cruiser was at the Ford dealer, left there for maintenance after he returned from his errand in Nevada. Since he was taking his POV, he decided to dress in civilian clothes. Might give him a chance to quietly assess the situation before deciding what to do.

He put on the Levi's and t-shirt that were folded on the chair next to the night table.

Esperanza sat up in bed and turned on the lamp.

"I'll make some coffee."

"No time, *querida*. This sounds serious."

He picked up the phone and dialed the station.

"Merle, Horse here. Who's on midnight tonight?"

"Andy, Jim, and Wally."

"Who's closest to town?"

"Andy. He's on cattle rustling patrol out in the river bottom."

"Have him meet me at 220 Valencia, corner of Valencia and El Paso. I'll be there first, so have him pull into the driveway behind my pickup. Tell him to come lights and siren until he's inside the city limits, then light bar only.

Tell him to leave the light bar on when he parks."

"Got it."

Horse hooked his short-barreled .38 in its clip-on holster over his belt. He lifted the lined, Levi jacket off the chair and shrugged it on. He sat on the edge of the bed and put on his socks and chukka boots.

When he was done, he leaned over and kissed Esperanza on the cheek.

"Go back to sleep."

"You know that's not going to happen. *Por favor, tenga cuidado.*"

He kissed her again.

"I'll see you when I'm done."

He stood up and hurried out of the house.

When he turned into his mother's driveway, she was standing on the porch, wrapped in her robe against the night air. She looked frail and worried. Horse suddenly realized how fast the years were slipping away. His mother was not supposed to be this old.

A crowd was gathered across the street in the Alvarado's yard. Some of the men glanced his way when he got out of his truck but turned back to join the other men in staring at Arturo Alvarado.

Arturo stood on his front porch, facing the men below. He had a baseball bat in his big hands, his right on the handle and his left wrapped around the barrel. The menace in his wide, defensive stance made a strange contrast with the multi-colored Christmas lights outlining the porch.

Horse climbed the steps to his mother's house. She turned and hugged him. She weighed very little, and he could feel the bones in her back through the robe and the nightgown beneath it. Something about the gathering across the street filled him with a need to protect her.

"*Gracis por venir, mi hijo.*" I called the Smoke Tree *policia*, but they didn't seem interested. *Como siempre.*"

Horse stepped off his mother's porch and was walking toward the street when Andy came around the corner with his light bar flashing. He pulled in behind Horse's pickup.

Andy got out of the car. The rotating lights flashed on and off, giving a strobe-like effect in the dim light. The men on the yard turned to look toward the patrol car

Horse changed directions and walked up to his deputy.

"I'm not sure what we've got here yet, but there have been angry words between Arturo Alvarado, the guy on the porch, and the men on the lawn.

I'm going to head over there. When I have their attention, get your shotgun and move to a position behind them."

Horse crossed the street. He pushed his way through the men and started up the steps. He stopped halfway and nodded to Arturo.

"*Buenas noches, Senor Alvarado.*"

Arturo did not take his eyes off the crowd.

"*Buenas noches, Teniente.*"

Horse turned sideways on the steps and leaned against the railing. From his position he could see both Arturo and the men in the yard. He recognized the man in front as Elias Pickett, a brakeman on the Santa Fe.

"I know I'm in civilian clothes, Mr. Pickett, but you and most of these other men know who I am. Since you seem to be the man in charge here, why don't you tell me why you and your friends are trespassing on Mr. Alvarado's property in the middle of the night."

The man stared at him. Elias seemed a little unsteady on his feet, like he'd had too much to drink.

He straightened and took a deep breath.

"Because his son is messin' with my daughter."

The words were loud in the still night air, but they came out a little slurred.

"Explain what you mean by, 'messing', Mr. Pickett."

"Last night, my daughter Elaine went to the basketball game with some friends. She asked if she could go to the sock hop after the game, too. I said okay, but she had to be home by eleven. That's her weekend curfew."

Horse was suddenly pretty sure where this was heading, but he wanted everything out in the open.

"What's that got to do with Mr. Alvarado?"

Elias swayed slightly again.

"That's what I'm trying to tell you, Horse. Eleven came and went and no Ellie. It made me mad 'cause I'm marked up on the board and need my rest, but I couldn't go to sleep until I was sure my little girl was home."

"Go on."

"At eleven-thirty, a car pulls up and Elaine gets out. It was that car right there."

Elias pointed at a pre-war DeSoto parked in the dirt driveway next to the house.

"When she came in, I gave her hell about missing curfew. I asked her who was driving the car that dropped her off. She wouldn't tell me."

Elias lowered his head. At first Horse thought the man was losing his balance again, but then he realized Elias was embarrassed.

"I lost my temper and slapped her."

The door to the Alvarado house flew open, and a handsome young man just over six feet tall stepped out. He was very lean, but there was a coiled muscularity to him.

"You hit her? You hit Ellie?"

A voice rose from the crowd.

"That's him. Get him."

The men surged forward. The sudden movement knocked Elias Pickett to his hands and knees on the bottom porch steps.

Mr. Alvarado lifted the bat.

From his position in the street, Andy Chesney racked a round into his shotgun and fired into the air. In the silence that followed the shot, his voice carried loud and clear in the night air.

"Everybody step back from the porch!"

He pumped another round into the chamber.

Good lad, thought Horse. Quick decision. Authoritative, calm voice.

Elias rose awkwardly to his feet and backed away from the steps.

The crowd behind him gave way and turned to look for the source of the shot.

Lights began to come on in houses up and down the street.

151

Horse had turned to face the crowd as it surged. Now he turned side-on again before he spoke.

"Javier, get back in the house."

The crowd in the yard turned back toward the porch.

The young man continued to glare at Elias Pickett.

"You touch her again and…"

"*Callate y volver a la casa.*"

The same voice that had called out "get him" called out again.

"Don't talk to him in Mex. Speak American."

"I said, 'Shut up and get back in the house.' And you, whoever you are, you shut up too!"

Javier turned reluctantly away, anger still etched on his face, and went inside.

Horse spoke to Arturo.

"Mr. Alvarado, what say you put down that bat?"

Arturo stared at him with hard, hot eyes. For just a moment, Horse thought he wasn't going to comply. Then the man shook his head slightly, as if he were waking from an unfortunate dream, and leaned the bat against the post at the top of the steps.

Horse turned his head toward Elias Pickett. As he did, he noticed men from the surrounding houses coming outside and walking toward the Alvarado home. There were no sidewalks in this part of Smoke Tree, and the newly-arriving men began to form their own group in the street. There were no streetlights in this part of town either, but the Christmas lights in the neighborhood blended with the flashing lights from Andy Chesney's patrol car to illuminate a strange tableau.

One group of men, all white, completely unaware of the quietly-arriving second group, stood on the lawn staring at Horse. The second group, all Mexican-American, was slowly sandwiching Andy and his shotgun between themselves and the white men. The early morning chill was deep, but the air was still, and the rising vapors exhaled by the two groups were rendered visible by the colored lights. The vapors blended and twisted and then mingled equally in a way the two groups themselves never would.

Andy, just like Horse, had turned in profile so he could watch both groups. Horse continued to survey the scene until he was sure the second group had stopped short of Andy's position.

"You were telling me before one of your friends tried to make this an even uglier situation…"

Elias, still embarrassed over being knocked to his knees, struggled to regain his composure. The surge of adrenalin must have sobered him slightly because he didn't slur his words when he spoke again.

"Ellie told me that Alvarado boy in there had brought her home."

"And you got your friends together and drove down here like a bunch of vigilantes because Javier Alvarado gave your daughter a ride home?"

"Hell no! Huh uh! That's not the half of it. She admitted to me she has been seeing that greaser for a long time."

"Watch it, Elias! You're in the part of Smoke Tree where that kind of talk doesn't wash."

"Well, damn it, it isn't right. Mexican boys ought not be sniffing around white girls!"

There were murmurs of assent from those behind Elias. The men in the street began to inch forward.

"Before this discussion goes any further, I need to know if any of you men are armed."

No one spoke, but men in both groups were shaking their heads.

Horse allowed time for someone to speak up.

"One of you men is not being forthcoming."

He waited again before he spoke.

"Are you, Officer Nichols?"

A stocky man wearing a dark jacket stepped out to stand at the side of the crowd.

"I'm a police officer."

"You're not in uniform. Are you telling me you're doing some kind of undercover work?"

"I'm off duty."

Horse kept his voice mild.

"And like all of us in law enforcement, you carry when you're off duty. For example, I have my personal firearm in a clip holster inside my jacket.

Am I right in assuming you have yours?"

"Sure."

"And you're part of this," and Horse purposely hesitated as if he were searching for the right word, "*posse* in front of this man's home?"

"I'm here to support my neighbor. I live next door to Elias Pickett."

"So, just to be perfectly clear, you're saying you're not here in your capacity as a law enforcement officer?"

"No, I guess not."

"Being part of a mob is not appropriate behavior for an officer of the law. Leave, right now! You're already going to be mentioned in my written report of this incident. Staying will only make it worse."

Nichols bunched his fists at his side. He stood that way for a few moments, not wanting to lose face in front of the crowd. Finally, he unclenched his fists.

"Aw, the hell with it."

He turned and walked toward a car parked on El Paso street.

Horse watched until Nichols got in his car and drove away before he spoke again.

"Here's what's going to happen. All of you men are going to get off of Mr. Alvarado's property and get in your cars and leave."

The same voice as before came from the crowd.

"Not until we teach that boy a lesson."

Horse pushed away from the railing and turned to face the men directly.

Those on either side of the speaker stepped away slightly, giving Horse a chance to see him.

"Mickey McCoury. I should have known. Mickey, you're on the verge of biting off a helluva lot more than you can chew."

"Yeah? There's only you and that deputy back there with the shotgun. I don't think either one of you has the guts to shoot unarmed citizens."

"You might want to take a look behind you and re-calculate the odds."

Mickey and the other men turned. For the first time they saw the increasing group filling the street behind them.

McCoury turned back.

"Just a buncha damn Mexicans. No Mex gonna stop us from doing what needs to be done."

"Okay, that's it. The next person who says something inflammatory is under arrest."

"What's the charge?"

"Inciting to riot. That's a serious felony. I guarantee you jail time."

There was some grumbling from those assembled on the lawn, but Horse could tell the equation had been altered.

"All right, Horse," said Elias, "we're going. But that Alvarado boy hasn't heard the end of this."

Singly, and then by groups of two and three, the men began to straggle away and head for the string of cars parked along El Paso.

Horse walked up on the porch and stood beside Arturo.

"Go on inside, Mr. Alvarado. These people won't bother you anymore."

"Not tonight. But what about later? You heard what Pickett just said."

"I don't know, Arturo. I really don't. I'm going to have a talk with Elias. Just not tonight. I want to do it when he's sober."

"And I'll talk to Javier."

"I'm not sure either of us will have much luck."

"Maybe not. Javier can be stubborn. And he's too big to whip."

"And you've already seen what Elias Pickett is like."

Arturo shook his head.

"Things are changing, Horse. When I was young, none of us would've ever even thought of chasing after a white girl. In those days, white people had their world and we had ours. Was it still the same when you were a kid?"

155

"It was. But I bet if you asked the kids at Smoke Tree High, Mexican and white both, most of them would say Javier and Elaine going together is no big deal."

For the first time that night, Arturo smiled.

"Maybe we're the problem. The guys in my yard tonight and the guys behind them in the street and me. Maybe there wouldn't be a problem if it was just the kids."

Arturo picked up his bat and started toward the door. He stopped and turned back.

"Thanks for coming, Horse. All this goes on and the Smoke Tree Police Department doesn't even show up, except for that Nichols guy.

You hadn't come by, somebody might've got bad hurt."

"Glad to help, Mr. Alvarado.

Buenas noches."

"*Hasta luego, Teniente.*"

Chapter 12

WILLY AND HIS GUN

Horse was in his office on Saturday morning as he often was. But this time he was there earlier than usual. He was carefully writing his preliminary report of the events in front of the Alvarado house the night before. The fact that one of his officers had discharged a firearm into the air above a crowd of civilians made it essential for Horse to clearly explain the circumstances so those who reviewed the report in San Bernardino would understand why pulling the trigger had been the necessary and appropriate response. The fact that he had personally been on the scene made writing the report easier but no less critical.

When Andy Chesney came in at the end of the graveyard shift, Merle directed him to the Lieutenant's office. He tapped tentatively on the frame of the open door.

"Come in, Andy, and sit down."

"Good morning, Lieutenant."

"How was the rest of your shift?"

"Quiet, sir."

"Well, I guess you had enough excitement at the Alvarado place to last you the rest of the night."

"Yessir."

"I'm writing the report about what happened, and I want you to know I thought you did a fine job. Just fine."

"Thank you, sir. That means a lot to me. That was the first time I ever fired a round in the line of duty. Would you have done anything different?"

157

"No. What you did had the desired effect. Everything came to a halt. And what you said after you fired and the way you said it was good too. It was no-nonsense, and you delivered it with a steady, calm voice.

But now comes the hard part."

"What's that, sir?"

"Before you go home today, I want you to write down everything you saw, heard and did, from the time you got the call from dispatch to the time the men got in their cars and left and you went back on patrol.

Any questions for me?"

"Just one, sir."

"Go ahead."

"Do you have a chainsaw I could borrow?"

Horse had no trouble writing his own narrative longhand, but his typing skills were not the best. It took him over an hour to produce a relatively clean original and two carbon copies. When he was satisfied, he locked everything in his desk drawer and went home to take Esperanza to the Christmas parade.

At ten thirty, Esperanza and Horse were on their way downtown. It was a beautiful day, the diffuse winter sun producing more light than heat from a pale blue sky dotted with fish scale clouds. A mild breeze was blowing out of the southwest.

Since the Sheriff's Department had provided the color guard for the Veteran's Day services at Santa Fe Park in November, the Smoke Tree Police Department was helping the Lion's Club with the Christmas parade. These events rotated between the two departments.

Horse parked his pickup two blocks east of Front Street. They walked down Gilead to Front Street where they found a spot on the raised sidewalk across the street from the Santa Fe rail yard. They spread their blanket between two of the rusted iron tethering rings embedded in the cement that were a reminder of Smoke Tree's horse and buggy days.

The parade was so amateurish, innocent and simple, it was a joy to watch. Just the kind of thing Horse loved about life in his home town. The leading unit was the Smoke Tree High School Marching Scorpions, complete with baton twirlers, cheerleaders and pompom girls. Then came Miss Smoke

Tree in a 1962 Corvette convertible provided by Riverbend Chevrolet. The Smoke Tree City Council was next, at least those who weren't out on the Santa Fe mainline. The council was followed by Boy Scouts, Girl Scouts, Cub Scouts, Brownies and a few equestrian groups interspersed between simple floats on the backs of pickup trucks.

When Horse saw the 1934 fire truck coming down the street, he knew the parade was ending. Santa Claus, aka William Milner, owner of the biggest grocery store in town and Mayor of Smoke Tree, was tossing candy canes to children. Some of the canes were caught before they even reached the ground. The ones that made it onto the street were snatched up and sometimes tussled over up by excited children.

Horse said, "What do you say we get on home?"

"Let's. And thanks for bringing me to the parade."

"My pleasure. I think I like it even more than you do."

They were folding their blanket when Horse saw the police chief's car, light bar flashing, bringing up the end of the parade behind the old fire truck. There was a man walking in front of the car. A man with no pants and no shirt, wearing what looked like a giant diaper fashioned from a bath towel. A large blue ribbon had been looped under his chin and tied in a big bow on top of his hairless head. There was a badge pinned to his makeshift diaper. He had a gun and holster strapped to his waist.

There was a crudely-lettered sign around his neck. It read: "The Last Man. Happy New Year."

It was Willy Gibson. He had walked all the way down Front Street in a pair of cowboy boots and was limping badly because of his damaged foot.

Horse turned to Esperanza. She was crying.

His voice quivered with anger when he spoke.

"Let's go get Willy."

They jumped down off the high sidewalk, and Horse hurried with their blanket to Willy's side. He took the ribbon off Willy's head and threw it to the ground. Then he wrapped the blanket around Willy's badly scarred torso and led him to Esperanza. It broke his heart to see the gratitude in Willy's eyes for such a simple act.

Horse smiled at him and patted his shoulder.

"I'll be right back."

159

He turned and walked back to the middle of the street.

Chief Rettenmeir pulled up beside Horse and rolled down his window.

"What the hell you think you're doing, Caballo?"

Horse moved to the door.

"Who said you could humiliate Willy Gibson?"

"Aw, hell. I was just having a little fun."

"Well, it isn't fun for Willy. And it's over. Now get your car moving and catch up with the parade, *pendejo*."

"Hey, you're interfering with me in the performance of my public duty. I told the president of the Lion's Club I was going to do this, and he thought it was funny. Now pick up that ribbon, put it back on Willy's head, and get the hell out of the way."

He started to open the door.

Horse leaned against it.

"You get out of that car, I'll knock you on your sorry ass right here in front of everybody. You can see how *you* like being humiliated. If you think I won't do it, just climb on out."

Horse stepped away from the door.

Chief Rettenmeir jutted out his chin and glared at Horse. Then his eyes cut away.

"You haven't heard the end of this. I'm going to call your boss on Monday morning."

"Go ahead. And be sure to tell him I called you a *pendejo*. Sheriff Bland, unlike you, understands a lot of Spanish. I'm sure he'll translate for you."

Rettenmeir jammed his car into reverse and cut the wheels sharply while stomping the accelerator. He lost control of the car and careened off the pavement into a road sign, bending it almost perpendicular to the ground. Without getting out to check the damage, he shifted gears and jammed the accelerator all the way to the floor, almost losing control again as he fishtailed down the street.

When Horse turned around, Willy was standing beside Esperanza. She had her arm around him.

The blanket Horse had wrapped around Willy had slipped enough to reveal his holster and revolver. Something about the revolver wasn't right. Horse walked over for a closer look. It was not the rusted piece Willy usually carried. It was a .38 police special, and while it could use a coat of oil, it looked like a functional firearm.

Horse couldn't believe the Smoke Tree Chief of Police hadn't noticed Willy was carrying what looked like a working revolver.

"Looks like you've got a new gun there, Willy."

Willy nodded eagerly.

"Where'd you get it?"

"Oun ih."

"You found it?"

"Ess."

"Where'd you find it? Out at the dump?"

Willy shook his head.

"Oeo."

Wheels began to turn in Horse's head.

"At the rodeo grounds? When?"

Willy shrugged. He knew his sense of time was not always reliable.

"Try hard to remember, Willy. It could be real important. It could have something to do with that dog that bit you."

Willy thought hard. If he had been capable of wrinkling his brow, it would have creased with concentration, but except for his eyes and lips, his badly burned face was incapable of expression.

Suddenly, he held up his one good thumb.

"Lah mon."

"If we drive out to the rodeo grounds, can you show me where you found it last month?"

"Ess."

Horse, Esperanza and Willy Gibson made their way up Gilead and across Broadway to Palestine Street and Horse's pickup. They got in, with

Esperanza in the middle, and drove Willy to his place at the landfill so he could change clothes.

When Willy got out of the truck, Horse asked if he could keep the holster and the revolver. Willy unbuckled it, no easy task for a man with only two fingers on each hand, and gave it to Horse.

When Willy disappeared into the little shack, Horse removed the gun from the holster. He put the hammer on half cock and rotated the cylinder. There were spent empties in the cylinder, but no live rounds.

He sat thinking.

Esperanza turned to him.

"Chief Rettenmeir is a cruel man."

"Yes, he is. I suppose I've closed my eyes to it in the past, but today proved it again. And he's not only mean. He's stupid. Can you imagine not noticing that Willy had this gun?"

Willy came out and closed the door to the little building. He was fully dressed in his usual outfit. He got back in the truck.

When they approached the mouth of Eagle Pass Wash west of the rodeo grounds, Willy held up both hands, palms out. Horse stopped the truck and the three of them got out, Horse carrying the gun and holster. Willy led them to a stunted smoke tree well off the two-track. He stopped and looked around. He moved a little farther and knelt down and began to push the sand aside with his damaged hands. It wasn't long before he unearthed the rusted revolver Horse had seen him carrying for so many years.

"Why'd you leave your gun here, Willy?"

Willy moved both hands up and down as if he were weighing two items.

"You traded yours for the one you're carrying now?"

Willy's eyes lit up with his unusual smile

"Did you find the one you're carrying on the ground right here?"

"No."

"Where was it?"

Willy led them back to the truck and pointed to a creosote bush next to the road. Over the next few minutes, with a combination of his garbled language and pantomime, he recreated the following story of how he had found the gun.

Late one night in November, when Willy was getting ready to go to sleep in the new spot Horse had found for him in the announcing booth, he heard a vehicle. He went outside and saw a pickup truck drive toward the soft sand at the mouth of the Eagle Pass Wash and stop. He saw the dome light come on, and someone stepped out. By the light of a full moon that had risen at sundown under a cloudless sky, he saw a man walk away from the truck and into the wash.

Willy sat down on the platform at the top of the stairs and waited for him to come back. A long time passed, but the man did not return. Willy decided to go wait by the dark-colored truck.

The moon was much higher overhead when the man came running out of the wash. Willy stepped away from the truck to talk with him.

Willy's sudden appearance startled the man so badly he veered off the road. Then he stumbled and fell. He scrambled to his feet before Willy could help him up. Pushing Willy out of the way, he climbed into the truck and started it. When the headlights came on, they shone directly into Willy's eyes. The truck backed down the dirt road and almost hit the steps to the announcing booth before turning and driving off toward Highway 66.

It took a few minutes for Willy's night vision to return. When it did, the moonlight revealed something lying on the ground near where the man had fallen. When Willy walked over, he found a gun, the gun he had been carrying ever since. While he stood looking at it, he suddenly realized the truck was coming back up the road from the highway.

Willy was an honest man. Normally, he would have waited and given the man what he had dropped. But something told him that would not be a good idea. Instead, he moved away from the road and deep into the creosote bushes to the south.

The truck stopped where the man had fallen. He got out and began to call for Willy, asking him to bring back his gun. When Willy didn't answer, the man began to offer increasing sums of money. When that didn't work, he began to make threats. The effect of the threats was to drive Willy deeper and deeper into the desert and farther from the rodeo grounds.

For a long time, he could see the headlights as the truck drove up and down the dirt road. Finally, the man went away. But something told Willy he wasn't really gone. Willy sat down in the dirt and waited. After about a half an hour, the truck came back, moving slowly with its lights off. The man got out with a flashlight and began to search for Willy. Willy got to his feet and crouched low as he moved even farther away. He did not come back to his sleeping place that night or for the next two nights, returning to his old sleeping place in the mesquite thickets by the river instead.

Late the third night he returned, carrying the holster and rusted handgun he always strapped on before he did his rounds. He watched the announcing booth for a long time but saw no one. When Willy climbed the stairs, he discovered the man had scattered his possessions around the tiny room in his search for the gun.

When Willy was sure the man was nowhere around, he buried his rusted gun about twenty yards from where he had found the new one. Satisfied with the trade, he put the new gun in his holster before going downtown for his nightly patrol.

When Willy finished his account, Horse had questions for him.

"Did you get a good look at the guy?"

Willy nodded, pointed to the sky and make a circle with the finger on his right hand.

"Full moon that night, huh?"

"Ess."

Esperanza watched and listened as her Carlos asked questions and Willy communicated the answers in ways that were unintelligible to her.

After a few more questions, Horse had a mental picture of a man in his fifties, average height, with brown hair. However, Willy could not give him much information about the truck beyond the fact that it was dark blue.

"Willy, you've been a big help. But I'm going to have to keep the new gun. I know you found it fair and square, but I think it was used in a crime. I need it for evidence."

Willy shrugged and pointed at the rusted revolver he had uncovered.

"Sure, you can have your old gun back. You helped me with a big case. You've earned a milk shake at the Foster's Freeze. How's that sound?"

Willy smiled with his eyes and lips.

"Ahhola."

"Chocolate it is!"

The man Chief Rettenmeir had dressed in a makeshift diaper and told to walk down the street in front of his car in the Smoke Tree Christmas parade could have avoided military service in World War Two. After graduating from Everts High School in Everts, Kentucky, in 1938, he went to work for the Harlan Coal Company. When the war broke out, he was classified IIA, deferred for critical civilian employment. Willard Gibson wasn't a particularly patriotic young man, but since he was unmarried he didn't think it was fair someone with a family had to go to war while he remained safely at home.

He enlisted.

Staff Sergeant Willy Gibson eventually served as a Sherman tank commander in the Third Armored Division. Movies made after WW II often depicted pitched battles between Allied and Nazi tanks in that war. Such encounters were actually rare. The usual job of the tank was to provide close cover and firepower for infantry units advancing on enemy positions.

Such had been Sergeant Gibson's experience until the Ardenne Counteroffensive during the Battle of the Bulge in Belgium in December of 1944. In the critical fight for Eisenhorn Ridge, his tank had the misfortune to encounter a German Tiger IV tank, known to Allied forces as a King Tiger.

His M-4 Sherman was faster and more maneuverable than the German giant, but no match for its armor or main gun. The M-4s' seventy six millimeter guns had to be within three hundred yards of a Tiger to be effective. But the Tiger's eighty eight was deadly from over a mile.

Not only that, a Sherman had to flank a Tiger to have any chance at all because its smaller gun, even at close range, could not penetrate the front armor of the Nazi monster, while a Tiger's tungsten-tipped round could burn through any part of a Sherman's armor with ease.

Sergeant Gibson knew he and his crew were in serious trouble when the Tiger topped a rise on a hilltop less than twelve hundred yards from his tank. The Tiger commander spotted the Sherman below and began to accelerate down the hill. The only thing Sergeant Gibson could do was give the two squads of infantry following his tank a chance to survive by drawing the enemy tank away before it got close enough for its MG-34 machine gun to be accurate.

He shouted at his driver to turn at an oblique angle to the left of the Tiger's line of travel.

The driver pulled hard on the lateral and applied full throttle. As he accelerated, he pushed and pulled the laterals to move in an evasive, erratic path that made the Sherman appear to be attempting to flank the Tiger. As if in a bad dream, Sergeant Gibson saw the Nazi tank commander bring his behemoth to a full stop and rotate the turret.

To Private Tom Dale's credit, his evasive maneuvers caused the first two rounds from the Tiger's eighty-eight to miss. But that was all the luck the American crew was to have that bitterly cold winter day. The third round hit the front of the M-4 at an angle, instantly killing the driver, the machine gunner, and the main gunner. The tungsten round ignited the ammunition supply and incinerated the loader. The resulting explosion blew Sergeant Gibson out the open hatch.

The Tiger, seeing the Sherman erupt in flames, turned to pursue the American infantrymen.

When Sergeant Gibson awakened from a coma in a hospital two weeks later, he was in terrible pain. He had second and third degree burns over most of his body. The doctors explained the second degree burns were the ones causing the most pain, but the third degree burns were the most dangerous and could not be adequately treated in a field hospital. A blinding headache made it hard to understand what they were telling him. It also temporarily spared him from the realization he had lost most of the fingers of both hands and part of his right foot. The pounding headache was the result of brain injuries so severe the doctors treating him were amazed he had regained consciousness.

In later years, he would have no memory of his time in the field hospital after that initial awakening, nor of the flight that evacuated him to an Army hospital in New England dedicated to the treatment of severe burns.

When he was discharged from that hospital and from the Army in the winter of 1946, he had in his possession a purple heart; a bronze star for valor, an honorable discharge, and a letter signed by an Army psychiatrist explaining that while Willard Gibson had suffered brain damage in the service of his country, he was perfectly sane and no danger to himself or to others. He also had the pay that had accumulated from the day he had been wounded until his discharge. The bulk of that money was in large bills sewed into liners inside his trousers by one of the nurses who had cared for him.

Willy had no desire to return to Harlan County, Kentucky. There was nothing for him there. His ruined hands would not allow him to go back to work in the mines. Besides, he dreaded the stares of people he had once known when they saw the freak he felt he had become.

And Willy now hated cold weather. The terrible cold he and the other soldiers had endured during the forced march of General Patton's Third Army to the Battle of the Bulge was something he would never forget. So when Willy stood shivering in the bitter wind outside the gates of the military hospital in New England on the afternoon he was discharged, the pale sun that gave off no warmth already sinking in the west, he made up his mind he was going to live somewhere warm.

The driver of his tank, Private Tom Dale, had hailed from Phoenix. On those freezing days in Belgium, Private Dale had talked about the dry heat of the desert southwest so much that the men around him sometimes wished he would shut up and let them suffer from the cold in peace. As Willy recalled those descriptions, he decided to head for the desert.

To conserve his money, he began riding the rails. Starting on regional freights, he beat his way west. Along the way, brakemen and railroad bulls who would have rousted other men took one look at Willy and left him alone.

Reaching Chicago in early March, he found his way onto a westbound Santa Fe flatwheeler. Arriving in Belen, New Mexico in the middle of the night, he climbed off. He stayed in Belen for a few days, but it was too cold for him there. He went back to the rail yard. Unable to find an open boxcar, he climbed into a gondola headed west.

He nearly froze to death before he reached Flagstaff, but at the base of the San Francisco Peaks, the train slowly began its descent from the Kaibab Plateau to the Colorado River. Ash Fork was not as cold as Flagstaff, Seligman not as cold as Ash Fork, and Kingman not as cold as either place but still too cold for Willy. It was, however, just warm enough for him to fall asleep.

When he awoke, the train was slowing to a stop in Smoke Tree for a crew change. With some difficulty Willy Gibson, stiff and sore, thirsty and hungry, climbed out of the gondola under the warm sun of an almost-spring day.

He tilted his face skyward and spread his arms to take in the warmth. He smiled his strange smile. Willy had found the place he wanted. He would spend the rest of his life there.

That first day, he walked away from town and away from the railroad tracks to a mesquite grove near the Colorado River. He lived there, venturing into town only to buy bread and crackers and cans of sardines, spam, and Vienna Sausages. These items, which could be opened by a man with little use of his hands by holding the key with his teeth while turning the can, were the staples of his diet. His drinking water came from the river.

There were times when Willy was not completely sure where he was or how he had come to be there. On really bad days he could barely remember his own name. These periods were made more tragic by the fact that he also had periods where he was lucid. During those times, he could remember everything that had ever happened to him and thus all that he had lost. It was during one of those periods of clarity that he met Mac, the former Marine Gunnery Sergeant who owned The Palms, a beer and wine joint on Front Street.

Over the years as his funds dwindled, Willy began to go into Smoke Tree at night and scrounge scraps of food from garbage cans in the commercial part of town.

Mac's specialty at The Palms was his torpedo sandwich. His torpedoes were made on fresh, foot-long buns with dry salami, provolone, capicola, mortadella, finely shredded lettuce, pepperoncini, and a carefully concocted mixture of vinegar, olive oil, basil, oregano and rosemary. Mac was a perfectionist and a stickler for freshness, so any of the ingredients that showed the least sign of being beyond their prime were thrown away at the end of the night.

Willy learned that Mac sometimes threw away what Willy thought of as perfectly good food, so he checked the lidded garbage cans behind The Palms every morning around 3:00 a.m. One night, Mac came out to the alley to find Willy searching through the trash.

In the dim light from the streetlight that shone into the alley from Zion Street, the two men looked at each other. Somehow, Mac knew immediately that this was a fellow veteran. Perhaps it was the thousand-yard stare that glinted in Willy's eyes, a stare Mac himself sometimes lapsed into when he could suddenly swear he heard surf from a Pacific island beach hissing as it receded through the streets of a dusty town in the middle of the Mojave Desert.

That chance meeting led to a friendship between the two. Willy often came into The Palms just before closing time, and he was the only person Mac would allow to remain inside after he closed the cavernous bar with its high, stamped-tin ceiling, ancient black fans and autographed murals of Lefty Frizzel and Ferlin Husky.

Mac was a patient listener, and over a number of months on those occasions when Willy's thinking process was functioning at a higher level, he gradually learned what had happened to Willy in the Ardenne and about his discharge two years later from the hospital in New England. Mac thought it was criminal that the army had cut loose a man who had served so valiantly but been so badly wounded he could never work again.

Once Mac knew Willy's entire story, he was determined to get compensation for the injured man. He convinced Willy to go with him to the Veterans Administration office in Las Vegas. Using the serial number on Willy's honorable discharge, a good-hearted clerk made application for disability payments. The clerk said Willy's case would be strengthened if he would undergo evaluation by a V.A. physician, but Willy refused to go near a hospital.

The clerk's persistent and determined efforts led to a small monthly disability check that was mailed each month to a post office box in Smoke Tree, a box Willy had rented with Mac's help. Every month, Mac would go with Willy to the post office and from there to the Bank of America where Willy cashed his check. The money allowed Willy to eat without scrounging through garbage cans and to buy simple clothing and other essentials.

And Willy now had a second friend in Smoke Tree.

But his first and always best friend was Carlos Caballo, initially as a young boy and then as a grown man.

So when Horse asked him at the parade to think as hard as he could about how he had found the new gun, he thought so hard that his head ached; ached as badly as it had the day he woke up from his coma. But he remembered! He was proud of himself. And when Horse said he had to keep the new gun for evidence, Willy did not hesitate to let him have it.

Because Horse was his first and always best friend

Chapter 13

LIFE IS LOOKING BETTER

It was a very tired Andy Chesney who drove his pickup truck to Christine Gehardy's rented house on River Road at noon on Saturday afternoon. He had only managed a few hours sleep after his midnight shift. When he knocked on the door, Christine looked at him and said, "You look like you could use some coffee. I've got some on."

After two cups of black coffee and a few of Christine's date and nut pinwheels, Andy went to work. There was a lot of work to be done. He filled the bed of his pickup with load after load of the junk that had been scattered northeast of the house: an old icebox; a refrigerator not much newer than the icebox; two washing machines, both with the wringers attached; a hot water heater; discarded couches and tables; and a small, pot-bellied stove. There were engine parts: starter motors; batteries; rusted, bulging radiators, shock absorbers; leaf springs; brake shoes; air cleaners and one transmission housing. There was also a collection of body parts: three fenders of indeterminate vintage; two hoods; several bumpers, rust pitting their chrome; and a lot of windshield frames and broken windshield glass.

While Andy loaded and hauled, Christine worked inside, putting together a big meal. As she worked, she glanced out the window from time to time to see how he was doing and took him glasses of iced tea.

By the time he had ferried the last of the big pieces to the county dump, the sun was dropping in a blaze of red and golden glory behind the Sacramento

171

Mountains. When he climbed wearily from his pickup, Christine came out of the house to meet him.

He waved toward the salt cedars.

"I should have cut the lower limbs off those trees first thing. They're probably the biggest problem. I thought I'd have time after I hauled the junk away. Common failing of mine: overestimating the amount of work I can do and the amount of time I have to do it in. It's too dark now, but I'll come back tomorrow and take care of it.

The same with that thing sticking out of the ground over there. It's the engine block from an old, six-cylinder Dodge. I'll never get it into the truck, so I'll just dig underneath it and bury it."

He turned and opened the door to the truck.

"Don't run off, Andy. The least I can do after all you've done is feed you dinner. I've fixed pot roast, mashed potatoes and gravy, home-baked bread, and apple pie for desert."

Andy smiled.

"That sounds a lot better than the canned chili that was on tonight's menu at my place."

When he followed Christine into the house, the Christmas tree was lit, and holiday music was playing on the radio. It took him quite a while to get his arms and hands clean of the day's accumulation of grease, rust and dirt, but eventually he felt presentable.

After the best meal Andy had eaten in a long time, he and Christine lingered at the table over apple pie and coffee. Then they did the dishes together in companionable cooperation. Afterward, they moved to the small living room and sat on the couch where they could see the tree and hear the music.

And all that time, they talked. Christine told of her life growing up in Brush Valley, Pennsylvania, and about getting her teaching degree at Indiana State Teachers College. The Indiana in this case being Indiana, Pennsylvania, and not the state of that name. And she told him the story of how she had ended up in Smoke Tree.

In turn, Andy told her about his early life in Birmingham, Alabama. And about how his father had moved the family to Fontana to work in the steel mill there when Andy was in elementary school. He told her why he had decided to be a sheriff's deputy and how he had been assigned Smoke Tree after completing his training.

"So," said Christine, "Seems like we're both sort of here by chance."

"Seems like. My boss says there are four kinds of people on the Mojave. First are the ones who were born here and don't like it but are afraid to leave or just plain lack the gumption to get out of town. Next are the ones who were born here and love it and never want to live anywhere else. Third are the ones who fell off 66 and stayed because of inertia. And last are the ones who came here for various reasons and fell in love with the place and made it their home.

He says people in the second and fourth categories subscribe to *Desert Magazine* and put up with its grainy, black and white photographs because it's loaded with information about the real desert. He says those people also go to Smoke Tree Corner Drugs and thumb through *Arizona Highways* so they can look at the beautiful, color photographs, but they never actually buy it."

Christine laughed.

"I guess I'm in the fourth category. I'm just a small town girl at heart, and I like it here. What about you?"

"I think I'm a new category. I'll have to tell the lieutenant about it someday. Someone who came here and hated it at first but then slowly began to change his mind."

The heavy lifting of the afternoon and the lack of sleep after his midnight shift began to take its toll. In spite of an extra cup of coffee, he began to yawn. He tried to conceal it from Christine because he didn't want the evening to end, but she knew he was very tired. She told him they could talk more when he came back in the morning for breakfast. He was happy to accept the invitation.

As he drove through the streets of Smoke Tree toward his little apartment on Antioch, he looked at the Christmas lights and decorated trees in the windows of the small homes he passed. He smiled as he thought about the new category of Smoke Tree dweller he had invented and how well it suited him.

Chapter 14
JUST ONE MORE THING

Late Saturday afternoon, Horse was helping Esperanza with the final harvesting in the garden. But as they worked, he kept thinking about what Willy had told him at the rodeo grounds about the pickup. Willy didn't know the make or model of the truck, but he knew it was dark blue. Horse was thinking of a way to narrow the search a little.

When he stood up and stared off into the distance for the third time, Esperanza laughed and told him to go to the office and deal with whatever was on his mind.

The weekend dispatcher nodded when Horse walked through the door.

"Couldn't stay away, huh Lieutenant?"

"Been thinking about something. Is Kael Parks tied up with anything right now?"

"No sir. He's headed back to town from the south. Should be near five mile about now."

"Call him in."

Horse went back to his desk and spent some time adding the information about the man Willy had described to his case notes. Under description of the vehicle he wrote "dark blue pickup, make, model, plates unknown." He was reading through the entire file one more time when Kael showed up in his doorway.

"You wanted to see me, Lieutenant?"

"Come on in and pull up a chair. I've got a chore for you to take care of before the end of your shift. It's part of the investigation into the murder of Caleb and Eunice Clovis."

"How's that going?"

"Things are starting to come together. We know the medical examiner in San Bernardino thinks they were killed around the Thanksgiving holiday. And yesterday, something came up that makes me think it's possible someone saw a vehicle other than Caleb's drive over the berm at the end of Edge Street and head up the dirt road toward Eagle Pass around that time.

I want you to go up to Edge Street and knock on the doors of all the houses that border on Edge. See if anyone remembers seeing a pickup, other than Caleb's old Studebaker, drive onto Eagle Pass Road Thanksgiving week. If they did, hopefully they'll be able to describe it. If we get really lucky, maybe they can even describe the driver. This is a priority. I'll have Mark give any routine calls to the other deputies."

"I'll get right on it, Lieutenant."

"Write up a summary of anything you find and leave it with Mark."

Chapter 15

ELIAS EXPLAINS

Horse and Esperanza attended early Mass on Sunday and then treated themselves to breakfast at the Bluebird Café. The regulars who came in for their morning coffee nodded to the familiar couple.

All except for one.

Rob Sanders walked in and headed for his customary seat at the end of the counter before he spotted Horse. When he realized who was sitting in the booth he was approaching, he turned abruptly and went right back out the door.

"What was that all about?"

"Rob was one of the guys in the Alvarado's front yard Friday night."

"Oh my! I never thought Rob was that way."

"That's because you're married to a man who wears a badge and carries a gun."

"And if I weren't?"

"Because you're a pretty Mexican woman, you'd probably get crude remarks. On the other hand, he might look right through you. I don't know which direction that one might be twisted."

"Do you think what happened Friday night is going to be the end of it?"

"I was hoping it would be. But the way Rob turned and almost ran out the door, something else might be in the wind."

Later, Horse was sitting in his favorite chair watching a game he had been waiting for all week: The New York Giants and the Philadelphia Eagles, both 9-3, were playing in Philadelphia. With New York trailing, Coach Allie Sherman did the unimaginable: he pulled quarterback Y. A. Tittle and put in forty year old Charlie Conerly, the oldest man in the NFL. Just as Conerly trotted onto the field for his first series, the phone rang.

"Carlos speaking."

There was no response.

"Hello. Who's calling?"

"This is Elias Pickett."

"Go ahead, Mr. Pickett."

"I want to talk with you. Can we meet at your office?"

"If it will put an end to the nonsense I saw at the Alvarado house on Friday night, I'll be there."

"I need to explain about what happened. I thought about it all the way to Barstow and during my rest period up there and then all the way back. That's a lot of thinking."

"All right. Be at my office at one o'clock."

As he hung up, Esperanza came in the back door. She was wearing Levi's and a flannel shirt, and she had a smudge of dirt on her cheek.

"I thought I heard the phone ring."

"You did. It was Elias Pickett. He wants to talk. I'm meeting him at the office at one."

She wrinkled her nose at him.

"You know, *mi carino,* there's only way you can ever get away from your job. Go away to a place where there are no phones and don't let anyone at the office know where you're going."

"You're right. When this Clovis case is wrapped up, let's take Canyon and Mariposa for ride out near the Turtle Mountains. I'd like to go out there before those winter winds start to blow every day."

"I'd like that. Remember the last time we were out that way?"

"Spring of 1960. The year the wildflowers bloomed all over the desert."

"Looked like a many colored quilt."

"We'll go out there again before Christmas, *querida*, I promise."

Just after one o'clock, Elias and Horse were in his office with the door closed.

"I'm listening, Elias."

"I want to explain about Friday night."

"I hope your explanation is better than the one you gave Arturo Alvarado."

Elias hesitated.

"Horse, you think he really would've hit me with that bat?"

"I don't doubt it for a minute. Arturo is a proud man, and you challenged him in front of his family at his home. If you'd walked up onto that porch, someone would've had to carry you down."

Elias nodded his head.

"What I said Friday night? That was the liquor talking."

"And that mob you brought with you? Was the liquor talking when you called those men and told them to meet you there?"

"That wasn't me."

"Who was it, then?"

"After I had the argument with Ellie, she was crying. My wife pleaded with me to go outside and cool off while she got Ellie into bed. When I went out, Vernon Nichols was standing in our driveway. I asked him why he was outside so late. He said he'd heard loud voices in our house and came out to see if we were okay.

So, I told him what happened."

"Did you mention Javier Alvarado?"

"I did. He seemed upset about that.

Anyway, when I went back in. I could hear Ellie crying in her room and Alice trying to calm her down. I felt terrible, Horse. I've never touched my little girl before, but she wouldn't tell me the name of the boy who brought her home, and I lost my temper."

"Elias, I didn't buy that on Friday night and I'm not buying it now. There's something more to this story, isn't there?"

179

Elias lowered his voice.

"Yes. If I tell you something about Alice and me that nobody else in Smoke Tree knows, can I count on you never to repeat it?"

"If it involves a criminal act, Elias, I can't promise you that."

"No sir. No crime."

"All right. You have my word."

Elias took a deep breath.

"Me and my Alice had to get married. She was in the family way."

"I see."

"Maybe you do, maybe you don't. We grew up over in Bagdad. Not the one on Route 66. The one in Arizona."

"Copper mining town."

"That's the one.

You think everybody knows everybody else's business in Smoke Tree? It can't hold a candle to that place. Bagdad is a company town. Dodge-Phelps owns it, lock stock and barrel. I mean every house, every street, every business, the whole ball of wax."

Elias hesitated a moment.

"My Alice and me started dating just after high school. We were both working for Phelps Dodge. Things went real fast. By the time she was sure she was going to have a baby, she was already about three months on. People can count. If we'd stayed there, everybody would've known. Her family lived there. My family lived there. We knew we couldn't stand the gossip and the looks. We had to get out.

A justice of the peace over in Casa Grande married us. We came to Smoke Tree because we thought it would be far enough away from everybody we knew. I was lucky enough to find work on the Santa Fe, and we started a life here. It wasn't long before we were just another married couple with a young child.

That's why I worry about Ellie. She can be a little wild. And headstrong. We ride herd on her pretty hard. Curfews and where's she's going and who with and all of that. I don't want her to end up having to get married like her mother and me. I've always been afraid if she did, she'd think she has to move away, just like we did.

180

So, when she wouldn't even tell me who had brought her home, I raised my hand to her for the first time in her life."

His voice quavered.

"I'll never forgive myself for that. I don't think she and Alice will either."

Elias sat without speaking. Horse let the silence stretch out.

Elias was still looking down when he said softly, "And then she told me it was the Alvarado boy brought her home. And how she's been seeing him for a while. Said she was in love and wasn't going to stop seeing him, either."

He lifted his eyes to Horse.

"I said some things at that house on Friday night, Horse. But you've got to believe me. I'm not that way."

"What 'way' is that, Elias?"

"You know, real bad prejudiced."

"Could've fooled me."

"Darn it, I wasn't thinking good. I'd been drinking and worrying.

I love my little girl, Lieutenant. I don't want her life to start out hard and maybe get worse. You know people in Smoke Tree. What kind of life would her and the Alvarado boy have here if they got married?"

"It wouldn't be easy."

"It sure wouldn't. You saw those men in the yard."

"Yes, Mr. Pickett, I saw them. And I heard them. But now I hear you trying to tell me you didn't bring them there. You want me to believe they decided all by themselves to show up in front of Arturo Alvarado's house?"

"That's not what I mean. Someone did lead them there.

It was Vern Nichols."

Horse started to speak, but Elias held up his hand.

"I'll admit I had been drinking before I set out to drive down there and tell that boy to leave off seeing my Ellie. But that's all I was going to do. When I walked out to my car, Vern came out of his house. Told me he had called a few people and they were going to meet us there.

Called them for what, I asked him?

181

For backup, he said. Said he knew a lot more about that part of town than I did. Said I might need help because things could go real bad for a white man on his own over there after dark. Said he would help out. For protection, see?

So, when I got there, there were already men there. Most of them were railroad men – men I know, but some of them weren't. I still don't know who they were. Then Vern showed up, and some more men came with him. He had a bottle of Southern Comfort he started around, and someone else had a bottle of Four Roses.

And, well, you pretty much know the rest."

"I do. Anything more you want to tell me?"

"Yes. There's been something on my mind of late, and it's another part of why I was upset Friday night."

"Go ahead."

"I've had a feeling that someone is sneaking around outside my house."

"Why do you think that?"

"Little things that don't amount to much by themselves, but when you put them together, they start to add up."

"For instance?"

"Like footsteps outside at night, but if I go out there's no one there, at least no one I can see. That has happened a few times.

And Ellie told me she thought she had seen someone outside her window, just caught a glimpse out of the corner of her eye. But when she turned, they were gone."

"What's that got to do with what happened Friday night?"

"I thought about it as soon as Ellie told me she'd been sneaking around with that kid. I thought maybe that's who has been hanging around the house. You know, trying to get a look at her without her clothes or something."

"The times you heard footsteps and went outside, did you ever hear a car door slam or a car drive away?"

"No."

"Well, if it was the Alvarado boy, he'd have to drive there. So, isn't it more likely it's someone who lives nearby?"

"Could be."

"Who lives next door?"

"On one side, we got a widow woman, Mrs. Kenton."

"And the other?"

"Like I said before, Officer Nichols."

"Have you ever mentioned this to him?"

"I did. He said he'd keep an eye out.

And that's another thing that's strange about this. When Vernon's working days, he brings his patrol car home at night and leaves it in front of the house. I wouldn't think anyone would have enough nerve to come creeping around a house with a cop car parked in the street. But the times I thought I heard footsteps and went outside? His patrol car was there."

"How about other people in the neighborhood?"

"No one I think would be likely to do something like that."

Both men were silent for a moment. Elias thinking about his family situation and Horse thinking about what had happened out on River Road.

Horse broke the silence.

"What's going to happen now, Elias?"

"What do you mean?"

"Well, first, are you going to try to stop your daughter from seeing Javier Alvarado?"

Elias bristled.

"I'm not sure that's any of your business!"

"Friday night made it my business. Answer the question."

"I'm going to try to talk some sense into her. Try to get her to see how hard life would be if she ever married someone like Javier."

"When you say 'like Javier' you mean Mexican, don't you?"

"Well yeah! I don't think the races should mix, Lieutenant. I'm sorry if you're offended, but that's the way I see it."

"The fact they are seeing each other doesn't mean they are thinking about 'mixing the races' as you put it."

Elias got to his feet.

"When I was dating Ellie's mother, we never even talked about getting married. And look what happened.

It wasn't easy at first. And we were both white. Can you imagine how hard it would be for a mixed race couple of kids?"

"Elias, you've only lived here seventeen years. I've lived here all my life. I know exactly how hard it would be. But from what I know about today's teenagers, if you fight your daughter on this you'll lose. You'll lose the fight, and you might lose your daughter."

"Maybe that's a chance I have to take."

He turned to leave and then turned back.

"Thank you for coming in on your day off to talk with me, Horse."

"You're welcome, Elias. Stay away from the Alvarado house. If you want to talk to Arturo, phone him and arrange a meeting on neutral ground."

"Let me think on it, Lieutenant."

"Think hard, Elias. Think hard. What happens from here on out is on your head."

After Elias had gone, Horse sat thinking about what Arturo had said about times changing. And about how Arturo and his friends and Elias and the guys who showed up in Arturo's yard Friday night were the problem. How the kids might work it out if everyone left them alone.

Horse thought Arturo was right about the kids. And he didn't think Elias and the men who had been with him were ever going to change.

Before leaving the office, Horse decided to take a quick look through the information Kael had turned up on Saturday afternoon. The report was in a folder on his desk. He opened it and began to read.

Nobody had remembered seeing any vehicle other than Caleb's driving onto Eagle Pass Road around Thanksgiving. As Horse read through the negative interviews, he began to worry the assignment had been a waste of time.

But then he found it. Steve Landis, who lived on Monte Vista, said he hadn't seen anything over the holiday, but he mentioned seeing a vehicle take that road a number of times in September. Kael pressed Landis for details. Landis described the vehicle as a dark blue Chevrolet pickup, out-of-state plates. He hadn't caught the name of the state. He only knew it was not California,

Arizona or Nevada because he would have recognized any of those. But he said he was pretty sure the plates had been white.

Unfortunately, he was not able to give Kael a description of the driver.

Horse called the Highway Patrol office in Barstow and asked the sergeant who answered what color license plates were in Missouri.

In a few minutes, he had his answer.

They were white.

Chapter 16

EVERY WHICH WAY

On Monday morning, Horse was in the office early. But apparently not early enough. There was already a message slip on his desk. It was from a Detective Scanlon at the LAPD requesting a callback. He dialed the Los Angeles area code and the number.

"Detective Scanlon, Hollywood Division."

"Detective, this is Lieutenant Caballo, San Bernardino County Sheriff's Department, returning your call."

"Thanks for getting back to me, Lieutenant. We had a hit and run in Hollywood early Sunday morning, and I don't think it was an accident. The man who was hit is in intensive care. His name is Clarke Clovis. He had your card in his wallet. Is he part of something out your way I need to know about?"

"He is. His mother and father were murdered around Thanksgiving but we only found the bodies last week. I interviewed Clarke and gave him my card in case he thought of something that might help us find the killer.

So, you think the hit and run was deliberate?"

"I do. He was crossing the street outside a jazz club when he was hit. One of the witnesses said she saw the vehicle that struck him, a dark blue pickup, late model Chevy or GMC, unidentified out of state license plates, parked down the street. She says it started up and accelerated away from the curb when Clovis came out of the club."

"That ties into our case. On Saturday morning, I found out the possible killer was seen driving a truck that might fit that description. At least the color was the same. The person who saw the truck also told us the driver may have dropped the murder weapon close to the vehicle. Later that day, we had a statement from a different witness placing such a vehicle in the area.

You say Clarke is in intensive care?"

"Yes. We haven't been able to talk to him yet. He's still unconscious, but the doctors expect him to come around anytime now. He also suffered some kind of hip injury and lots of contusions.

It looks like only a quick reaction on his part kept him from being killed. According to a witness who was standing near the impact point, Clovis seemed to sense the approaching vehicle and tried to jump out of the way. He managed to get his feet off the ground before he was hit. Probably saved his life. Instead of going under the truck, he went up over the hood and bounced off the windshield before he hit the ground and sustained the head injury."

"Did any of this make the paper?"

"Do you get the Los Angeles Examiner out your way?"

"We do, but not until afternoon. It comes out on the train."

"The incident happened too late to make the Sunday edition, but it's in today's. Apparently Clovis is an up-and-coming musician in the Los Angeles area. A reporter who picked up the hit and run from the police blotter recognized his name and wrote a short piece about what happened."

"Did the article say anything about Clarke's condition?"

"No. Just that he'd been taken to a local hospital."

"Did it say which one?"

"No, but anyone familiar with Los Angeles will know which one it is."

"I'm pretty sure the driver of the truck is from rural Missouri. I'm betting he has no idea which hospital that would be. I'm going to call Missouri and see if I can get some more information about the truck. I'll get right back to you with anything I learn."

"Appreciate it."

"Detective, do you have any pull with the Examiner?"

"The usual. The crime beat reporters rely on us for stories and comments. We can call in a favor now and then."

"Can you get them to plant a story hinting that Clarke's not expected to recover?"

"The Examiner might be concerned the story would cause Mr. Clovis's family a lot of mental anguish."

"Not a concern in this case. Clarke's only surviving family member is his uncle, Tyler Clovis, the same man who probably killed his parents and just tried to run over him. Clarke's not married or divorced and has no fiancée or serious romantic attachment. That's what he told me when I interviewed him."

"It would sweeten the pot if I could tell this reporter there's an interesting story here and you would be willing to give him an interview if you arrest this guy."

"Sure. You can promise him that."

"Okay, Lieutenant, I'll give it a try."

"Thanks. If Tyler thinks his nephew is not going to make it, he may leave Los Angeles and head our way. He has a loose end to tie up out here."

Horse hung up and walked out of his office.

"Fred, get me the phone number for the Sheriff's office in Livingston County, Missouri."

"Will do."

"Then find me an off-duty deputy who wants to get some overtime driving to San Bernardino to deliver a possible murder weapon to Captain Hardesty."

Horse went back inside and set to work updating his case notes. He put in the details about the attempted murder early Sunday morning. Then he went to his poster and wrote "Hollywood" on the far left side.

When he went back to the dispatcher's desk, Fred had the phone number for the sheriff in Missouri.

"Thanks, Fred. How about a deputy?"

"Jim Harkness is on his way in. He says if the department will let him take his POV, he and his wife would like to do some Christmas shopping at the Harris Company before he drives back."

Horse smiled.

"If I know Lorraine, he's going to be late getting back. She'll shop until the store closes. Anyway, tell him he's got a deal. But remind him the overtime will just be for driving. We're not paying him while Lorraine looks at everything in that store."

"I'll pass that on."

"When he gets here, tell him the gun is in the evidence room.

I'm going to call Missouri. If I get what I'm looking for, I'm going to be on the phone with some other people. Tell anybody who calls that I'll call them back."

"Yessir."

Horse went back into his office and closed the door before sitting down at his desk.

When he dialed the number, someone answered on the first ring.

"Livingston County Sheriff's Department."

The heavy accent made "sheriff's" sound more like "shuruff's" to Horse's ear.

"Is the Sheriff in?"

"Who's callin'?"

"This is Lieutenant Carlos Caballo of the San Bernardino County Sheriff's Department in California."

"California, huh? Give me a minute. I'll see if I can scare him up."

Horse was on hold for a while before someone came on the line.

"Sheriff Sprague here."

"Sheriff, I'm Lieutenant Caballo of the San Bernardino County Sheriff's Department in California. I'm calling from Smoke Tree."

"Smoke Tree. Smoke Tree. I've heard that name."

He paused a moment.

"Oh yeah, that's that place I see on the news in the summertime. Hottest place in the U.S. of A. some days."

"That's us, sir."

"Say, let's drop all this 'sir' stuff. Call me Bobby."

"All right, Bobby. I'm Carlos.

We're working on a murder. Couple of local people were found shot dead in the desert outside of town. It looks a man from your neck of the woods was involved."

"Be glad to help."

"The man's name is Tyler Clovis. Do you know him?"

"Carlos, I've been sheriff here nigh onto twenty years. Probably know every wrongdoer in the county, man, woman and child."

"So, has this Tyler Clovis ever been in trouble?"

"Oh, hell yeah. Mean, nasty fella. Liked to pound on his old lady. At least he did until Molly got tired of it and lit on out of here. We made quite a few calls at his place. Lives over to Ludlow."

"Do you happen to know what kind of vehicle he drives?"

"Not off the top of my head, but I sure can find out."

Sheriff Sprague pulled the phone away before he shouted.

"Lyle? Hey Lyle! Get on the horn to the DMV. See what kind of a vehicle is registered to Tyler Clovis in Ludlow."

He came back on the line.

"Shouldn't take long. Anything else?"

"Can you give me a description of him?"

"Ferret-faced guy. Eyes too close together. Nose too small for his face. Sandy hair, what there is left of it, brown eyes. Five nine or so. Medium build. Guy you'd forget the minute you met him. And you'd do well to be shut of him."

Horse was writing as fast as he could as the sheriff spoke.

"What's he do for a living?"

"Owns a little machine shop. Turns brake drums, mills heads, does small engine repairs, fixes appliances, sharps chain saws. That kinda thing."

"Do you know anything about his finances?"

"Hear he does okay. He's not rich or anything, but he makes a decent living out of the place. That's why it surprised me."

"What surprised you, Bobby?"

"Week or so back? He put his shop up for sale. Told some old boy over that way he wasn't going to need it any more. Said he was gonna come into some money. I wouldn't know from where. His daddy was poor as a church

191

mouse when he passed some years back. Doesn't have any other family that I know about."

"He had a brother."

"News to me. Never seen him around."

"He lived out here."

"Hold on a minute, Carlos. Got something for you on that vehicle.

Here we go. Blue, nineteen fifty nine Chevrolet pickup. Missouri license plate thirty one dash nine twenty two. And here's more on Tyler. Date of birth September eleven, nineteen and fourteen. Height: five foot nine. Weight, one hundred seventy. Brown hair, brown eyes. Residence address on Milwaukee Avenue, Ludlow. "

"I don't suppose you'd have any information on a handgun registered to him?"

"Well, Carlos, we don't register handguns here in Missouri. Now, if he wanted a concealed carry permit it would've come through this office, but I've never seen an application from him."

"Thanks for all that, Bobby."

"My pleasure, Carlos. So, you think this old boy's gone and murdered someone?"

"His brother and his brother's wife."

"So, that's why you said he *had* a brother. When was this murder?"

"Around Thanksgiving, as far as the medical examiner could tell, but we didn't find the bodies until last week."

"Why heck, Carlos. I've seen Tyler here in the county since Thanksgiving."

"Did you see him last week?"

There was a pause.

"Now that you mention it, the last time I drove by his shop it was closed."

"We think he's back in California. Tried to run over his brother's son in Los Angeles early Sunday morning."

"Good lord. A regular killin' spree.

What would you like me to do on my end?"

"We're going to pick him up out here if we can. If he gets by us and shows up there, take him into custody for us."

"Be glad to. Never liked that weasel anyway."

"Thanks again, sheriff."

"If you get him, let me know so we can stop looking for him."

"I will."

Horse disconnected the call, got a dial tone, and put in a call to Detective Scanlon.

"Detective Scanlon, Hollywood Division."

"Lieutenant Caballo. I've got a full description of Tyler Clovis and the vehicle registered to him."

"One second. Let me get a pen.

Okay, shoot."

Horse ran through all the information from the Missouri DMV and the description from Sheriff Sprague, pausing from time to time to give Detective Scanlon time to catch up.

"Got it.

Lieutenant, we'll put this out across the city along with the information the driver is a possible suspect in a murder case and has also attempted to kill someone in a hit and run. But don't get your hopes up. This Tyler Clovis must know there were witnesses. Easiest thing in the world to steal a set of California plates and put them on his truck."

"I understand."

"But I do have some good news for you. Reporter gave me more than I expected. Tomorrow's Examiner will report that Clarke Clovis has not regained consciousness and doctors think he never will."

"Perfect."

"Also, just in case, we have a uniform on the ward. We'll pass this description on to him. If your suspect shows up, he'll have a hard time getting to Mr. Clovis."

"I think if he sees the story, he'll head back this way if he hasn't already. I'll alert the Highway Patrol, but I think your comment about the California plates is correct.

And detective, thanks for all your help."

"Glad to assist. When this is over, you'll be getting a call from Larry Stevens at the Examiner."

"Okay. I'll do right by him. I owe you both."

When Horse hung up, he walked over and wrote "Ludlow, Missouri," on the far right side of his poster board. Then he updated his case notes with the information from Sheriff Sprague.

When he was finished, he dialed Captain Hardesty in San Bernardino.

"Hardesty."

"Good morning, Captain. Carlos Caballo calling about the Clovis murder."

"Getting closer to a suspect?"

"Bearing down on one. We've had some breaks."

Horse summarized everything about Willy Gibson finding the gun and the information Sheriff Sprague had provided about Tyler Clovis. When he was done, the captain asked him how soon he could get the gun to San Bernardino for testing by ballistics.

"A deputy will leave here with it within the hour."

"That's great progress, Horse. Anything I can do to help?"

"Yessir, there is. I'm beginning to think this is all tied to that Geiger counter we found in Caleb's truck. I took it up to Las Vegas and talked to a guy who knows his stuff. He told me it was a piece of junk that gives out false readings.

Here's my theory. I think Tyler Clovis bought it from some mail order outfit. He came out to the desert to meet up with his brother and get in on the uranium boom. They went prospecting. They came across something that caused the faulty device to go crazy. They thought they were going to be rich.

I think they staked a claim. According to the fellow in Vegas, they would have had to file that claim in San Bernardino County to make it official. If you send someone over to the County Recorder's Office and have him go through the records from August forward, he might find that claim"

194

"I'll get someone over there as soon as we hang up.

What happens after the claim gets to the County?"

"It takes about a month for the County Recorder to process the claim and mail a letter making it official.

I think Tyler went back to Missouri to wait. And the more he thought about that claim, the more he thought there was no reason for him to share the money with Caleb and Eunice, or with Clarke Clovis, who would inherit.

Around Thanksgiving, he drove back out here to kill them. He didn't want his truck to be seen driving out there the usual way, so he parked down by the rodeo grounds north of town and walked across the desert to the shack. Full moon that night. It wouldn't have been hard. But when he got back to his truck, he ran into Willy Gibson.

Willy showed me where the guy fell and dropped the gun next to a big creosote bush. There are holes all around the bush. Holes like that are dug by all kinds of little rodents: kangaroo rats, grasshopper mice, white footed mice and a bunch of others. They lead to networks of burrows.

I think Willy startled Tyler bad enough that he lost his balance and then stepped down hard as he caught himself. That made the little tunnels under the ground collapse and down he went.

When he fell, he either dropped the gun or it came out of his pocket. But he didn't realize he had lost it until he got on the road. He came back to look for it, but Willy had picked it up and disappeared into the desert."

"So, Tyler went back to Missouri to wait for the dust to settle. See if anything came out about the killings or Willy finding the gun."

"That's right. And he was pretty sure nobody was going to look in that miserable shack for a long, long time, and when they did the bodies would be long gone. He figured whoever picked up the gun would just keep it. And sure enough, nobody came looking for him.

So, he came back to California to get rid of Clarke."

"All over a worthless claim!

What do you think Tyler Clovis will do next?"

"Detective Scanlon has put out a BOLO. He doesn't think it will do much good because Clovis has probably already stolen some California plates for his truck. The only question is, will he see the story in the Examiner and believe Clarke isn't going to survive the hit and run?"

"How will we know one way or the other?"

"If he buys the story, I think he's going to show up in Smoke Tree. I think he's going to return to where he dropped that gun and try to find the guy who has it. In his mind, the gun and the guy who picked it up are the only things that can tie him to any of this.

When he comes, Tyler Clovis and I are going to meet face to face, most likely after dark."

"Be careful, Horse. This guy's killed two people and tried for one more."

"I'll be ready. I intend to have the high ground."

Horse said goodbye, got out of his chair, and walked out of his office.

"Any calls come in for me?"

"Just one. The Mayor. I told him you couldn't be disturbed but you'd call him back."

"Where is he, the store or City Hall?"

"The store."

He went back in his office and made the call.

"Milner's Market."

"Lieutenant Caballo for Mr. Milner."

"One moment."

"Good morning, Lieutenant."

"Mr. Mayor."

"I'd like to talk to you about something very important to both of us."

"Sure. My place or yours?"

"Neither. This is official city business. Can you meet me at City Hall after lunch?"

"Certainly."

"See you there at one."

Chapter 17

OUT OF LEFT FIELD

Just before one o'clock, Horse walked into City Hall and asked for the mayor.

"He's in his office," said the City Clerk. "Very unusual. Most of the time we only see him on days the council meets. Whatever it is he wants to talk to you about, it must be very important to get him down here."

She looked expectantly at Horse.

He said nothing.

She sighed and said, "Go on back."

Horse walked down the hall and stopped in front of the open doorway of the Mayor's office. William Milner was at his desk.

"Afternoon, Lieutenant. Come on in."

"I have an idea what this may be about."

"Some of it, maybe. But I think I have a surprise for you. A big enough surprise that it would be best if you closed that door before you sit down."

Horse shut the door.

"And it would help if you brought that chair to this side of the desk."

Horse picked up the chair and carried it to a spot next to the mayor.

"I want to keep this discussion very quiet," he said, as he angled his chair toward the one Horse had set down.

"If you hear a popping sound while we're talking, it will mean somebody came in the front office and Norma Sue had to pull her ear off my door."

He leaned toward Horse and spoke in a soft voice.

"I've had two calls since Friday morning from Chief Rettenmeir."

"I take it that's not the surprise."

"No. The first call concerned something that happened out on River Road. The chief claims you tried to tell him how to run his department. The second call came this morning and had to do with the Christmas parade. He said you threatened to punch him."

"I did. I would have if he'd stepped out of his car."

"And this had to do with Willy Gibson?"

"It did."

"Before we go any further, I want to tell you I didn't know what was going on behind me in the parade. I was sitting up in the front of the fire engine saying 'ho ho ho' and tossing candy canes to kids."

"I'm sure you know by now that he had Willy walking in front of his car wearing a diaper and a big blue ribbon tied in a bow on top of his head."

"I didn't find out about that until I climbed down from the truck. But I promise you Lieutenant, had I known about it, I would have put a stop to it. Willy doesn't deserve to be treated that way."

"I'm glad we're in agreement on that."

"So, what happened out on River Road?"

Horse explained the events of Wednesday night that had led to his phone call to the chief on Thursday morning and Rettenmeir's unwillingness to cooperate.

When he was finished, William Milner sat quietly for a minute.

"Horse, I'm going to share some serious concerns with you, but I'd like you to keep this discussion under your hat."

"Certainly, Mr. Mayor, I can do that, with one exception."

"It's just you and I here, so you can drop the 'Mr. Mayor.' It's Bill. What's the exception?"

"Anything that affects my job, I discuss with my Esperanza, my wife. She won't reveal anything that I wouldn't."

"Understood.

For some time now, I've been extremely disappointed in the performance of the Smoke Tree Police Department. I don't think Chief Rettenmeir is in control. He's got some bad apples over there. In fact, he's got more bad ones than good ones. Do you agree with that assessment?"

"I do."

"Okay, here's the surprise I mentioned. I would like you to put together a proposal to have your substation take over the policing of the City of Smoke Tree.

I wasn't going to talk with you about this until after the first of the year. I would have waited until then, even after the incident on River Road. But then I found out what happened at the Alvarado's home on Friday night."

"Not much goes on around here you don't hear about."

"Not much. When I heard about it, I knew this discussion couldn't wait."

"Bill, such a proposal, which would include a budget for salaries and new hires and buying new equipment, is not something I can do on my own hook. I'd have to talk to my immediate boss, the undersheriff, and he'd have to take it to the sheriff himself."

"Understood, but let's talk about it off the record."

"All right."

"From your perspective, what would be the biggest challenges involved in such a move?"

"First, we would have to have twice as many deputies. That's a lot of new hires."

"Are there any of the current officers at the STPD you would be willing to keep?"

"A few could come in as lateral transfers. Sergeant Kensington, Corporal Lattimore, Officer Sutcliffe, Officer Lambert, perhaps one or two others. A solid patrol sergeant like Kensington would be a lot of help."

"What are the other challenges?"

"The east end of the county is different. I don't want to bring in supervisors from outside who don't know Smoke Tree and the unincorporated areas out here. That means promoting some of my current people into supervisor's slots. Not something I have the authority to do."

"But you could make recommendations."

"I could."

"Horse, I have reason to believe your recommendations would be well received. I'm not sure you realize how favorably your performance is regarded in San Bernardino."

"Assuming that's true, I have a question for you."

"Go ahead."

"Do you have the votes on the council for this?"

"I'm sure I can get at least two of the council members to agree with me. That would give us the majority we need."

"Something this big, unanimous would be better."

"It's very likely I could get a fourth. One of the councilmen likes to sit on the fence until he sees which way the wind blows. Once he sees there are three of us in concurrence, he'll vote with the majority."

"And the fifth?"

"The fifth will not be with us. He was on the phone to me early Saturday morning. A good friend of his was in the crowd you read the riot act to in front of the Alvarado house. The councilman thinks you overstepped your authority."

"What my deputy and I did Friday night was keep a bunch of drunks from starting a riot."

The Mayor nodded his head.

"I agree.

By the way, do you know why the STPD didn't show up?"

"I know at least one person called. But the STPD ignores the east side."

"And you know this person who called?"

"My mother."

"This is exactly the kind of thing we have to correct. If it has to be three two or four one, so be it. We can't have serious incidents like this where the police department fails to respond. This is one community, not two."

"I have another question, Bill. This would have to be approved by the Board of Supervisors. Will you have support there?"

"I think we will. I've spoken, off the record, to our representative on the Board. She agrees it would be much better to have the sheriff's department take over. And she tells me the Board usually concurs with the recommendation of the district representative in cases like this."

"Last question.

If you have all this support lined up, why talk to me about it? Why not go straight to my boss?"

"Because, Carlos, you are the absolutely essential element. You grew up here. You know everybody. You have the confidence and respect of the local people. I'm well aware that many people in Smoke Tree already call you instead of the STPD. If you don't want to take on this added responsibility, I won't pursue it. The whole idea will die a quiet death"

Horse gathered his thoughts before speaking.

"I need time to really think this through, but I'm short on time right now. The murders of Caleb and Eunice Clovis are my first priority."

"Of course."

"When we make an arrest and assemble the evidence to convince the District Attorney to take the case to trial, I will come to a decision. That's assuming some other crazy thing doesn't happen."

"You think an arrest might come soon?"

"Off the record still?"

"Certainly."

"I think so."

"That's a relief. People are nervous because of the story the local paper wrote about the killings. Made it sound like some maniac was roving the desert.

And what do you think will happen next with the Alvarado situation? I've got my fingers crossed that story doesn't show up in the Smoke Tree Weekly."

"Elias Pickett was in my office yesterday. We talked for a long time. If I can believe him, and I think I can, he never intended for the situation to escalate the way it did."

"Then why did it?"

"Elias blames it on Officer Vernon Nichols of the Smoke Tree Police Department."

"But the STPD didn't respond."

"Nichols was there in civilian clothes. He was off duty. He lives next door to Elias and heard the dust-up between Elias and his daughter when Javier Alvarado brought her home after her curfew. According to Elias, it was Nichols who put together the group that showed up in front of Arturo's house."

"So, we're right back to the STPD rotten apple problem."

"We are. But by the way, I wouldn't worry about the local paper writing about what happened."

"Why not?"

"Because The Smoke Tree Weekly is like the Smoke Tree Police Department. If it happened east of the railroad tracks, it doesn't matter."

When Horse returned to the substation, Fred handed him a message slip.

"Captain Hardesty says he has some information for you."

Horse went in his office and placed the call.

"Hardesty."

"Horse, returning your call."

"You were right. A claim was made by Caleb Clovis and Tyler Clovis. A copy of the recorded claim was mailed out the week before Thanksgiving."

"Mailed where? There's no mail service out where Caleb and Eunice lived."

"It was sent to Tyler Clovis on Milwaukee Avenue in Ludlow, Missouri."

"Well, that's another link in the chain."

"Also, your deputy dropped the gun off here a bit ago. Ballistics will have the test results by tomorrow."

"Good. Too bad there won't be any useful fingerprints. The guy who picked up the gun carried it around for almost two weeks."

"And just so I'm clear on this, you're sure the guy who had the gun didn't do the shooting?"

"I am. He couldn't have. He has two fingers and no thumb on his left hand an only a thumb and middle finger on his right."

"That would make it impossible to rapidly cock and fire a revolver."

"Yessir. And thanks again for all your help on this."

"Anytime.

I'll be in touch as soon as I hear from ballistics."

Chapter 18

TALKING IT THROUGH

Late that afternoon, Horse and Esperanza were in the pickup truck heading through Smoke Tree. They crossed the Santa Fe tracks just north of the depot and drove the short stretch of paved road that passed the east side recreation center and baseball field. The baseball field was deserted, but they could see a pick-up basketball underway on the blacktop court. When the pavement ended, the dirt road continued on through thickets of mesquite and quail bush before it dead ended into the dike road.

Horse turned south on the dike and stayed on it until he turned toward the Bureau bridge spanning the Colorado River. He paused on the apron at the top of the ramp to be sure no one was coming across the single lane from the Arizona side before he drove onto the bridge. The planks rattled and trembled beneath the truck. The clatter became more pronounced in the middle section, the section that could be disassembled so the Bureau of Reclamation dredge could pass through on the river below. The smell of the creosote that coated the pilings drifted into the cab.

In Arizona, they turned north on the dike road until it intersected with another dirt road coming in from the east. They turned off the dike and drove through miles of mesquite thickets, quail bush, chamisa and tamarisk in the river bottom. The cool winter air was filled with the smell of dust, alkali and evaporating water from the irrigation ditches that watered the farm lands leased by corporate farmers from the Fort Mohave Tribe of Mojave Indians.

The rich bottomland had been laid down over thousands and thousands of years by the meandering river. Upstream, soil from Colorado, Utah and Arizona had been dumped into the main stem by the Gunnison, San

205

Juan, Green, Paria, Escalante, and Little Colorado Rivers and then scoured as it flowed through the Grand Canyon. By the time it settled out of the river in the Lower Colorado River Basin, it was as fine as powdered sugar.

Dust billowed high into the sky behind Horse and Esperanza as they drove. Dust that would settle out on the mesquites and bushes and ditches and wandering cattle where it would be joined by still more dust kicked up by the next passing vehicle.

Before up-stream dams and constant dredging had imprisoned the river in what was little more than a glorified flood control ditch, the Colorado had flooded the Mohave Valley every spring when water from the melting snows of the western slopes of the Rocky Mountains and the Wind River Range in Wyoming took the river to flood stage. Those floods had constantly re-arranged the landscape of the valley as the mile-wide, braided river wandered at will through the broad Mohave Valley between the foothills of the Black Mountains on the east and the Sacramentos on the west. When the floods receded, the rich, damp river bottom soil left behind had provided fertile planting areas for the Mojave Indians. The tribe planted beans, squash, corn and pumpkins to supplement their diet of fish from the river and game from the bottom lands and nearby foothills.

But that had been in pre-contact times. The Mojaves who had survived the invasion of white people were but a sad remnant, their numbers reduced by disease, design and misfortune. The inevitable result of the Indian School at Fort Mohave punishing children for speaking their own language had been the gradual loss of their culture. The stories and history of the tribe, never written down but passed on orally from generation to generation, were being lost and forgotten, drifting away like the dust of the river bottom, carried on the winds of change, worn down and reduced like the eroding mountains surrounding the valley that carried their name.

The road Horse and Esperanza were travelling began to curve northeast before it forked with yet another dirt road. This one cut directly to the east. Horse turned onto it, and soon the land began to rise. As it did, the screw bean mesquites that dominated the bottom closest to the river began to give way to the hardier honey mesquites that could shoot tap roots deeper into the soil. Before long, even the honey mesquites dwindled, replaced first by stands of rabbitbrush giving up the last of their showy yellow blossoms and then by creosote, white bursage, varieties of yucca, and the pink barrel cactus that glowed pinker still as the sunset flared in the west.

They rose slowly on the badly washboarded road that cut through a broad, uplifted plain tilting toward the Black Mountains through miles and miles of blue-black volcanic basalt, porphyritic andesite, gabbro, scoria and rhyolite. It was rough country, unkind to hikers and horses alike; mastered best by burros.

As they drove, Horse explained what he had learned that day about the murder case, including Horse's discussions with Detective Scanlon in Hollywood about the hit and run

"Is Clarke going to be okay?"

"I'll know more tomorrow. Scanlon said the doctors think Clarke will wake up soon. I'm not sure about his other injuries. Maybe the docs aren't either."

Boundary Cone loomed above them as they drove on: a dark, heavily eroded volcanic remnant rendered purple and slate-blue in the remaining light of the dying day. When their dirt road intersected old highway 66, Horse turned south on the road, traversing the face of the Black Mountains. He continued on the former Gold Road until he came to a badly eroded track that turned off and climbed up the hill toward long-abandoned mine works. A hundred yards off the highway, he stopped the truck and got out. As Esperanza climbed out the other door, Horse reached behind his seat for two blankets.

Horse dropped the tailgate and padded it with a folded blanket. He lifted Esperanza to a spot on the blanket and climbed up beside her. They wrapped up in the other blanket. Horse put his arm around Esperanza. She leaned against him. They quietly watched the light go out of the winter sky as bats flew out of the old mine shafts behind them and fluttered and flared overhead, hunting insects as they moved down slope toward the bug-rich air above the river bottom and the lights of Smoke Tree.

Venus rose in the darkening west. Far off, a pack of coyotes howled at the slivered crescent of the waxing moon. Stars began to appear in great numbers throughout the sky like ice crystals tossed onto a black satin sheet. A different pack of coyotes began to yip somewhere below them, signaling the beginning of the evening hunt.

They could see a steady stream of headlights descending toward Smoke Tree from South Pass on the other side of the valley below. The stream was intersected south of Klinefelter by a trickle from highway 95 that merged into the Mother Road like a side stream in the distant canyon country spilling into the Colorado.

Horse and Esperanza sat without talking for a long time, taking in the dying of the day and the fall of night. It was peaceful on the mountainside. The air was still; the silence profoundly deep.

Horse was the first to speak.

"Thank you for driving up here with me, *querida*."

"I love it here. *Tan tranquilo, tan especial.*"

"I wanted to get away from the house and the office. I want to talk to you about something important without being interrupted."

Esperanza laughed.

"I don't think they'll find us up here."

"Hard to tell. One of my deputies might chase us over the state line."

"And this thing you want to talk about, it is beyond what you told me about the case?"

"Beyond that."

"*Y mas alla de la fealdad en la casa de Arturo Alvarado?*"

"Beyond even that."

"You've had quite a day, *mi corazon.*"

"I have. This afternoon I met with Bill Milner."

"*Y lo que queria el Alcade?*"

"He wanted a lot."

Horse relayed the entire conversation.

Esperanza listed until he was completely finished. Then she sat without speaking for a few minutes.

"Did you think this would happen sometime?"

"*En verdad, no pense que lo haria.* Smoke Tree has been putting up with a bad department for years. I thought they should have fired the chief a long time ago."

"*Quizas.* They have probably talked among themselves about offering that job to you."

"Perhaps. They've never approached me."

"That's because they know you would never leave the sheriff's department."

"No, I wouldn't. My debt to Captain Hardesty and Sheriff Bland is too great. I would not be in law enforcement if it wasn't for them."

"So, the Mayor is coming at it a different way."

"I guess so. It's smart thinking on his part. It would get rid of a whole bunch of bad cops once."

"*Ciertamente.*"

"But the important thing, *mi amor*, is not what Bill thinks. It's what we think. Do we want to do this thing?"

"It would be a huge change."

"*Enorme.*"

"Well, let's take our time. *Es mucho que pensar.*"

"*Claramente.*"

They fell silent again, looking down at Smoke Tree below them. Even within the lights of the town, they could clearly see the brightly illuminated ribbon of 66 as the traffic pulsed relentlessly through the little community.

"Hey, *gran chico*, let's go home. You must be starving."

"I am, *querida*. I didn't have time for lunch today."

"Well, I made *chili verde* and fresh tortillas today. Just have to heat them up. And there's flan for desert."

Horse laughed.

"You know how to get a guy off a hillside!"

They drove back they way they had come through the deep darkness of the desert night. Occasionally their headlights picked up the ruby eyes of a kit fox out for its nightly hunt. When they reached the mesquite thickets, no more foxes were seen, but occasionally the hot eyes of a coyote flashed as they passed by.

Just before they reached the dike road, a feral boar charged across the road in front of them. In the headlights, its short tusks gleamed like ivory before it disappeared into the brush. The sight of the huge, dangerous animal made Esperanza shiver.

Chapter 19

ROUGH JUSTICE

After dinner, Horse and Esperanza were spending a quiet evening reading in front of a mesquite wood fire. The sweet smell of pine needles filled the room and the lights on the Christmas tree glowed red, blue and green in the corner, and Christmas music played softly on the stereo. Horse was so comfortable and content he was growing sleepy and thinking of going to bed when the phone rang.

Esperanza looked up.

"Do you have to answer it?"

"I guess not. Just this once."

The phone rang eight or nine times and then stopped.

"See, not an emergency."

But the phone began to ring again.

Horse sighed and got to his feet.

"I'd better take it, *querida.*"

When he picked it up, his mother was on the line.

"*Terible problemas, mi hijo. Tienes que venir, y rapidamnete.*"

"*Que es, mama?*"

"I was out in my *pequeno patio delantero* looking at the Christmas lights on the neighbor's houses when I saw Javier Alvarado walking down El Paso. He was walking *muy despacio* and sort of, of, *oblicuo, ya sabes?* When I asked him *que esta mal, el dijo un policia* beat him up real bad. That one you sent away on Friday night. He went in the house. I stayed outside trying to decide whether to call you. *No me gusta molestarte por la noche, mi hijo.* You work too much.

Entonces Arturo salio de la casa. He ran to his car and drove away *muy rapidamnete.*

Tenia una pistola."

Horse's mind kicked into overdrive.

"Cruce la calle. I knocked on the door. Delores answered. *Ella dijo* Javier told Arturo he was walking from the recreation center when Nichols pulled up and shoved Javier against the car and handcuffed him. He drove Javier to the rodeo grounds *y lo golpeo con las punos.* Everywhere but the face. He told him to stay away from white girls and drove off and left him there.

Delores said Arturo went to the closet and got *la gran pistola* he brought home from the war."

"A forty five?"

"Si, that's what she called it. Forty five. Arturo said he was going to kill this Nichols. *Creo que lo dice en serio."*

"He probably does, Mama. Tell Delores I'll take care of this."

He hung up. Esperanza was looking at him with questioning eyes.

"Take care of what? And what's this about a forty five?"

Horse headed down the hall to get his gun. Esperanza followed him.

As he strapped on his weapon, looped his handcuffs through his belt and put on his Sheriff's Department jacket, he told Esperanza what his mother had said.

Esperanza took in the angry expression on his face.

"I know you're going to go, but answer one question first. Who are you really looking for? Arturo or Nichols?"

"Whichever one I can find first."

He kissed her on the forehead and hurried to the door.

Esperanza walked out onto the veranda and watched as he started his car and sped away. This was the kind of thing she hated. And what she hated most was that there was nothing she could do but wait.

Horse made a quick pass through town. He saw neither Arturo nor Nichols. He knew he had to find one of them, and quickly. The gun Arturo was carrying, the Colt 1911, was a murderous weapon with incredible firepower, but it was not an easy gun to master. Horse had qualified with it in the military, and while he was an excellent shot with a revolver, he found it difficult to be even basically proficient with a .45.

Horse had no doubt that Arturo would open fire on Nichols if he found him. If Arturo tried to shoot at Nichols from his car, his chances of success would not be good. If Arturo was out of his car and got close to Nichols, the officer was a dead man. So there were two probable results if Arturo found Nichols, neither of them good. Either Arturo would miss and get shot himself, or he would gun down Nichols and go to prison for the rest of his life. That was a given if you killed a peace officer in California.

Horse completed a second pass. He concentrated on those areas the STPD usually patrolled: Highway 66 itself and the white neighborhoods closest to 66. There was still no sign of either Nichol's patrol car or Arturo's '56 Ford Fairlane. Horse was hesitant to alert his officers about what was going on because he had no idea what Arturo might do if pulled over. Because he was sure Arturo posed no threat to civilians, Horse decided not to endanger his own deputies. And he sure wasn't going to notify the STPD. That bunch would love to have an excuse to gun down an armed Mexican who was driving around town looking for one of their own.

He keyed his mic.

"Dispatch."

"Can anyone tell me where the STPD guys usually go for beans or on break during swing shift?"

For a moment there was no response.

Then, Stuart Atkins answered.

"Lieutenant, they almost always go to the Best Bet Motel and Café. The owner comps them. Not just for coffee but for meals too. Also heard he lets them take women to the motel rooms in return for, well…in return. But you won't see anyone if you drive by. You have to get off the highway and drive around back. They usually park under that big old salt cedar behind the café.

You want me to go by and check? Over."

"Thanks Stuart, but no. I'm near that location. I'll go by. Just something I need to take care of. And no back up required."

I'm clear."

He knew he was breaking every rule of procedure and perhaps even risking his career, but this was something he had to take care of himself. He hung the mic on the hook and flipped on his light bar as he sped south through town. The Best Bet was at the southern end of Smoke Tree near where 66 started up a steep hill toward the 66/95 split.

When Horse hit the stretch that paralleled the Santa Fe Railroad tracks, he turned off the light bar. Approaching the Best Bet, he pulled off the highway, slowed to a crawl, and angled his car toward the big salt cedar between the motel and the café. There was a Smoke Tree Police Department patrol car parked beneath it. The nose of the car was almost against the trunk. Horse parked his unit perpendicular to the rear of the black and white so the patrol car couldn't be moved.

When he walked into the café, the only customer was a man at the counter drinking coffee. A tired-looking waitress was swiping half heartedly at the counter with a rag. She gave Horse a bored glance as he walked toward her.

"Anywhere you like."

"I'm looking for the officer who belongs to the patrol car parked out back."

"Haven't seen him. Might try the motel."

Horse turned and left.

The Best Bet Motel was a sad assemblage of broken down cottages crowded in a crooked line that backed against the hillside bordering the mouth of the gully behind them. They were usually rented to truckers looking for a cheap place to bed down, but Horse knew there was more than sleep available at the Best Bet. He also knew he would have to deal with the situation if the sheriff's department took over patrolling Smoke Tree. One more thing to worry about.

Horse walked into the office: a small, wooden building with a *porte chochere* on the side. When he rang the bell, a man came out of the door behind the counter.

He didn't seem happy to see Horse, but he made a brave attempt at a welcoming smile, revealing a set off ill-fitting false teeth he adjusted with his tongue before speaking.

"Help you, Lieutenant?"

"Where's the cop?"

"Excuse me?"

"The cop attached to the car over by the tree."

"I'm not sure…"

Horse interrupted.

"I don't have time to dance with you, Frank."

The smile disappeared from Frank's face.

"He's in number seven. Please don't tell him I told you."

"Wouldn't dream of it. And keep your hands off the phone. In fact, go back in your room and stay there for a while."

Horse walked out and headed down the row of ramshackle cottages to number seven.

He tried the door. The knob wouldn't turn.

He knocked.

"Yeah?"

"Manager."

"Piss off, Frank. I'm busy."

Horse pulled his gun. He took a short step and slammed the sole of his right boot into the door beside the knob. The ancient jamb splintered. The door banged off the interior wall.

Horse followed his gun inside.

A woman with mousey brown hair was undressing near the foot of the bed. She was down to her bra and panties. She was crying. Vernon Nichols was sitting in a chair watching her. His shirt was partially unbuttoned, and his gun belt was hanging over the back of the chair.

He looked at Horse but made no move to get up.

"Well, well, if it ain't the famous lieutenant.

Why the gun? You afraid my girlfriend will attack you?"

Horse spoke to the woman without looking at her.

"Start getting dressed. You'll be out of here in a minute. What's your name?"

"Amy. Amy Kressler."

"Why are you here with this crud, Amy?"

Her voice trembled as she spoke, putting he clothes back on as she talked.

"I was coming into town on 66. This cop pulled me over. Said I was doing sixty five in a forty zone. No way I was. He took my license and registration and said he had to go to his car to call something in. When he came back, he had a bottle. The one on the nightstand.

He splashed whiskey on me and said I was under arrest for driving drunk. Then he told me I could either spend the night in jail and go to court in the morning or follow him to this motel.

There's no way I can afford to pay a DWI fine. I barely got enough money to get to L.A."

"She's lying, of course. She came on to me."

"Where were you coming from, Amy?"

"Grants, New Mexico. Looking for a better life in California."

She laughed a bitter laugh.

"Some life."

She sat down on the bed to put on her shoes.

Nichols started to speak.

"Shut up, Vernon."

Horse was silent until the young woman was completely dressed.

"Miss Kessler, you can be on your way. This man won't bother you again. I'm very sorry this happened to you, but he's not going to get away with this. I'll see to that."

She picked up her purse from the nightstand and turned to go. Then she stopped. She turned and picked up the bottle of whiskey and threw it as hard as she could at Nichols.

She missed. The bottle hit the wall behind Nichols' chair but did not break.

"You fat shit!"

She was crying again.

She went out the door.

Horse waited until he heard a car start up in the parking lot and drive away. He walked over and took Nichols' gun belt off the chair and threw it on the bed.

"Get up and assume the position against the wall. You know the drill."

Nichols smiled but didn't move.

"What's this about, Lieutenant? A little hanky-panky between two people attracted to each other is against the law now?"

"Get out of that chair and get against that wall, or I'll pistol whip you where you sit."

"You don't have the nerve."

Horse said nothing, but something in his eyes drove the smile from Nichols' face. He slowly got to his feet, walked to the wall and leaned against it, catching his weight on his outstretched palms.

"Feet and hands wider!

Now, listen carefully and do exactly what I say. Step back a little farther and then lean forward until your forehead is against the wall."

"Come on…"

"Do it!"

Nichols complied.

"Take your right hand off the wall and put it behind your back.

Good.

Now your left."

"Hey, I'll fall down."

"No you won't. You're a strong guy."

When Nichols was in the awkward position with his hands behind his back and his forehead against the wall, Horse reached behind himself for his cuffs.

He quietly holstered his gun and stepped forward.

When he looped the cuff over Nichols' right wrist, Nichols suddenly tried to turn. Horse kicked his right leg out from beneath him. The policeman fell face first to the floor. Horse followed him down and planted his knee in the small of Nichols' back. He snapped on the other cuff. In one smooth motion, he stood up and pulled Nichols to his feet

Nichols suddenly realized he had greatly underestimated the lieutenant's strength.

"Feet wide and head against the wall again."

Horse patted Nichols down.

He removed a throwdown .32 with electrical tape on the grips and the serial number filed off from an ankle holster. He put the small gun in the pocket of his Levi jacket.

"Handy."

"You never know."

Horse continued the pat down.

He put his hand in Nichols' right pocket.

"Easy there, Lieutenant. We hardly know each other."

Horse pulled out a large folding knife, a set of brass knuckles and the keys to Nichols' patrol unit. He put those items in his other pocket. Nichols was carrying nothing else but some loose change.

Horse picked up Nichols' gun belt and looped if over his shoulder. He pulled the handcuffed man away from the wall and pushed him to the door. He shoved Nichols outside onto the small porch.

"Try to run, I'll shoot you."

Horse guided Nichols across the dirt lot to his sheriff's department cruiser and opened the back door.

"Duck your head."

When Nichols bent down, Horse shoved him sprawling into the back seat. He got in front, started the car and drove out of the lot. He turned south on 66.

"Where we going?"

"Someplace quiet."

Nichols kept up a string of complaints as they drove up the hill. When Horse took 95 south, Nichols fell silent. Horse drove to the five mile road cutoff and turned east on the narrow stretch of abandoned and badly deteriorated blacktop. He continued until a broad, open space loomed on the right side of the road. He turned off the blacktop and drove south across a large section of desert pavement.

Horse stopped and got out, leaving the headlights on and the engine running. He opened the back door and pulled Nichols out. He pushed him ahead to a spot twenty yards in front of the headlights. Insects, attracted to the lights, flew in and out of the beams.

Horse grabbed the bulky policeman by the collar of his shirt and pulled him backward. Simultaneously driving his knee into the back of the man's leg, he took him to the ground.

When Nichols was sprawled on the rocks, Horse stood up.

Nichols turned his head sideways.

"What the hell, Lieutenant…"

Horse moved forward and squatted directly in front of Nichols so the policeman had to strain to lift his head so he could see the lieutenant.

Nichols tried to roll over.

"Stay on your stomach."

Nichols ceased his efforts.

"Let's you and I have a talk."

Tired of trying to hold his head up, Nichols spoke to the rocks.

"About what?"

"Let's work it backward. Begin with the woman you coerced."

"What about her? It's my word against some whore."

"Funny, I didn't take her for a whore. But let's talk about Javier Alvarado next."

"That little punk."

Nichols turned his head sideways and spat in disgust, but fear had made him cotton-mouthed and white spittle stuck to his chin.

"What made you think you could handcuff and beat a young boy and get away with it?"

"You can't prove it. I didn't leave a mark on that boy. So there's nothing you can do about it."

"And yet, here you are, face down in the dirt in handcuffs."

"All I did was teach that boy a lesson he needed to learn."

"What lesson's that?"

"That Mexicans should keep away from white girls."

"And that's what you told the crowd you rounded up and got liquored up in the Alvarado's front yard."

"What if I did?"

"Did you tell those men you thought the Pickett girl was your property?"

The policeman did not respond.

"I know you've been prowling around outside the Pickett's house, peeping in Elaine's window. What do you think Elias Pickett will say when I tell him it was you his daughter caught a glimpse of out there in the darkness?"

"That's bullshit!"

"And the young woman out on River Road?"

"What are you talking about?"

"My deputy saw you. And then he saw you again at the Alvarado's house. Shouldn't have worn the same clothes."

"Can't prove it."

"No? Another of my guys saw your car pull out of the wash on the dirt road just west of her house and turn onto 66. That's outside the city limits. No reason for a Smoke Tree patrol car to be out there. And when my dispatcher called your dispatcher, your guy said there were no cars out that way."

"Hey, lots of the guys take their cars home at night. No telling who it might have been."

Horse decided to run a bluff.

"Only one that night. At least that's what Chief Rettenmeir says."

Nichols laughed.

"Rettenmeir! Rettenmeir's a hundred pounds of shit in a fifty pound bag. All the stuff I've got on that clown, he would never testify against me."

Horse rocked back on his heels and looked into the sky. Bats and nighthawks had appeared to chase the bugs flitting through the lights. He watched them for a while: the hunters and the hunted.

Then he turned back.

"You should be grateful. I saved your life tonight."

Nichols grunted.

"How's that?"

"Javier's father is out looking for you."

"I can deal with him."

"Really? He's carrying a forty five."

"Some officer of the law you are, Lieutenant. Someone's out driving around with a weapon gunning for a sworn policeman, and you're hassling me? You should be arresting him."

"Had to find one of you to keep Arturo from ruining his life. Found you first."

Horse looked into the sky again, framing what he wanted to say.

"Nichols, I'm going to give you a chance to make things right. Resign from the department in the morning. Leave Smoke Tree and never come back."

"No way. You can't prove any of this crap."

"And that's your last word on it, huh?"

"Damn straight."

Horse stood up and walked back to his car. He unbuckled his gun belt and put it on the front seat. He put Nichols' throwdown, knife, brass knuckles and the keys to his patrol car on the seat next to it.

He walked back and squatted beside Nichols again.

Nichols stared at him, his eyes filled with hatred and rage.

"Nichols. I'm going to give you more of a chance than you ever gave Javier Alvarado. My gun, your gun, your car keys, your knife and your throwdown are all in the front seat of my unit. My keys are in the ignition and the motor's running.

I'm going to unhook you. If you can whip me, you can drive away and leave me here, just like you left Javier. If you can't, you're going to leave Smoke Tree."

"What's the trick?"

"No trick. Straight up, clean fight. No weapons. Hand to hand. See how you do with someone who can hit back.

I know your word isn't worth a helluva lot, Nichols, but for my own satisfaction, I want you to give me your word you agree to those terms."

Nichols was silent for a moment.

"Sure. I agree."

"That's not good enough. Say, 'I give you my word.' "

"I give you my word."

Horse stepped behind Nichols and knelt down. He removed the cuffs and tossed them outside the circle of light. He stood up and stepped back. Nichols rolled onto his hands and knees and got to his feet. He stood for a moment, rubbing his wrists and stretching the kinks out.

"You've made a big mistake, taco bender."

He balled his meaty hands into fists and moved toward Horse in a crouch.

Horse was an experienced boxer. He knew immediately what kind of fighter he was facing. A brawler. A man who would tuck his chin into his chest and bull his way forward, letting you bust up your hands on his thick skull until he got close enough to rip you apart.

Horse stepped lightly away to his left.

A grin split Nichol's face.

"This is going to be…"

Which was as far as he got before a left jab exploded on his eye. He pawed at his face and laughed.

"Is that the best…"

And another left jab landed. This one squarely on his nose. Blood gushed over his mouth.

Nichols decided he didn't want to talk anymore. He dropped his head lower and shuffled forward. But no one had punched him in a long time, and the pain and the blood running into his mouth made him stupid. He swung a huge, angry, looping right hand that would have been devastating had it landed.

It didn't.

Horse twisted his head away from the punch. Leaning forward after it went past, he pivoted his weight and drove a vicious left hook to Nichols' right side midway between his belt and his rib cage. Nichols dropped his hands momentarily. Horse pivoted his hips the opposite direction and drove a straight right directly to his heart.

Nichols' heart skipped a beat. His eyes went wide and he began to fall back and to his right. Horse stepped in closer and hooked him hard to the other kidney as Nichols went down. He collapsed completely, falling hard to the ground with no attempt to break his fall. His head bounced off the desert pavement. He lay there without moving for a long time.

Horse stepped back and watched, just in case the man was playing possum.

Finally, Nichols groaned. He waved his left hand weakly.

"Okay, okay. I'm done."

"And you'll leave Smoke Tree and never come back?"

"Yeah, yeah. Tired of this jerkwater town anyways."

Horse walked into the desert and retrieved his handcuffs.

Nichols struggled to one elbow.

"What about my stuff?"

"I'll leave it with your dispatcher. I don't think you'll want to go by to pick it up, but who knows? Maybe you'd like to explain how you misplaced your service revolver and your car."

"Hey, wait a minute. Take me back to town."

Horse laughed.

"Walk back. Javier did. And when you're pissing blood in the morning, remember, you gave me your word you would leave. If you don't, I'll come for you.

Count on it."

Horse walked back to his car. He got in and turned around and headed back toward highway 95.

He made another slow pass through town. He spotted Arturo's car close to some salt cedars on the vacant lot next to the Mobil station. He pulled in and parked alongside the Ford Fairlane so the driver's side door of his cruiser was opposite Arturo's.

He turned off his engine and rolled down his window. Arturo rolled down his.

"*Senor Alvarado.*"

"*Teniente.*"

"You can stop sitting here with that unpermitted .45 in your lap now. Officer Nichols is leaving Smoke Tree."

"I can fight my own battles, Horse."

"Not this time."

"You didn't see what that *cabron* did to Javier."

"No, but I heard. That's why I went looking for him. Had you found him before I did, no good could have come of it. No matter what had happened, Javier would have been without a father and Delores *habria sido sin marido.*"

Arturo did not respond.

Horse waited.

"Horse, in my head I know you are right, *pero in mi corazon…*"

"I know this is a bitter pill to swallow. This man came to your house with bad intentions and then attacked your son without provocation. *Pero tragarlo es necesario hacerlo. El es un hombre malo, Senor Alvarado, pero no se le puede matar* without destroying your own family.

This is over now. Agreed?"

Arturo sat for a long time. Finally, he nodded.

"Take the gun home and put it in a safe place."

Arturo started his car.

"You will understand, *Teniente*, if I don't thank you for doing something I should have done myself."

"It's my job, Arturo."

When Arturo had gone, Horse drove to the Smoke Tree police department and gave Nichols' service revolver, throwdown piece, knife, brass knuckles and patrol car keys to the to the dispatcher.

The dispatcher asked a lot of questions.

All Horse told him was where to find the patrol car.

When Horse got home, it was after midnight. Esperanza came out to meet him.

"I'm so glad you're back, *mi novio*," she said as they walked to the house together."I've been so worried. Are you all right?"

"Got a sore hand. Otherwise fine."

She opened the door for him.

"Did you find Arturo?"

"Yes, but I found Nichols first."

"Where was he?"

"At the Best Bet with some woman he was going to force to have sex with him."

"Where is he now?"

"Out by five mile somewhere."

They sat down at the kitchen table and Horse went through the evening's events with Esperanza. When he was done, she shook her head.

"That was dangerous, taking the handcuffs off and giving him a chance. He could have hurt you.

Why would you do such a thing?"

"Sometimes it's the only way to send a message guys like Nichols understand."

Esperanza took his left hand in hers and looked at the broken skin on his knuckles.

"No wonder I worry about you every time you go out the door. I prayed for you the whole time you were gone. Now that you're home, I can quit worrying, At least until tomorrow."

Chapter 20

DARKNESS COMES IN DARKNESS

In the pre-dawn hours, Horse took his usual walk around the property. His left hand was swollen and sore from the jab that had caught Vernon Nichols on the forehead above his right eye. After his walk and a few minutes feeding Canyon and Mariposa, he joined Esperanza for breakfast. They ate on the couch in front of a fire rekindled from the previous night's embers. A big omelet with some of the last tomatoes from the garden and two big cups of coffee chased the cobwebs from Horse's brain. He headed off to work.

By nine o'clock, he had talked to the deputies coming in from the night shift and read through the overnight log. He went into his office and closed the door and wrote a lengthy memo for his eyes only. It detailed everything that had happened the previous night. He wanted to get it all down before memory altered the experience.

He was locking the memo away in his bottom desk drawer when his intercom buzzed.

"Yes."

"Captain Hardesty for you on line one."

"Horse here, Captain."

"Ballistics confirmed the gun your deputy brought in fired the bullets that killed Caleb and Eunice Clovis."

"Thanks for the information, sir. I'll call Detective Scanlon in Hollywood and tell him he's looking for a murder suspect now."

"Okay."

Horse disconnected the call and dialed Detective Scanlon's number.

The desk sergeant who answered said the detective was not at his desk. He promised to have Scanlon return Horse's call as soon as he came in.

Horse called the Askew Funeral Home. Donny, the oldest son, answered.

"Lieutenant Caballo here, Donny. I'm calling you about the Clovis funeral."

"Yes sir. I have it down for Wednesday afternoon, just like Clarke wanted."

"He's going to have to re-schedule. He's been badly injured and can't make it out."

"Do you have a new date for me?"

"Clarke will get back to you on that."

By one o'clock, Detective Scanlon still hadn't returned his call. Horse tried the number again and got the same desk sergeant.

"Still not back, Lieutenant, but he'll get the message as soon as he walks in the door."

"Probably a few others on his call-back list."

"There are."

"Then take me off. I'm going to be away from my office for an hour or more. I'll call again when I get back."

"Thanks, Lieutenant. Appreciate that."

Horse plucked his hat off the rack and headed out his door.

"Going to lunch, Fred. Be at the Bluebird if you need me."

He drove downtown. He parked on Front Street and went into the Smoke Tree Corner Drugstore. He bought a copy of the Los Angeles Examiner and walked the three blocks to the Bluebird Café, thinking about everything that had happened since a week ago Monday. It seemed in Smoke Tree that nothing much happened, but when it did it happened all at once.

He slid into his usual booth. When Robyn came by, he ordered the daily special. He opened the Examiner and found the story in the metro section. It explained the prognosis for Clarke Clovis, the rising jazz trumpeter who had been badly injured in a hit-and-run early Sunday morning in Hollywood, was grim. Doctors did not think he would ever regain consciousness.

When Robyn put his food in front of him, she lingered.

Horse looked up.

"Something, Robyn?"

"Remember that guy who was in here with you last week?"

"Clarke Clovis?"

"Yes."

"I've been thinking about him."

"Oh?"

"You heard him say we went to school together. We did, but I never even saw the guy, Lieutenant. I mean, he was there, but it was sort of like he was invisible."

"That kind of thing happens with kids sometimes, Robyn."

"But kids grow up. And sometimes when they do they realize how mean they were."

"Go on."

"What I'm trying to say is, I'd like to apologize to him for being such a stuck up ninny. Do you think he'll ever come back to Smoke Tree? I mean, I wouldn't blame him if he didn't."

"Yes, I think he will. You do know his mother and father were murdered, right?"

"Sure. I read about it in the Smoke Tree Weekly."

"Well, Clarke wants to bury his mother at Desertview Cemetery. He'll be back to do that."

"Would you do something for me?"

"If I can."

"If you find out when it's going to be, will you let me know?"

"Certainly."

"I'd feel better if I could tell him how sorry I am. And not only about his parents but about the way my friends and I treated him."

When Horse returned to the office and called Hollywood, Detective Scanlon answered.

"Good afternoon, Detective. Lieutenant Caballo here. I wanted to bring you up to date on the guy who tried to run down Clarke Clovis. Our ballistics guys confirmed the gun Tyler Clovis dropped fired the rounds that killed Clarke's parents. So now the charge is definitely murder"

"So, you've made your case. Congratulations."

"But we still don't have Tyler Clovis."

"We put out the BOLO on him and on the vehicle, but nothing's turned up."

"I just saw the article in the Examiner. That might get him moving our way."

"It might. The patrolman we put on the door reports nothing unusual."

"Did Clarke wake up?"

"Yes. Last night."

"Any information from the doctors?"

"A concussion. According to the doc I talked to, other than a nasty headache that should go away in two or three days, no brain damage or anything like that."

"If I call the hospital, will they let me talk to him?"

"Sure. There's a phone in his room."

Scanlon gave Horse the phone number for the switchboard at the hospital.

"Thanks for your help, Detective."

"You helped me too. Always nice to clear a case. Let me know if you catch the bastard."

"Will do."

Horse dialed the hospital and asked for Clarke's room. When he answered, his voice sounded reedy and weak.

"Hello."

"Clarke, this is Lieutenant Caballo in Smoke Tree. Glad to hear you're awake. Do you feel well enough to talk with me?"

Clarke's voice got stronger.

"I'll try. I've got the worst headache I've ever had. Hard to think."

"I wanted to let you know some things. First, the truck that hit you was driven by your Uncle Tyler. You remember anything about the accident?"

"Flash of light and then up in the air and banged into something and then nothing."

There was a moment of silence.

"Why would he want to run over me? I don't even know him."

"It's a long story, Clarke. I'll give you the details when we meet again."

"You think he killed mom?"

"I know he did. And your father."

Clarke's voice dropped to a whisper.

"Have you caught him?"

"Not yet. We're working on it. Us, the LAPD and the sheriff of the county where he lives in Missouri. We'll get him. In the meantime, there's a police officer stationed outside your door."

There was another long silence.

"I can't talk any more. My head hurts too bad."

The call disconnected.

Horse was adding to his case notes when there was a knock on his door.

"Come in."

Andy Chesney stepped inside.

"Got a minute, Lieutenant?"

"Sure. Pull up a chair."

Horse had been worried about this moment, more so now that he would have to decide whether he wanted to add the town of Smoke Tree to his responsibilities. Andy was a good deputy. Horse didn't want to lose him.

"Any progress on the Clovis case while I was off?"

231

"We know who pulled the trigger. It was Caleb's brother. He also tried to run down the son, Clarke Clovis, in Hollywood early Sunday morning."

"Does L.A. have him in custody?"

"No such luck. They're looking for him, but they're not real optimistic. It's a big city."

Andy cleared his throat and shifted in his chair.

"I came in early because I wanted to talk about that transfer."

"I figured that's what it was."

"I've changed my mind, Lieutenant. I'd like to stay in Smoke Tree. I mean, if that's okay with you."

Horse smiled.

"I was hoping you'd stay, but I didn't think you were going to."

"Well, sir, I've decided this desert's not so bad after all. It's sort of starting to grow on me"

He stood up.

"I guess that's it, Lieutenant. I'd better get ready for my shift."

"Thanks for letting me know, Andy. And be alert out there this evening."

"I will, sir."

"One more thing."

"Yessir."

"Did that chainsaw work out okay for you?"

"It did fine, sir. Just fine."

Horse had a very strong feeling Tyler Clovis would return to Smoke Tree under cover of darkness to try to find the murder weapon and the man who had picked it up. Horse was pretty sure Tyler had no idea he had been identified as the man who had killed Caleb and Eunice and tried to run down Clarke. But that's all it was. A feeling. A hunch. He knew he could be completely wrong about Tyler returning and when he might come. Horse didn't want to interrupt normal patrols or create a lot of overtime on a hunch. But he was going to keep watch.

The sun dropped below the Sacramento Mountains at four thirty that afternoon as Horse drove north out of Smoke Tree. He turned off the highway onto a dirt road that led to the sad remains of the lagoon just north of the Mojave Village.

The lagoon had been one of the nicest spots on the river before August of 1959 when a huge flash flood hit Smoke Tree. The muddy water pouring out of Eagle Pass wash took out Highway 66, stranding travelers. It also filled the lagoon with uprooted desert plants, rocks, mud, and trash. The mud and debris plugged the inlet at the east end of the lagoon, completely cutting it off from the river.

Had the lagoon been frequented by the wealthy, the Bureau of Reclamation would undoubtedly have brought in bulldozers, cleared the inlet, and used their huge dredge, *The Colorado*, to restore it. But since it was mostly used by the poorest of the poor, the Mojave Indians, the ruined lagoon was left to stagnate, breed mosquitoes and slowly begin to evaporate under the desert sun.

Horse drove down the road into the mesquite thicket bordering the foul waters. When he was sure his unit couldn't be seen from the highway, he pulled his shotgun from its holder and got out of his car. Carrying the gun and a five cell flashlight, he walked back down the road to the shoulder of 66 and waited for a break in the traffic.

When there was a momentary gap, he hurried across. As the deepening twilight bathed the Sacramento and Dead Mountains in constantly shifting shades of purple and blue, he cut southwest through the creosote toward the rodeo grounds.

When he reached the bleachers surrounding the empty rodeo arena, he moved on and climbed the steps leading to the announcing booth. He sat down on the landing, leaned back against the crude railing and pulled his knees toward his chest and settled down to wait.

A quarter of a mile from where he sat, a river of cars and trucks flowed in both directions. People who were in his area, but not of his area. Thousands and thousands of people every hour. People he would never meet unless they did something stupid or were in the wrong place at the wrong time and ended up dead or lost or broken down in the desert. Or committed a crime or were victims of a crime.

Horse was a patient man. He was also a man who knew how to keep watch during the hours of darkness. Night watch in Korea during a terrible retreat had taught him to stay alert lest he and his comrades not live to see the sunrise. He was sure that even though he was tired after a nearly sleepless night he could keep the required vigil.

And in fact, for the first few hours he had no problem staying awake. He had a lot to think about. He thought about the Clovis case, about a man so stupidly and malevolently greedy he would slay his own brother, as Cain slew Abel. And, not content with that abominable sin, had also slaughtered his brother's wife and tried to kill his brother's son over something that was almost assuredly without value. And even if the uranium claim had been worth millions, it would still not have kept the moral and spiritual vacuum of his actions from sucking out his very soul: a loss that was, to Horse's way of thinking, beyond recompense.

Horse thought about the fact that every day he worked in law enforcement he came in contact with people who lived their lives on the same moral plane as Tyler Clovis and Vernon Nichols. As a result, Horse was becoming more and more distrustful of his fellow human beings. More disappointed, and therefore more cynical. More suspicious of their motives, more aware of the gap between what they claimed to be and what they actually were.

But then there were people like Esperanza and his mother and Mr. Stanton and Chemehuevi Joe and young Andy Chesney. Good people. Loyal people. Reliable people. Horse hoped that the sheer weight of their good will balanced out the evil intentions of the bad people. He didn't know if that were possible. And he worried his job was distorting the lens through which he perceived the world so much that his perspective would always be skewed toward suspicion and skepticism.

Strange thoughts for a man waiting for a killer on a cold night in December as the earth churned relentlessly through space, bound on the same journey it had made for millions upon countless hundreds of millions of years, streaking toward the solstice and deeper darkness.

But even such thoughts can keep a man fully awake only so long.

When the sliver of the waxing moon slipped behind the Sacramento Mountains, Horse knew it was approaching ten o'clock. He hadn't expected Tyler Clovis to show up this early, but it was better to be too early than too late. His eyelids were beginning to droop, but Horse knew how to deal with the problem.

He dug a shotgun shell out of the pocket of his sheriff's department jacket. He put the butt of his shotgun on the ground and pulled the barrel against his chest with his left hand. He draped his right hand over his right knee with the shotgun shell held loosely between his thumb and finger and continued his vigil.

Sometime close to midnight, he nodded off. His grip on the loosely-held shell relaxed and it fell to the boards that formed the floor of the landing. He was instantly awake. He listened carefully to the sounds of the distant highway and the desert around him before getting up and walking a few circles around his waiting place.

When he nodded off and awoke for the third time, it was very cold. But that was good because it might make it easier to stay awake. He took his third walk around the landing and sat down to wait again. It wasn't long before he heard the sound of tires rolling slowly across dirt, but he could see no headlights. His heart rate quickened. This would be his quarry. A hunter who did not realize he had just become the hunted.

Horse quietly laid the shotgun and the flashlight on the wooden planks. He moved to the middle of the landing and got up on one knee. He reached back and picked up the shotgun with his left hand. He picked up the heavy flashlight with his right and turned his head to the side to bring the rods in his eyes responsible for night vision into play.

The wheels of the vehicle stopped turning.

Everything was quiet.

Then he heard a soft click and picked up a brief flare of light out of the corner of his eye.

The driver had forgotten to disconnect his dome light!

The door clicked again as it was pulled closed.

It stayed closed for a long time. Horse thought Tyler was trying to regain his night vision.

When the door opened again, the dome light had been disabled.

"Nothing like closing the barn door after the horse has run off," thought Horse.

He heard feet on the ground as the driver stepped out of the vehicle. He did not hear the door close. He thought perhaps the man had left it open.

Horse had to give the man credit for moving quietly through the darkness. He listened intently but couldn't tell if the man was heading for the steps or the mouth of the wash where he had dropped the gun. Then he felt a small vibration as the bottommost stair took the weight of a tentative step.

Horse kept his head turned to the side but put his thumb against the on/off switch of the big flashlight. He felt each step in turn subtly react as the man climbed the stairs. Then, even in the darkness, his peripheral vision picked up slight movement as the top of a head began to rise above the level of the landing.

Horse simultaneously, rose to his feet, switched on his flashlight and stepped forward with the shotgun in his left hand. The piercing beam hit the startled man squarely in the eyes. Involuntarily, he raised his right hand to shade his eyes.

It was Tyler Clovis. The hand he raised held a small automatic.

Dropping the flashlight, Horse gripped the barrel of the shotgun with his right hand. He took one long step and slammed the stock against the side of Tyler's head, relying on the afterimage burned on his retina for a good sense of the target. Tyler grunted and went over backward. Horse picked up the flashlight and clattered down the stairs after him, the shotgun back in his left hand.

Tyler was lying stunned on his side in the dirt as Horse descended. Tyler's gun lay several feet from his body. He groaned as he tried to get to his feet. Horse knew Tyler could not see him on the other side of the cone of white light.

Horse spoke for the first time.

"Get up and you're a dead man. There's double aught buck in this shotgun and it's pointed at your head."

Horse came off the last step and moved around Tyler, careful to stay well clear of his legs.

"Roll onto your stomach."

Tyler did not move.

Horse took a short step and kicked Tyler in the buttocks.

Tyler screamed.

"Get on your stomach, now!"

Tyler hurried to comply.

Horse put the flashlight on the ground with the beam pointed toward Tyler, all the time keeping the gun pointed at the prone man

"Put your hands behind your back."

Slowly, one hand and then the other moved to the demanded position.

Horse pushed the muzzle of the shotgun against the back of Tyler's head.

"That's the bore of my .12 gauge. The safety is off. If you move, me and my deputies are gonna have to scoop up your brains with a teaspoon."

Still standing, Horse pulled a set of cuffs from his jacket pocket. He dropped to the ground while keeping the shotgun against Tyler's head. He snapped the cuffs on first one hand and then the other and stood up and stepped away.

"You can move now. Get up."

Tyler managed to get his feet under his body and stand. Horse pushed him over to a place in front of one of the four by fours supporting the landing above.

He pulled another set of cuffs from his belt and looped them through the cuffs on Tyler's wrist. Horse pulled Tyler back against the post and hooked the second set of cuffs around the post. He snapped the second set of cuffs together. Tyler was tethered to the pole.

Horse walked over and got his flashlight off the ground. He pushed the safety on his shotgun to the "on" position and leaned it against the steps. He picked up the gun Tyler had dropped and walked back and stood directly in front of him.

He pointed the flashlight at the ground.

The reflected light faintly illuminated both men.

"Tyler Clovis, I am Lieutenant Carlos Caballo of the San Bernardino County Sheriff's Department. I am placing you under arrest for the murder of Cable Clovis and Eunice Clovis, and for the attempted murder of their son, Clarke Clovis."

He waved the small automatic in Tyler's face.

"This is the second gun you've dropped out here, but the first one you dropped is going to send you to the gas chamber."

"I didn't do nothin'. And I'm going to hire me the best lawyers in California to prove it."

"With what?"

"You'll see."

"You mean your uranium mine? There isn't going to be any uranium mine, Tyler. The claim is worthless. The Geiger counter you bought is a piece of junk."

"That's what you think. You wasn't there. You didn't hear all them clicks!"

Horse put the small automatic in his pocket. He walked over and got his shotgun and turned off the flashlight.

Horse and Tyler Clovis and the rodeo grounds were swallowed in darkness.

Horse stood for a while, waiting for his night vision to return.

When it did, he moved off across the desert. The Great Bear was slipping behind the Dead Mountains.

False dawn would not be far away.

Chapter 21

DECIDING

By Friday afternoon, the fifteenth of December, Horse's part in the case against Tyler Clovis was wrapped up until the trial. Tyler was in jail in San Bernardino and all the reports necessary for his prosecution had been turned over to the San Bernardino County District Attorney. Horse was looking forward to the weekend he had promised Esperanza. They had decided they would use the days alone to decide whether they should take on the responsibility of policing Smoke Tree. They were also going to make one other major decision about their future.

On Saturday morning, he and Esperanza were up in the dark. Horse made the coffee while Esperanza cooked a skillet of *huevos a la mexicana* with Serrano peppers and Jalisco cheese. By false dawn they were on the veranda, wrapped in blankets against the morning chill. They had their coffee, the skillet of eggs and a basket of homemade corn tortillas. They ate and talked and watched the morning light come slowly into the sky. They lingered and drank coffee until the pale sun was completely above the rim of the Black Mountains across the river.

After breakfast, he hitched the horse trailer to his Chevrolet pickup and led Canyon and Mariposa inside. He and Esperanza drove south on Highway 95 to Vidal junction and turned west on Route 62 to the tiny wide spot in the road named Rice. They pulled off the highway and stopped next to three ancient, silver railroad cars parked on the Santa Fe siding. While he and Esperanza unloaded and saddled the horses, two of the Mojave Indian men from the Santa Fe track crew came out of the cars and greeted them and praised the horses. Horse asked if they would keep an eye on his trailer and his pickup until they returned the next day. The men assured him they would.

239

He and Esperanza mounted up and rode due west out of Rice. As they moved, the Turtle Mountains rotated on the northern horizon. They picked up the Colorado Aqueduct, incongruously blue against the brown desert. They crossed and re-crossed the highway twice as they followed the canal. Once they crossed it for the last time, the highway fell behind.

They paralleled the aqueduct for miles, the horses moving at a walk as they talked through the decision about accepting Mayor Milner's request for Horse to take over the policing of Smoke Tree. During the long discussion they stopped from time to time to get down and inspect the Colorado Desert from ground level. Whenever they dismounted, Horse would use the canvas bucket from his saddle bags to take water from the channel for Canyon and Mariposa.

They made camp before sunset. Horse collected matchweed and gamma grass for kindling and built a fire of dried and punky palo verde branches. Then he gathered small pieces of fallen ironwood from beneath an old tree heavily infested with parasitic mistletoe that was slowly but inevitably sucking the life from the tree. When he added the ironwood to the fire and it took hold, he knew he had a fire that would last for hours. He unsaddled Canyon and Mariposa, and he and Esperanza brushed them lightly, the horses turning their heads to watch them, as if to be sure they did it right. Both horses, their ears relaxed and loosely forward, grunted with pleasure. Horse then fed them grain and apple pieces and hobbled them for the night.

He put three cans of Olympia beer in the canvas watering bag and lowered it into the cold water of the aqueduct. He tied the rope holding the bucket to the stanchion supporting the fencing along the waterway. By that time, the fire had burned down to a bed of coals. Horse put two, foil-wrapped, twice-baked potatoes into the fire to heat. He punched holes in the top of a can of black beans and put the can in the coals with the potatoes. When the juice began to bubble, he wrapped a rag around the can and opened it with the p-38 he always carried on a chain around his neck.

While Horse retrieved the three cans of beer from the aqueduct, Esperanza pulled the potatoes from the coals. She spread homemade flour tortillas on paper plates, spooned them full of beans and potatoes, and rolled them into burritos. As they ate their dinner, they watched the sunset flare over the Coxcomb Mountains. The first quarter moon was well above the horizon in the eastern sky behind them. By the time they finished, bats and nighthawks were taking insects out of the air above the water in the channel, the nighthawks sometimes pulling out of dives that made the peculiar roaring sound that gave them their other southwest name: bull bats.

It was twilight by five o'clock, and the temperature was dropping fast. Venus was the brightest object above the western horizon. Horse and Esperanza sat side by side, looking into the night sky. Slowly at first, and then with increasing speed, despite the light of the first quarter moon, the sky was filling with stars, so many and so dense they seemed to bleed into the earth. Moonlight obscured the Pleiades in the east, but Cassiopeia and Pegasus were almost directly overhead. Horse and Esperanza stared without speaking, content with each others' company, sometimes pointing when a meteorite streaked to a spectacular, fiery death against the glittering backdrop. Horse built up the fire against the night chill. Canyon and Mariposa occasionally sighed or snorted softly, their eyes gleaming in the flickering light of the fire.

After a time, Horse and Esperanza began to talk again about adoption. They both felt a child was the one thing lacking in their lives. Because of a case of mumps after puberty, Horse could not father children. They had both known that before they married. And they both agreed there were many children across the border in Mexico in desperate need of a home. On their last visit to an orphanage south of Tijuana, they had met and talked to a young boy and his sister. The children had been at the orphanage since shortly after birth and were almost four years old. The director was concerned they were getting so old they might not be adopted: everyone wanted babies.

Horse and Esperanza had fallen in love with both children. Horse pointed out that if he took on the increased responsibility of a larger substation, it would probably entail a promotion. The additional money would ease the financial burden of adopting both children.

They talked late into the night. Horse kept adding fuel to the fire as the air grew steadily colder. They were glad to have the undisturbed time to talk about both important decisions. When the time the fire burned down for the last time, they were very sleepy. They agreed they would make both decisions the following day.

Horse spread their double sleeping bag on the ground. He circled the bag with a horsehair rope. He had always heard that rattlesnakes would not cross a horsehair rope, and whether it was true or not, and even though he was convinced it was too late in the season for rattlesnakes, the presence of the barrier made Esperanza feel better.

They undressed. Horse hung their clothing in a nearby palo verde tree. They climbed into the bag. Wrapped in each others' arms, they drifted off to sleep. Horse awoke a few times in the night. Each time, the only sounds were Esperanza's peaceful breathing, the shuffling of the horses and the soft gurgle and swirl of water in the aqueduct. And each time, he thought about the brother and sister in Mexico slowly losing hope that anyone would ever take both of them home.

Sunday morning they slept late, not getting out of the big sleeping bag until an orange sun climbed above the McCoy Mountains. Horse could not remember the last time he had not been up before sunrise. The temperature was in the mid thirties, and he shivered when he climbed out to check their boots for bugs. Finding none, he slipped his boots over his bare feet, put on his Stetson and walked to the palo verde tree to get their clothing.

Esperanza watched him walk away in his boots, hat and jockey shorts. She usually thought he looked like an Aztec warrior, but she'd never seen a painting of an Aztec warrior decked out in the outfit Horse had on that morning.

She put two fingers in her mouth and gave out a loud, wolf whistle.

"*Nice culo, mi esposo . Muy lindo!*"

Horse laughed. "Glad you enjoy the view."

When Horse brought their clothing back, they dressed side by side on the unzipped sleeping bag, then stood up and warmed each other with a long hug. He started a fire and went for water for the horses. Then he took the enamel coffee pot back to the aqueduct and filled it. Esperanza added coffee and set the blackened pot in the fire.

While Horse unhobbled the animals and gave them their morning feed, Esperanza put bacon slices into a black skillet and set it on the fire while she cut potatoes into thin slices. Just as she added the potatoes to the skillet, a gust of wind kicked up, flaring the fire and blowing sand through their campsite.

"*Oye, vaquero! Va a tener arena en tu desayuno.*"

"That's okay. Cleans my teeth."

After breakfast, they burned their paper plates and buried the remains of their fire. Then they saddled up and rode off to the north. They reversed the route they had ridden the day before, stopping only to water the horses. They were approaching Rice by one in the afternoon. Instead of riding back to the truck, they continued north and rode into the foothills of the deep reds and browns of the Turtle Mountains. They passed ghostly smoke trees and desert willows and palo verde infested with mistletoe in the washes. Honey mesquites and cholla cactus and cheesebush clustered on the hillsides along the way. And everywhere, rock. All kinds of rock: blue gray rocks of basalt, eroding boulders of andesite, chunks of black obsidian, rocks the color of rusting iron and rocks the color of spoiled liver. Rock all around them as they rode.

They watered the horses at Mopah Springs beneath the desert fan palms and let the horses rest. When they remounted and rode back toward Rice, that special, desert light of late fall and early winter came into the sky. It was beautiful and peaceful. By the time they got to the tiny town, both decisions had been made. They would take the job, and they would adopt the brother and sister.

It was dark by the time they got to Smoke Tree. Horse unsaddled Canyon and Mariposa and turned them out into the corral. He brought them grain. Before he rubbed them down, he gave them each a handful of molasses balls for being such good horses. When he went into the house, Esperanza had a fire going and big pieces of French apple pie with cheddar cheese on the table along with coffee.

When Horse finished his pie and coffee, he got up to take his plate and cup to the sink.

"Sit down on the couch and take a load off, big guy. You get special treatment for feeding and currying the horses."

Horse walked over and sat on the couch. He could hear Esperanza clattering dishes in the sink. It wasn't long before she returned from the kitchen.

She turned out the table lamp and sat down beside him. Her eyes glistened in the flickering firelight, and her jet-black hair took on added luster. When she smiled at him, his heart filled with so much love it caused a tightening in his chest. He knew he would never be able to put his feelings for her adequately into words. He hoped she knew what was in his heart.

"Thank you for a wonderful weekend, *querida.*"

"It's not over just yet. Come take a shower with me, and I'll show you what happens next."

When they got off the couch, she hooked her finger through a belt loop on his Levi's and led him down the hallway.

Chapter 22

GATHER

Most winters on the Mojave Desert, the vicious north winds that mark that season remained in abeyance until early January. But On Wednesday, the twenty seventh of December, 1961, the wind blew hard and cold out of the northeast all day long. It scoured sand and bits of coarser matter from washes and hillsides and hurled it all at the people and buildings of Smoke Tree. It was the beginning of Horse's least favorite time of the year on the Mojave. The time of the dry and bloody nose. The time of the nasty shock when crossing a carpet and reaching for a doorknob. The time of the pitted windshield and the constant accumulation of dust inside buildings no matter how tightly sealed the windows. The time when even good friends got irritated with each other to the point of coming to blows, and domestic violence calls spiked.

Horse thought Clarke Clovis could hardly have had a worse day for the service for his mother. But as the mourners gathered in the cold at the Desertview Cemetery, just as the sun dropped toward the peaks of the Sacramento Mountains, the wind suddenly died and the air turned calm and gelid.

There were only a few people: Carlos and Esperanza, Lonnie and Jean Jenkins and Clarke Clovis. Clarke, wearing a black suit and no overcoat, was still having trouble staying on his feet for long periods because of the pain in his left hip. Standing slightly off kilter, he held a golden trumpet that gleamed in the light of the descending sun. He was just about to speak when an old Ford with a bad muffler rattled slowly up the Afghan pine-lined gravel road to the cemetery.

Robyn Danforth, elegantly dressed in a simple black dress in spite of the cold, got out of the car and walked toward the group over the dormant, brown Bermuda grass. Her high heels wobbled occasionally as she moved across the hard but uneven ground.

245

Esperanza smiled at her as she approached.

If Clarke was surprised to see her, he hid it well, simply nodding to her from his position near the head of the casket suspended above the waiting grave.

After she had joined the group, he began to speak.

"My mother had a hard life. A terrible life. A life unimaginable to most people.

She deserved much better. She never got a break, but she never complained. Just lived as best she could, day after difficult grinding day, taking care of me and suffering constant abuse from the horrible, disgusting, worthless hunk of inhumanity that was Caleb Clovis."

He lifted the horn in his right hand shoulder high.

"Mr. Jenkins introduced me to the trumpet. He gave me lessons for free. He and Mrs. Jenkins were the bright lights in my life.

I owe them a debt of gratitude that can never be repaid. But even that enormous debt is not as great as the one I owe my mother for her love and encouragement."

He paused and wiped tears from his face with his left sleeve.

"Mother loved music. There was no phonograph or radio in our house because there was no electricity. She once brought home a small transistor radio, but Caleb smashed it to bits. He was determined there would be no beauty in my mother's life.

She loved Frank Sinatra most of all. She heard his music played on jukeboxes at the places in Smoke Tree where she worked as a cook. And she had a favorite among the songs he sang. That favorite was, 'My Funny Valentine'.

Mom, this is for you."

He put the trumpet to his lips and began to play. The clear, haunting, melancholy notes of the song came with heartbreaking clarity from his horn and rolled over the coffin, across the cemetery, and out into the desert beyond. The sound was beautiful beyond description.

Toward the end of the song, the sun dropped beneath the distant horizon and produced a desert moment as magnificent and mysterious as it was rare. For one minute, or perhaps two, those gathered there and everything around them: the sky, the mountains, the river, the entire visible landscape and the very air, became suffused with a ruby colored light. It gathered softly and seemed a separate, palpable and living thing.

The exquisite and delicate light began to fade with the last notes of the song. The ruby glow remained reflected from the bell of the trumpet one moment longer than it lingered elsewhere.

And then it was gone completely.

The world returned to its normal colors.

Clarke lowered the horn to his side.

Everyone stood, wordless and transfixed, until Robyn detached herself from the group and walked to Clarke's side. She stretched up on her tiptoes and whispered in his ear for some time before easing herself back to the ground.

He looked at her and nodded.

She rose up again, kissed him on the cheek, and turned and walked away.

THE END

If you enjoyed this novel, the author would be very grateful if you would write a review. Independent Authors lack the resources of the publishing houses. They rely on readers to promote their books by posting reviews. Please locate the book on Amazon. Near the bottom of the page, just above the "More About the Author" Section, you will see a gray button that reads "Write a customer review." Please click on it and leave your thoughts about the book.

Cover Photo by Ginny George

Other Books by the Author

The House of Three Murders

Horse Hunts

Mojave Desert Sanctuary

Made in the USA
Coppell, TX
14 July 2021